PRAISE FOR *NOW THEY WILL KNOW I AM HERE*

"*Now They Will Know I Am Here* offers readers a thrilling ride through the world's terrorist hotspots as Tom Rivers of the CIA tries to stay alive long enough to thwart an ingenious plot against the homeland. With nonstop action and a savvy grasp of the darker machinations of our democracy, Tim McQuay has written an engaging page-turner that fans of Tom Clancy and modern espionage novels will love."

— PETER PRICHARD, AUTHOR OF
*KILLING GRACE, A VIETNAM WAR
MYSTERY*

"A riveting spy tale that delivers a CIA hero fighting Islamic terrorists. ... Umm is not the typical Islamic terrorist found in spy thrillers, and she's highly motivated to boot. Considering her ferocity, readers will wonder what it will take to finally stop her. ... The fact that Rivers is not a rampaging gunslinger who can act with impunity whenever he wants lends the story believ-ability."

—*KIRKUS REVIEWS*

"Reminiscent of Alma Katsu's *Red Widow* and Daniel Silva's fabled Gabriel Allon series, Tim McQuay delivers a terrific thriller jammed with revelations and reversals that carries the ring of truth."

—TIM WENDEL, AUTHOR OF *REBEL FALLS*

Now They Will Know I Am Here is both a riveting thriller and a cautionary tale ripped from current news stories and intelligence reports. Tim McQuay has crafted an original and gripping account of international agents racing to stop a terrorist plot hatched in a real-life Syrian detention camp that is the breeding ground for the next generation of ISIS. With characters and plot twists equally vivid, complex, and surprising, it's a read that reels you in and doesn't let go.

— SEAN CARBERRY, AUTHOR OF *PASSPORT STAMPS: SEARCHING THE WORLD FOR A WAR TO CALL HOME*

NOW THEY WILL KNOW
I AM HERE

A CIA THRILLER

TIMOTHY MCQUAY

HOT TYPE PUBLISHING LLC

Print ISBN: 979-8-218-37480-8
Paperback and eBook available via Amazon and its Kindle Direct Publishing

For Cathy and Mark,
who are my happiness

"Civilization is like a thin layer of ice upon a deep ocean of chaos and darkness."

- FILMMAKER WERNER HERZOG

PART ONE

1

Stealing is a sin, or so Philippe had been taught by the morally constipated Catholic nuns, but he always savored the feeling that working the early Sunday shift was really stealing a day's pay from his bosses.

"V*as-y mollo*" was his motto for Sundays. *Take it easy.*

He was driving a civilian van, white and unmarked like so many others, delivering two briefcase-size parcels from the Charles de Gaulle Airport to the U.S. Embassy and then to the National Police on the Île de la Cité. Afterwards, he'd park by a café and enjoy coffee while monitoring his radio for pickups, normally slim to none on this day of rest.

Philippe knew the rhythm of the highway into Paris, driving in the slipstream between the first and second waves of flights that started arriving near dawn. Traffic was light.

The van suddenly lurched and shuddered. Philippe reflexively straightened it from a skid out of its lane. His guess: a blowout, left rear tire. A nail, a piece of metal on the roadway?

Philippe radioed dispatch that he had pulled onto the shoulder and a repair truck was needed. He'd call back shortly after checking the damage. As he got out to inspect the rear tire, he saw a van had pulled in behind him, and a motorcycle that had just passed by as the lurch occurred was motoring back toward him on the shoulder.

Amazing, people stopping to check on me. Really must be the holy day.

Philippe saw the blown tread and gave a small wave to the other van that all was OK. He turned toward the motorcyclist and stared right into clear blue eyes in the opening of the helmet and felt a handgun jam into his ribs. A current like electricity—fear—ran through him.

He was shoved to the far side of his van, away from the lanes, and saw two figures in black ski masks opening it with a key liberated from his belt. The motorcyclist stood behind him as he was forced to kneel. They moved quick and wordless.

Philippe then heard a voice, his own, surprising him. A low, choked recitation of the Hail Mary, a prayer he had learned as a child but not uttered in decades.

"Stop!" one of the thieves shouted.

In a moment, Philippe realized the command wasn't to him. It was for Blue Eyes behind him, who had drawn a knife upon hearing the prayer and now thrust it into his neck, cutting violently until his head came off.

"Why?" screamed a stunned thief.

The killer trembled with rage and muttered: "The infidels and their prayers betrayed me."

"Now they will know I am here."

2

The unmarked car moved between six-story buildings that blocked most of the morning sun, and the street shadows matched Tom Rivers' mood.

He didn't like being played.

His boss, Angelos, was supposed to be a straight shooter, but he had given Rivers an assignment that was akin to sending a dog to play in traffic.

Here he was, dropped into Paris, and told to scoop up information on the theft of U.S. and French passports and the beheading of a van driver that hit global media a few days ago. His presence was bound to intrude into ongoing investigations by the French police and its intelligence apparatus, as well as Interpol, the FBI, and the State Department. Last on that list was the CIA's Paris Station, which greeted Rivers unexpected arrival as if he carried the plague. And he couldn't blame them.

From their point of view, Rivers was, at best, an unwelcome oversight from headquarters, a spy on spies—or, worse, a troublemaker sent by Angelos against a rival heading Paris Station. Probably both.

"You look in a dark mood this morning," said his driver, Paul Laurent.

"I am trying to count my friends," said Rivers.

Laurent smiled; he already liked this young man who seemed to have an appreciation for the absurd, a quality found in abundance among French cops like him.

"Well, I have just the thing to perk you up," said Laurent. "Nothing like a fresh murder."

"Where are we going?"

Laurent glided the car deftly through traffic. "To Saint-Denis, where crime is a livelihood. A former colleague called me and told me to come quick. And so we are."

"You know, Paul, an everyday murder isn't in my job description," said Rivers.

"This one likely is."

Laurent had volunteered to be his guide-watcher when Rivers made a courtesy call on French Intel. Angelos sent the skinny on him when Rivers inquired: "You've lucked out. Laurent is old school. A solid man."

Angelos added some details in the encrypted text: "Paul Laurent, 52, works for the General Directorate for External Security as its liaison to the Paris police. Former Paris police captain. Suddenly hired to current position of DGSE Inspector after starting a Paris police investigation into political corruption. Without him, the investigation went nowhere."

The promptness of the reply told Rivers as much as the information.

"How long have you known Angelos?" asked Rivers as they drove away from the city center.

Laurent didn't take his eyes off the road. "Your Angelos was an operations officer like you twenty-some years ago here, and he showed an interest in what was happening on the street. Smuggling, drugs, human trafficking. His colleagues were not too interested in crime, as if criminals did not know the shady things that people and governments do. He wanted to sip directly from the sewer, and I was happy to help him."

"So Angelos wants me to sip from the sewer," said Rivers.

"So it would seem," said Laurent.

Laurent offered, and Rivers accepted, a dab of menthol under his nose to blunt the smell of the sprawled body on the floor in a pool of darkened blood. Laurent's colleague filled him in with a torrent of words as Rivers was left unintroduced. They had driven to a worn-down warehouse on a street cheered by old garbage and graffiti, and this room with the body in it already was seedy decades ago.

The corpse was in that early stage when the body still remembered being alive; he was a young man, perhaps in his mid-twenties with an athletic build, broad face frozen in shock. His chest featured two holes that had streamed blood.

"Live wrong, die wrong. Meet the former Aslan Baseyev," said Laurent, pointing at the body. "Last night he joined the list of suspects in the passport heist. This morning the police received a call that there was a murder here."

"Why was this guy on a list of suspects?"

"There are always suspects in Saint-Denis," said Laurent. "In his case, a drug runner was hauled in unrelated to the van hijacking and tried to work a deal by pointing to Baseyev. He said Baseyev was a drug runner like himself but known to take part in hijackings, and he hadn't been around in the past week. It was considered a promising lead."

"Who called it in this morning?"

"A woman's voice. A burner phone."

"We didn't have to come here to learn this," said Rivers.

"No, but we had to be here to see this," said Laurent.

He held up two clear sealed plastic evidence bags, each containing a passport.

Rivers picked up the one that had an open U.S. passport and stared at the photograph of an attractive young woman with the name Meriem Dahar. The pages looked real to him, but what did he know? The second bag held a French passport in the name of Zahia Boutella. The same attractive young woman stared back at him.

"Murder and passport theft are not new to Saint-Denis," said Laurent. "But my colleague saw, as I do, two curiosities here: Someone called in this killing so it would be discovered immediately, and someone left these passports in rather plain sight."

Rivers was silent.

"You have no comment?" said Laurent.

Rivers shrugged. "Someone is killing people and intentionally leaving clues behind. To what end, how would I know? I'm not even sure why I'm here."

"Didn't Angelos tell you?" asked Laurent.

"He just said to look for the 'loose ends.'"

Now Laurent shrugged. "He does tend to be cryptic."

Rivers took photos of the two open passports and sent them and the name of the deceased directly to Angelos. He then took a deep breath and sent the same to Paris Station's deputy chief with a note outlining what had transpired.

Back in the car, Laurent—who knew too well the politics and infighting of bureaucracies—suggested Rivers may want to consider looping Paris Station into what was up.

"Already did," said Rivers.

Two miles down the road, Rivers got a text to stop by the office of Harry Dalton at "your earliest inconvenience."

3

He was a manicured man in a tailored suit and for the moment was very well-mannered. That didn't make him less dangerous. Rivers had heard that Harry Dalton, chief of CIA Paris Station, was well known to serve a stiletto with a smile.

"I really appreciate, Thomas—you don't mind me calling you by your first name, I hope," said Dalton, then continuing without pause, "that you contacted Paris Station with your whereabouts and the passport information.

"When my French counterpart called to ask why you were at a crime scene a few moments after we received your text, I wasn't left in the awkward position of not knowing what a CIA officer was doing in my area of responsibility."

It was a nice opening from Dalton, and Rivers appreciated that he hadn't raged or threatened, although he knew that his own answers now would determine if the atmosphere remained civil. He chose his words carefully.

"I'm here, as you know, at the direction of Operations

Director Angelos, assigned to—as he said—look for the 'loose ends," said Rivers. "And he said I would report directly to him and not to Paris Station."

"Loose ends. Rather a murky tasking," said Dalton.

"Without a doubt, sir."

"Considering his instructions, why send your text to Paris Station at all?"

"I reported directly to Mr. Angelos, as he ordered, but I don't recall him ever specifically barring me from communicating with Paris Station thereafter," said Rivers. "I think Paris Station has a need to know what is happening in its own backyard.

"Plus, if I need help, you are the closest."

"Hmmm, independent thinking," said Dalton. "Not always desirable. But perhaps that's why Angelos picked you for a 'loose ends' assignment."

"Personally, I think it's because I'm easily disposable," said Rivers. "This is only my second year with the agency."

"I wouldn't rule that out," said Dalton. "But never underestimate Angelos. I never do. I am disturbed that he's put someone in Paris without following proper procedures. But he's been successful managing operations his way."

Dalton leaned in, as if taking Rivers into his confidence, although what he said was widely shared gossip in the agency: "Do you know that he and I are considered the frontrunners for the vacant CIA deputy director post?"

"Above my rank to know, sir," said Rivers, who knew.

"Well, I'd appreciate it if you kept Paris Station informed, after directly informing Angelos," said Dalton. "I am a good friend to have and a bad enemy.

"Also, please try not to get killed here. The paperwork would be tiresome."

"I will keep in touch," said Rivers. "And endeavor to spare you unwanted paperwork."

It was late-afternoon, and Rivers was back in the car with Laurent. "Check your phone."

A text had arrived while he was meeting Dalton:

Dear Monsieur Rivers,
Please accept this invitation to a cocktail party at La Maîtresse at 7 p.m. Business attire.
Martin Lyons, Deputy Director, DGSE

Rivers looked at Laurent, who laughed. "You're a curiosity, and the power brokers would love to unwrap a mystery CIA man on an unfathomable mission: you," said Laurent.

"It's a small gathering of influential intel and police officials and good liquor," he added. "I know because I once was invited."

"I was a police captain and had begun an investigation into political corruption. It was made clear to me that my work had to end," he continued. "I resisted, but then was offered a better job as a DSGE Inspector. I'm sure I was invited to the cocktail party to gauge my reaction. They saw, as I had on reflection, that I didn't have the makings of a poor martyr. So, new job for me and, poof, the investigation quietly died under my successor."

Rivers considered Laurent's words a confession of sorts, made matter-of-factly, just stating the terms of his professional survival. More a bend to reality than of the weak to the powerful, at least in his telling.

He responded with no judgment in his voice, "I'm not here to play politics."

"Just remember to be flexible, Thomas," said Laurent, who steered the car toward dropping him off at his hotel. "We are all playing a game whether we know it or not, much less whether we like it.

"And I think you know it and are far better at it than you let on."

4

Rivers spotted security in the street and more upon entering La Maîtresse, where he was quickly ushered to a back room. There, Martin Lyons, the deputy DSGE director who had invited him, seemed to materialize like a genie.

A quick count was ten men and a woman standing and chatting in the room.

Power brokers, Laurent had called them.

And while a table along the wall held a selection of hors d'oeuvres and top-flight liquors and wines, Rivers had no doubt he was the main course.

Most of the assembled were studiously ignoring his arrival— appearing too eager to dissect him would be gauche, after all— but the woman met his gaze. She was, in a word, classy. Stylish in an expensive blue blazer, a silk cream blouse, and slim black trousers. With the figure of a dancer; brown hair hung to her shoulders. And marvelous blue eyes that held his own. Then, in an instant, she looked away, and suddenly the room felt colder.

"Ahh, Mr. Rivers, so pleased that you could join us," said Lyons, who moved with the easy grace of a man well-oiled by power and money.

He blocked Rivers from the room with an unobtrusive step and dropped his voice.

"Every four to six weeks a few of us in our shared community meet at a different location to talk shop, nothing specific— that is taboo—but about trends, people in the news, even sports, although that can spark such arguments. All not to be shared. Occasionally we invite a guest, like you this evening. Now let me introduce you."

"A moment, everyone," said Lyons. "Here is our guest, Thomas Rivers, a colleague from across the Atlantic."

Thus began an excruciating hour for Rivers, as the assembled diplomatically tried to unwrap this young man in their midst without directly asking: Why in the hell are you in Paris? Rivers dodged and diverted.

He asked a police official the brand of the luxury watch on his left wrist and sparked a ten-minute conversation with three of them about Patek Philippe, Panerai, and Rolex watches. They saw Rivers's scarred Luminox, a watch favored by men in the trenches, so to speak, a fact added to their inventory of him.

Finally, one asked, "How long will you be with us?"—which perked up many ears—and he answered with an uninformative, "As long as I can. Anyone would want to stay in Paris forever."

Rivers moved on, trying to work toward the intriguing woman, and chatted about the Paris Saint-Germain football club, downtown Paris vs. downtown Washington traffic, and French thinness vs. American obesity.

The Panerai watch owner—an official with the French military ministry—sidled up and spoke during a lull in the conversation. "I was thinking," he said, "when I saw your Luminox, that it's a favorite of some of your military's special forces. Is that your background?"

Rivers continued to smile. Such an awkwardly put question. As it was, the watch had been given to him by a girlfriend at a Christmas past, and he had worn it thoughtlessly ever since.

"The Luminox has been with me for a while. Back to the days when I was a U.S. Army captain in military intelligence. Nothing special to it—or me."

The man nudged further.

"Isn't that an unusual background for your current assignment? That background is more in line with a paramilitary job."

Rivers shrugged amiably: "My best intelligence work; I got a job that didn't involve carrying a weapon."

Another asked, at last, "Are you working with Mr. Angelos on the passport case?"

Of course, they all knew this, or at least suspected, and perhaps even of the Angelos-Dalton competition. They were fishing for an answer, a hesitation, an evasion.

"I was in touch with both Mr. Angelos and Mr. Dalton earlier today. I'm sure they'd both want me to say 'hello.'"

His questioner persisted. "There have been several passport robberies. Why is Mr. Angelos especially interested in this one?"

Lyons looked aggrieved that the rat-a-tat-tat of questions had reached the taboo stage.

Rivers simply answered, "Isn't everyone? After all, a head was chopped off."

After too many exhausting minutes, Rivers arrived at the corner that held a tall man and the attractive woman, who had both remained on an outer orbit of the small gathering. Rivers stepped before them but, in the moment before introductions, the woman simply smiled and slipped away, apparently for a refill of her glass of red wine.

For the next ten minutes, the tall man engaged him in a serious conversation, one-sided but still fascinating, and quite oblivious to Lyon's mandate against talking shop. Adam Barnes of Interpol was in charge of investigating the influx of a drug called Captagon into Europe from Syria. "First Assad's butchery of his own people sent a wave of refugees to Europe, now this amphetamine. He's turned Syria into a mega-narco state. Your country should take a bit more interest in this, for this situation is aided by Russia and Iran."

"We should," said Rivers, agreeing to be agreeable. "But fentanyl from Mexico, China, and now Canada, has our more immediate attention."

Barnes brushed aside the comment and continued his monologue. "With the Captagon, of course, comes the human smuggling, particularly women forced into prostitution. And the threat of terrorists among them."

"I'll keep that in mind during my brief time here," said Rivers, who had turned his body diagonally to Barnes and stepped back, working to diplomatically disengage.

"And what about your companion? Is she Interpol too?" asked Rivers, changing the topic.

"Raz Jackson? Oh, no," Barnes answered. "Raz is CEO of a private intelligence firm that provides security services to high-end hotels and travel businesses. I think she stayed by me in this corner because she knows my intensity keeps most people away."

"Time for a refill," said Rivers, raising his glass in salute and moving toward the table with drinks.

"Do you want another Perrier or something stronger, like whiskey or wine?" said Raz Jackson when he arrived.

"I'll have what you're having, Raz," said Rivers. And she filled a glass with Bordeaux and handed it to him. "You've earned it."

She had sized up Rivers as the type of man who could catch the eye of a discerning woman. He was medium height, with medium brown hair—nothing notable there. It was the way he moved. Relaxed, assured. A wisp of a smile. A man comfortable in a rough-and-tumble world.

Before he could speak, Raz pointed her chin at the assembled and added, "They've scanned you, and you them. Who is the most dangerous man in the room?"

Rivers took his time answering. "I wouldn't want to make enemies of any of them, but perhaps Martin Lyons. He didn't speak to me much but observed me closely. He let the others do the work."

"What do you think they saw in you?" asked Raz.

He wanted to ask her questions, but she was a step ahead.

He paused, and Raz jumped in: "They saw that you were elusive. A quality the French value."

"And you? What did you see?" said Rivers.

"The jury's still out. But we may find out more when we meet for dinner tomorrow night. I'll text you," she said.

At that, Raz put down her glass and turned to the door.

Rivers spoke as she turned. "Actually, you are probably the most dangerous person in this room."

Raz glanced back, her blue eyes taking him in for a moment.

"You noticed."

5

"How was the get-together?"

Dalton, the Paris Station chief, was calling on the encrypted phone as Rivers sat at an outdoor café nursing a glass of Bordeaux, appreciating its robust finish and the evening air. He was two blocks from his hotel and looking forward to calling it a night.

"You tell me," said Rivers. "You're the eyes and ears of everything here."

"Well, I do have the participants on speed dial," said Dalton. "Except for one."

"And who would that be?" asked Rivers, following his lead.

"Raz Jackson. Who I assume you met and, if halfway intelligent, will meet again."

"I did meet her and am marginally intelligent. But why," Rivers continued, "is Raz Jackson not on your speed dial?"

"She's an independent sort," said Dalton. "And then there is her past association with our Mr. Angelos."

"Oh," said Rivers.

"Oh, indeed," said Dalton. He let a few seconds tick by. "Razanne Jackson was an operations officer like you until about five years ago. She worked the Middle East, probably during some of the same time you were in Iraq and Syria with the Army.

"You guys didn't compare fun times in the sandbox?"

"We barely spoke," said Rivers.

"Well, I'm sure you'll make up for lost time when next you meet."

Dalton finished by sending along a ten-page memo summarizing the reams of investigative and intel reports, thousands of pages collected from the past few days.

Lord, how the bureaucracies churn out galaxies of words.

Thankfully, the first page was a bullet summary of the summary.

After the long day, Rivers was up for the shortest version. He'd scan the rest in the morning after coffee cleared his wakening fog.

At the top of the email, Dalton had added a note: "Nothing from the Angelos regime."

A bit snarky.

After all, law enforcement was in charge of the investigation, and that wasn't CIA's bag. Gathering intelligence was. And if Angelos was onto something, he sure as hell wouldn't be putting it in the soup for all to feast.

Rivers read the five bullet points:

- Passport theft: Inventory records show the van carried 301 U.S. and 416 French lost or stolen passports that were recovered in Europe. The transport was from a secure collection point at CDG airport. National authorities have locked the passport numbers. Threat exists that forgers could make high-quality alteration to French passports that might allow entry to more secure nations like the United States. U.S. passports are rigorously controlled for border entry but have value for obtaining internal identification like driver's licenses.
- Forensics: There is a lack of fingerprints and DNA evidence. Video and speech captured by van devices are inconclusive. Van tire was punctured by 9mm bullet, probably fired by motorcyclist observed on video from van. The bullet was recovered and possibly could be matched to a weapon, if one is recovered.
- Suspects: Nothing specific at this time. Investigation continues in the murder of suspect Aslan Baseyev in Paris. Two forged U.S. and French passports with identical photographs of a woman were recovered at the scene. The woman in the passport photographs remains unidentified. Search of internet and dark web were also inconclusive.
- Baseyev profile: The twenty-five-year-old resident of Saint-Denis in Paris was known to police and suspected to be part of criminal rings involved in drug smuggling (Captagon) and human trafficking, but he had no criminal convictions. He entered France from Ukraine in 2020. He was considered a low-rung

member of shifting Chechen criminal networks in Paris, with known members claiming the van theft with a beheading was not their work.

- Beheading: Video shows one of the thieves decapitating the courier and other thieves appear agitated by the event. Beheadings are a hallmark of ISIS. DSGE officials state that the list of suspects includes ISIS-inspired criminals who are home-grown or are refugees in France and Europe.

Rivers shook his head. No viable leads. But he did have two questions, one for Angelos and one for Laurent.

6

Rivers finished reading the email and looked up from his seat at the outdoor café, its small tables clustered on the sidewalk, the evening crowd thinning. At one table, a twenty-something woman held the hand of a graying man, perhaps a student with a teacher, a lecherous romance. At another, an older couple tired from a long day, perhaps at the Louvre. For a moment, he wondered how they would describe him at his table: Lonely? Jilted? Tired?

Simmering.

His frustration with Angelos was cresting. He texted the operations director at CIA headquarters, asking for a time when they could talk. Angelos had made it clear that Rivers was to speak to him directly. Unusual, and not working in Rivers's view. It wasn't like he was asking to have his hand held.

He sighed and remembered a line from a favorite HBO series, *Deadwood*, something like, "Your boss isn't always right, but your boss is always your boss."

His phone buzzed when he arrived back at his hotel room.

"You're beginning to irritate Mr. Angelos," said the voice. The phone ID showed it was an Angelos line, but it was not Angelos. The person behind the voice heard the pause and Rivers's uncertain intake of breath over the phone.

"It's Mike Cowen. You know who I am, right."

It wasn't a question. It was an expectation.

"Go on," said Rivers.

Cowen was the guy who always hovered around Angelos, his assistant or something. A HQ veteran who Rivers had beers with had warned him not to think of Cowen as a gofer but as Angelos's hammer.

"The boss has a lot of things in motion," his beer buddy said. "He needs someone like Cowen to help push things over the goal line."

"How am I irritating Angelos when I'm not in much contact with him?" said Rivers.

"Don't be a wise guy, Rivers."

"You've reported no meaningful information," Cowen continued. "But you apparently want to take up some of his valuable time."

Rivers cut to the chase with his question: "What prompted Angelos to send me here, *three days* after the crime? Why the time lag if it's so important?"

Now it was Cowen's turn to pause.

"Mr. Angelos doesn't have to explain himself."

"True. So, you answer."

"I am not one to try to read his mind," said Cowen.

"Well, I'm out here in the field. Not that Paris is a hardship assignment. But if Angelos wants me to shine a light on something, I need a little guidance where to look in a very dark room with my solitary flashlight."

Rivers's sharp tone and lack of using Mr. before Angelos was unmistakable over the phone.

Cowen realized Rivers wasn't going to shy away like a meek or even career-conscious employee. Instead, he saw that Rivers was just trying to make sense of things to do his job.

Rivers repeated, "What prompted Angelos to send me here *three days* after the crime?"

"I don't know what was on his mind," said Cowen. "Mr. Angelos is beset with issues with Israel, Ukraine, Iran, Russia, and China. But I can say it did suddenly arise after our forensics lab sent in a report. Our analysis of sounds picked up on a van monitor identified words seemingly spoken by the person who beheaded the driver: 'Now they will know I am here.'

"That seemed to mean something to Mr. Angelos."

"Last question, then," said Rivers. "Why did Angelos select me?"

"That I know," said Cowen. "He thinks you're street-smart and can handle yourself."

Just as the call went dead, Rivers heard, "Now prove him right."

7

Back in the car. Morning shadows in the canyon of old buildings in Paris. Better mood than yesterday.

"Bonjour, Monsieur Rivers. How did the cocktail party go? Were you the toast of the evening?" asked Laurent, prying with a playful tone in his voice.

"A good time was had by all," replied Rivers.

"So let me see how sharp you are," said Laurent. "What did you think of Martin Lyons?"

"Your boss, right?"

"Yes, a man on high," said Laurent.

"Lyons is smooth and sharp, a politician," said Rivers. "But you'd have to tell me how capable he is in running the day-to-day of your agency."

"High marks," said Laurent. "After all, he hired me."

"And how about Adam Barnes?" said Laurent.

Rivers smiled, wondering if Laurent would go through the entire guest list. "Barnes was intense."

"Yes, zealous," said Laurent. "But a man of amazing knowledge and skill. A good man to know."

Then there was silence in the car.

"Aren't you going to ask me about Raz?" said Rivers.

"Too late and too early for that," said Laurent. "Your mood suggests immediate infatuation. Quite understandable. So too late for a clinical assessment. Too early in that you haven't really been in her company … yet."

"Well, I do have a clinical assessment," said Rivers. "She's smart, beautiful, and dangerous."

"Maybe that knowledge will help you withstand her charm … if you wish to remain clinical."

Rivers didn't answer.

Then Rivers asked, "Did you know that she once worked for Angelos?"

"Of course."

Again, silence in the car. Laurent clearly wasn't saying more, for now.

"Don't take this the wrong way, but why are you working with Angelos?" asked Rivers.

"Our interests seem aligned in this matter," said Laurent. "And showing you around takes me out of the office and back on the street. That's the best of me." A simple answer to a lingering question for Rivers.

"Anything on the girl in the passport photos?" There had been nothing in the memo from last night.

"She's a ghost," said Laurent. "With luck, not a real one."

They had plowed through traffic to the outskirts of Paris and arrived at a high-rise in a sea of high-rises. This one, a tan building, eight stories with retail at the street. Residences above with balconies, many populated by welcoming plants.

The street and sidewalk were spotless; the surrounding buildings graffiti-free. Different from some of the neighborhoods they had passed through.

Above one door was a sign: Dudayev Centre.

"We have arrived," said Laurent. "It's a social club for the Chechen community. If we want to know more about the departed Aslan than the police report, there's an elder here who may help. I've known him for years."

The police file on Aslan Baseyev said he was a Chechen refugee who washed up in France around 2020. Never arrested but a person of interest in some cases dealing with drug and human smuggling, particularly women for prostitution.

"Too small to be a target of an investigation and too nimble to be the fall guy for the targets," said Laurent, who had summed it up during the drive. "Nimble until he was dead."

Inside the center to the right was a small room with the musty smell of old books and an equally musty fellow sitting in an easy chair, a book in one hand and a drink in the other. Two canes leaned against a side table that balanced a lamp and the bottle and spare glasses.

"*Ahh, je me demandais quand tu serais la,*" said the man. He did not rise.

Laurent went to the man, leaned forward and greeted him with *la bise*, a slight air kiss for each cheek.

The man motioned to offer a drink from the open bourbon bottle, but Laurent waved his hand gently to decline. It was, after all, quite early.

Laurent introduced Rivers and asked if they could speak in English, which resulted in the man giving an approving though displeased nod.

"I said, 'I wondered when you would be by,'" said the man to Rivers.

Laurent introduced the man as Musa Gugaev. He looked just like a lot of old men lost to age and drowned by alcohol and memories. But his watery eyes were still searching. His gaze bore into Rivers, noting a man in his early thirties, fit with a soldier's posture, eyes that searched back at him. A bit of danger in that look. A fitting colleague for Laurent.

Laurent had told him that he seemed to have gained Gugaev's trust after declining to arrest his then thirteen-year-old nephew for a minor crime, releasing him instead to familial discipline. Thereafter, he visited him at least twice a year, for many years now.

They spoke for several minutes of pastimes. Then the matter at hand.

"I thought my friend would come around to hear about the departed," said Gugaev. "The police are turning everything upside down. And all they have to do is think about it: the Chechen gangs here do not decapitate. Bad for business. It was an outsider."

"Do you know who the outsider is?" said Laurent.

"We can guess," said the old man. "Aslan Baseyev arrived in a recent wave of our diaspora."

He turned to Rivers and said, "I count them in waves. First, my own. We fled after Russia tried but failed to crush our home-land of Chechnya. Then, the second, when Putin turned our country into rubble. The last—Baseyev's wave—were the few Chechens who had joined ISIS and survived.

"Baseyev came here a few years ago and seemed to have left his ISIS leanings behind. He was, I am told, not a fanatic. He was a follower. But I heard that a few weeks ago he fell under the spell of a young woman who was part of an ISIS gang. He was part of the robbery with this woman and gang, but he fled the group afterward, disturbed at the beheading.

"Of course, ISIS is a hard group to leave," said the old man. "So, he is dead."

He chuckled. What mirth in all this Rivers did not see.

Laurent and the old man chatted some more and then a natural end came to their reunion.

Gugaev turned to Rivers and pointed to his two canes: "The Russians came to my town, and we fought them. Old Kalashnikov rifles against helicopters and tanks. Some of our wounded were shot as they lay, others beaten to death with iron pipes. I had a head wound that bled richly and was lying there, and one came and broke both my legs with a pipe. He must have been tired from killing so many; I can only guess that he left me unfinished thinking I would die in agony with the rats finishing me off.

"But I survived."

"America, and your generation, doesn't know the cruelties of the world."

He grabbed and shook a single cane in Rivers's direction. "If you find these ISIS dogs, take care not to be broken by their cruelties. Kill them all first."

8

They were one step out the door of the Dudayev Centre when Rivers blurted out, "Back, back, back," and grabbed Laurent's arm to pull him back inside.

Laurent instead gripped Rivers's arm and pulled him forward, saying, "Do not resist. Do not fight back, no matter what."

They were bracketed by men who looked like thugs.

Laurent and Rivers walked toward their car, parked at the curb in the next block. Two men followed about ten feet behind, one whistling to drive their threat home. Two men across the street matched their pace and locked them with their eyes.

As Rivers expected, three men suddenly appeared as they approached the corner of the block at the intersection.

Seven to two. At least.

Laurent stopped and greeted the man in the middle of the trio to their front. Rivers stood at an angle, so he could more easily peek behind him.

The whistler had moved within striking distance.

Laurent and the thugs' leader spoke in French, quick sentences. After a bit, Laurent turned to Rivers to give him an abbreviated version: "Our friend here and I have had some dealings in the past. He's asked me to get my police captain friend to stop hassling his enterprises. It is hurting his business. And he gave me some information in trade.

"He says Baseyev was a member of his group but vanished about two weeks ago. Seems he went to work with a group of women to do the heist of passports after falling for one of the girls. He says Baseyev knew a security guard at the airport with a drug problem who identified the van and its contents. A friend of Baseyev said he ran away from the gang with one of the women after the beheading.

"He doesn't know who killed Baseyev. And the women are gone now. His guess is that they are ISIS. Who else goes around cutting off people's heads?"

Rivers was listening when the whistler stepped forward with a punch that caught him to the side of his face, sending him to his knees, dizzy and pained.

At least no punches or kicks followed.

Laurent helped him up as the gang departed.

"Why did they hit me?" asked a hazy Rivers.

"You are obviously an American," said Laurent, as if that explained everything.

Rivers stumbled back to the car with Laurent. "We didn't get much that we didn't already know," he mumbled.

"Oh, we did," said Laurant. "While you were down, he told me that Baseyev told a friend that the women had come from Al-Hol in Syria."

Rivers looked up as if a splash of ice water was thrown in his face.

"Al-Hol," he said. "Damn."

9

Rivers sat at a table for two at the small restaurant that was in Raz's text invite. It was a narrow space on a narrow street with the day's specialties chalked on a board—grilled chicken and lamb, seafood, and vegetables that filled the air with a spicy aroma—adding to the delicious smells already eternally seeping from the old woods of the room.

Raz arrived and was hugged by the grayed owner at the front. Her bodyguard—a woman who had the lethal look of ex-Mossad —took a discreet position that angled the door and the room. Raz saw him and gave a polite smile.

A waiter held out her chair for her before Rivers could dislodge himself from his tight space to do it, and Raz thanked the man by name.

Her blue eyes searched his face, then she reached out and gently touched the angry welt on his right cheekbone. He trembled at her touch.

"You might need one of my bodyguards if you're going to antagonize people," said Raz.

"I can use all the help I can get," Rivers said.

"Yes, you can," said Raz.

A bottle of red wine appeared with two glasses, Raz guided him through the menu, and they ordered.

"Maybe we should talk shop first to get it out of the way, if that's possible," said Rivers.

"Not a very seductive line," she said. "Maybe that will come later."

She was toying with him, he knew.

"Angelos," he said. "You worked with my current boss."

"Yes, I was an operations officer in Cairo when I worked for him," said Raz. "He was back at Langley, the deputy operations director at the time. Our relationship was professional. At the end, though, I had had enough of things—and, my God, the GS pay-scale.

"So, I resigned and started my own business, providing security systems to boutique hotels and businesses and bodyguards as needed. I cashed in on my connections."

"You seem plugged in with the intel crowd, considering last night's cocktail party," said Rivers.

"Ahh, such a stale male crowd," she said. "Of course, they allow an attractive woman in their social mix occasionally. And I am not beyond using my charms for my benefit."

"Do you still deal with Angelos?" asked Rivers.

"Yes, on occasion, when our interests merge," said Raz.

"Like now?" said Rivers, remembering Laurent used the same wording to describe his relationship with Angelos.

Raz didn't answer, taking a sip of wine.

She sounded honest to Rivers; honest, though elusive.

"Is there anything you can tell me that I should know?" said Rivers.

Raz took another sip of wine, her eyes staring into him over the rim of the glass.

"The usual in your line of business," she said, putting down the glass. "Be careful; be very, very cautious."

"And you can tell me," said Raz, "about your time in Iraq. I heard an interesting story. Is it true?"

His answer would tell her a lot: Was he a braggart? The hero of his own story? Was it true?

Rivers had a set response to avoid the story of the incident in the rare instances it came up: simply saying, "It's fiction." And he wished it were. The last time he had spoken about it was when Angelos interviewed him.

"It's fiction," he said.

Raz wasn't going to let him dodge away. "I heard you're the Army guy who beat up two Navy SEALs."

"It's fiction," repeated Rivers softly.

"But what part of the story is true?" she said. "Some of it must be, certainly."

Rivers sat back and sighed. He looked into the beautiful eyes searching him. He reminded himself that she had been an intelligence operative and was still in the business. So, he ought to be wary. But if he was going to break through her cool reserve, he'd have to earn it.

"It's not a pretty story," he said.

"My job with Army intel was to work with the Peshmerga, the Kurdish fighters who were key to halting ISIS. I worked out of Mosul after it was liberated. One night, a woman came to our building crying that her son had been abducted. 'Not our problem,' said my commander. But then she said American soldiers had done it," said Rivers. "'Check it out,' he told me."

He paused and then continued in a monotone.

"I followed her to a building about a mile away and, leaving her outside, walked in. I had a sergeant with me, thank God. I walked in on two Navy SEALs having a little party. Booze, a teenage girl naked and showing signs of being beaten, the boy unconscious and naked below the waist. Raped. Both of them."

Anger and sadness rippled over Rivers's face.

"I was stunned. Disgusted. My sergeant put his weapon right in the face of one of the SEALs. I should have done the same to the other, but I was too slow. The guy jumped me, and it was a brutal fight. If he wasn't drunk, I wouldn't have stood a chance. I got lucky and hit him in the throat, and he went down.

"That's all, folks,' as the saying goes," said Rivers.

A long silence. He looked shaken by the memory.

"So, as I said, not a pretty story," he said.

Raz had tested for bravado and found humanity. She reached across the table and took his hand.

With her touch, something unlocked in Rivers, and he continued, "I try not to think about it. But the faces of those kids, the girl and the boy, they haunt me."

Now he looked sheepish, surprised at finding himself letting his mask drop.

This wasn't what she'd expected at all. Raz looked closely at Rivers and felt a man still wounded by what he had seen while just doing his job. She knew about such things.

She squeezed his hand and joined him in silence.

A silence shared.

10

They held hands as they strolled along the bank of the Seine, the lights of the Eiffel Tower in the distance, an early spring breeze resisting giving up its chill. Raz guided them to a few tight streets of restaurants and clubs, one a simple black door and a stone stairway down.

They both were surprised by their sudden comfort with each other.

Raz told him that she had grown up in New York City, with frequent trips to Paris. Her father was an FBI agent dealing with organized crime; her mother a translator at the United Nations who was born in Beirut and raised in Paris before moving to the United States. Raz, as a result, spoke English, French, and Arabic, and, as an honor student in economics at Columbia, she had found easy entry into the CIA.

There were as many silent pauses as words, which seemed natural to both.

Her company was headquartered in the Le Marais neighborhood, and Raz said creating a company was the best thing she could have done. It gave her financial freedom and, she laughed, now she was a demanding boss rather than a difficult employee.

"Oh, I have trouble seeing you as difficult," said Rivers.

Raz frowned. "I'm very difficult," she said. "Most of all with myself."

The jazz club's stone stairway was twenty-five irregular steps into what once was a large wine cellar and now had a stage at one end and tables and seating surrounding a dance floor. A sax sounded a deep, lazy blare over a bunch of couples hooked over one another in slow motion. The place had a seductive scent of wine, perfume, and sweat from the bodies moving in tight quarters.

Their wine arrived, and Raz and Rivers sipped and then moved to the dance floor as the band took up a swing number from the '40s. They moved fast to the music, then slow to the next as the music alternated in tempo. Fast, then slow.

A slow number started, and Raz seemed to melt into Rivers. Their bodies moved slowly as one. He could feel her through her dress. Warm and close. He kissed her on her neck. She bent her neck to welcome his kisses. And then she broke into a giggle. And Rivers bent back to look into her beautiful face, and he saw a woman completely happy in the moment.

Later, they moved back to their table, and Raz motioned with her head toward the restrooms and moved in that direction.

Rivers waited, and a waiter arrived. He said the woman he was with had paid the bill and there was a note for him. Rivers read the note several times, and then put it in his pocket. He was confused.

Raz's note read, *Don't be smitten, but don't be a stranger.*

11

So, Rivers was moving back to the sandbox. Destination: Al-Hol.

Angelos's alter ego, Cowen, responded to Rivers's information about the ISIS camp in a phone call at 3 a.m.

"You're on a flight this morning to Dubai, then onto Erbil, Iraq, one of your old Army haunts," said Cowen. "Find the identities of this gang of women that may have come from the detention camp."

Rivers wasn't too sleepy not to point out the obvious: "There's CIA paramilitary in the area. Wouldn't it be faster to task them?"

Moving from Paris to the sandbox and Al-Hol in particular wasn't something to eagerly accept—not once you'd spent time there, as Rivers had.

"The boss wants you to go."

Enough said.

Al-Hol was in the middle of nowhere, a detention camp in Syria just over the line from Iraq. Endless rows of white tents ringed by barbed wire on a desolate patch of high desert. Water had to be trucked in. No small task for the estimated 55,000 women in black burqas and children, surviving families of ISIS fighters left after the caliphate was crushed.

No one wanted them, and years had passed. And almost all the guards had memories of murdered family and razed villages at the hands of the Islamic State.

Rivers had been there twice as an Army intel officer, observing as guards and Kurdish forces combed through the miles of camp for weapons and deadenders: hidden men and maturing teens being groomed for a new fight.

He remembered his last time, when a tunnel and a dugout cave were discovered, with three women chained inside, two newly dead and one dying. She told her rescuers their crime: approaching the camp administration to help weed out the hard-core ISIS.

These white tents offered no white flag of surrender by the ISIS fanatics.

Rivers daydreamed on the flight into Dubai, a bad dream from his last time in Iraq.

He had worked closely for months with a young Kurdish officer named Alex Nuri. Together, they collected prisoners at the front, with Alex questioning the ISIS members and translating for Rivers, who then fed the information to command HQ. They traveled, ate, barracked, and hit the deck together when mortar or sniper fire was incoming. Rivers went with Alex on visits to his family. And then, like the snap of the fingers, they were joking one day, with Alex's handsome face open in a laugh, when a sniper round cracked through the air and slammed into his head.

In that moment, Rivers entered a secret society of men and women who had touched death and loss at the level of wearing a comrade's blood splatter.

While on the flight, Rivers contacted Alex's father, Daryan Nuri, in Iraq. He had misgivings but knew Nuri would be hurt if he didn't call. He had been embraced by the Nuri family at lunches and dinners, and forever was an honorary part of it after Rivers bore Alex's body back from the Mosul frontline. If anyone had inroads into Al-Hol, it would be Nuri.

Rivers called during his flight into Dubai, and Nuri instantly nixed the offer of dinner in Erbil, where Nuri's businesses were centered. Instead, Nuri insisted that Rivers visit him at the family estate. He would make the arrangements.

Who was Rivers to argue with one of the Kurd's richest men, with vast holdings in oil, media, and finance?

Rivers flew on Nuri's business jet from Dubai to Sulay-maniyah, his hometown and a jewel of a city tucked away in the mountains along Iraq's border with Iran. A Bentley picked him up at the airport, and the driver informed him that Mr. Nuri would see him in an hour for cocktails at the main residence.

He was dropped off at a guest villa, one of several styled as modern-cast stone and concrete buildings that seemed to flow from the mountains that were their backdrop. A small stream burbled through the large property, which also held a swimming pool, tennis courts, garages with apartments for the help, and a slew of guards who were practiced in being unobtrusive. And a ton of security and surveillance gadgets.

Rivers dropped his go bag on the floor of the nearest bedroom and gazed out a wide window at a looming mountain, gray in the early shadows of evening. He had been good at walling off so many memories, only occasionally lapsing into staring in the dark some nights, sometimes triggered by a laugh that sounded like Alex's or the face of a certain child.

Now, here, gazing through a window at a jagged peak—exactly as he had done before—he thought of his friend, the Nuri family, and even his own family, which he no longer had.

Nuri arrived outside the guest villa in a Mercedes convertible and said, "Get in. We'll have drinks later."

He motored away, the heater on, but with the cool mountain air blasting their faces. Rivers had put on a heavier jacket like Nuri's, which his host had thoughtfully provided.

Nuri took delight in driving Rivers around Sulaymaniyah to show off its rich menu of culture and enterprise. It had just shy of a million people, with four museums and three universities, all nestled in a valley among the towering mountains. Rivers had taken the tour in earlier days, but with Alex it had included a roll through nightclubs.

Nuri stopped the Mercedes at Sarchnar Park, which had tree-lined walkways and benches along a river, the water clear, and the air shockingly fresh.

"Let's walk," said Nuri. Which they did in silence for quite some time, until Nuri eventually spoke.

"Thomas, I am happy to see you, and sorry that you have not visited since Alex's death. You always will be part of our family," said Nuri. "But I do understand. It is painful, isn't it?"

"More distant now but never gone," said Rivers. "And certainly not the pain of a father losing a son."

Nuri nodded and said, "I assume you are back to help finish the business with those devils. I would be happy to help you with that."

"I need to talk to someone who knows the inside of Al-Hol," said Rivers.

"I know of such a person," said Nuri.

Later, they had Irish whiskey in Nuri's den with one wall of glass looking out at a mountain. Family photos stood on a table. Alex by himself and with his brother Shvan in their Peshmerga officer uniforms. He now ran Nuri's Erbil main office. A younger brother, tall in a suit, now represented the Nuri family interests in Athens. And Leila, last seen by Rivers when she was in high school, when Alex told him that she had a crush on him. Now in a slim dress with bare shoulders, Leila was a student at New York University.

They toasted Alex, and Nuri picked up his picture and began to say something, then paused to collect himself.

"A sacrifice to protect his family, to save our Kurdish people," he finally said. "The Peshmerga were the wall that ISIS broke against."

Nuri paused again, a faraway look in his eyes. And Rivers turned aside, discreetly wiping a tear from his eye.

12

By Rivers's second cup of coffee the next morning, Nuri had already set things in motion. One of his employees in Erbil had checked with Nadia Hatami's organization—a combination women's refugee center, community grocery, and shelter—and was told she was visiting her sister at the Al-Hol detention camp in Syria for several days, something she often did.

This was followed by Nuri personally calling Nadia on her cell phone to arrange a visit for Rivers. She knew Nuri personally as a longtime contributor to her efforts in Erbil.

"She will see you at Al-Hol," said Nuri. "She stays in housing provided by the UN when she visits. Be warned, Nadia views Americans as fools and doesn't suffer fools well."

"Any particular reason?" asked Rivers, who could think of several.

"Nadia is Yazidis, who suffered particularly at the hands of ISIS," said Nuri. "She sees the United States as a superpower that did nothing to protect the Yazidis and have contributed little since. You have to realize who she is: she was about fifteen when most of her family were executed before her eyes and then endured months as an ISIS sex slave. She told me that she escaped after stabbing her latest ISIS rapist in the throat with a sharpened wooden stick and then dodging through the streets of Mosul to the Kurdish battle lines.

"Nadia is tough," said Nuri. "She is only in her mid-twenties now but a leader in her community in Erbil. Many who have endured what she has are shattered here and here." He pointed at his head and heart. "Not Nadia.

"I have arranged to get you to Al-Hol," said Nuri. "My people can be trusted but be careful. It isn't particularly dangerous anymore—but it is not *not* dangerous."

It took a half day to get to Al-Hol, first taking what Rivers thought of as Air Nuri—in this case a prop four-seater—from Sulaymaniyah to a militarized airport just over the border in Syria. It had been a main staging area for the U.S. Operation Inherent Resolve and then was turned over to the allied Syrian Democratic Forces. Somehow Nuri had the OK to use the airport.

As soon as he landed, Rivers was met by Jack Rojas, the leader of a CIA paramilitary team working out of the airport. Rojas handed over a SIG Sauer handgun and his best wishes.

"They told me you were coming in and going to Al-Hol," said Rojas. "Better you than us. That place gives me the creeps. Killers roaming inside and kids staring at you from behind the wire. There's your guy." He pointed to a dirty but well-maintained Toyota SUV with a guy named Murat at the wheel, Nuri's pick to drive him two hours to Al-Hol.

Murat looked less than happy. "We're leaving late for the camp. We shouldn't be out on the road at night for a return trip," he said.

"I doubt my meeting there will take long," said Rivers.

"That will work. I can go fast."

"I thought this was a safe area," said Rivers.

"It is, until it isn't," said Murat.

He pointed to the back seat, reached back and pulled loose a canvas cover, and Rivers saw two AK-47s, magazines in the weapons.

"In case it isn't," said Murat.

———

Rivers listened, for Nadia was not a woman to be hurried.

She was dressed in the bright colors favored by Yazidis women. The right side of her face was the smooth skin of a young woman, but the left had mottled scars from cigarette burns. And her look cut right into him.

A young woman who worked for the UN sat with them and translated. "I have heard that your Western internet sometimes refers to Al-Hol as 'All Hell,'" said Nadia. "But this camp is far better than the graves of my family."

Nadia gave a roll call of horror.

"ISIS executed our men, boys over twelve, adult women. They rolled their bodies into ditches. Boys and girls were beaten, raped, and flogged with whips. Girls like me and younger—I was 15—were sold or married to ISIS fighters as sex slaves or put into houses for continual rape. I was one of those.

"So many of us killed ourselves."

Rivers had heard and seen signs of the brutality before, but it was different hearing it from Nadia, who spoke with a spit of anger and bitterness in her voice. He shifted on the hard bench outside an administrative building.

"So why are you and your sister here with these hated people?" asked Rivers.

"There are Yazidis women in the camp, several dozen. They could have left long ago or walk out with me today, but the rules say their children are ISIS and would have to be left behind," Nadia said. "Stupid rules. They are afraid the children have been trained as terrorists. Some have been, but not the Yazidis children. These women will not leave their children. My sister and her children are behind that barbed wire. So, I come to help with food and money and hope."

"There are a group of women in Paris who came from here," said Rivers, stating it as fact rather than question. "They killed a man and stole passports…"

Nadia cut in, "I am not surprised and you shouldn't be. Most of the women and children in the camp are harmless. They were brought here by their husbands or taken as slaves. But there are evil ones in the camp," she said. "My sister told me that the worst ones were smuggled out. I have told the UN this, and some women came forward. Nothing happened, except those women were murdered in the camp."

"Who did you tell at the UN?"

"The security chief Sykes," said Nadia. "He did nothing except, I am sure, tell the evil ones."

The UN translator was a friend of Nadia's and now looked pale and frightened. His questioning had flipped the lid open on a dangerous situation.

"When we're done here," said Rivers, looking at the translator, "get out. Say there's a sudden illness with someone at home. Leave in the morning." The young woman nodded in understanding.

"Do you know the names of the people who left?" asked Rivers.

Nadia nodded. "Some. I gave them to Sykes, but I remember clearly the two most feared: Dogu Matsoy, a Chechen, and a woman simply called Umm, who was said to have trained girls to be suicide bombers. Matsoy left almost a year ago; Umm perhaps a month back."

"Why don't you come back with me?" said Rivers to Nadia.

He had checked in with Sykes when he arrived, showing identification as an inspector with the U.S. State Department on a routine check. He had the feeling they were being observed, and his asking for Nadia could have put her in the crosshairs.

Nadia smiled for once, or at least the smile her damaged face was capable of. "I have been too scared to be scared anymore," she said. "I will remain here.

"We Yazidis believe evil is created by man and not God, and that there is no Satan and no hell, just people doing good or bad here on earth," Nadia said.

"But I now pray now that there is an eternal hell, just for these evil ones."

13

Murat checked the early evening sky and looked aggrieved at how long Rivers had taken. Then he winked and said, "We'll be all right, but we're going fast." Still, he exacted some measure of revenge by cranking up the music in the car and lighting up a foul cigarette, while gripping the wheel with one hand and shoving down on the accelerator.

The white rows of tents blew by and then they entered a hazy world, the sun's last rays lighting up sand and dirt blown up by an evening breeze. The world outside the windshield was a light brown mist on a desolate landscape.

Rivers drifted a bit, relaxing after his wearing conversation with Nadia. He was writing his memo in his mind, readying to type and send it on the encrypted satellite phone that Rojas had given him back at the airbase. Umm, Matsoy, Sykes. The CIA could access the UN files on them and move the investigation ahead. His work here was done.

"What did the Yazidis woman tell you about that awful place?" said Murat.

Rivers ignored the question.

"What do you know about the smuggling around here?" asked Rivers.

"Your smuggling is someone else's livelihood," said Murat.

"Have you heard of ISIS women being smuggled out?"

"ISIS are evil, and there are bound to be evil smugglers," said Murat. "And there are a lot of ISIS supporters not in the camp."

One moment these words; the next, Murat and Rivers saw the danger.

As the SUV sped over a small rise in the highway, a white truck blocked the road.

"Jesus," yelled Rivers.

Murat slammed on the brakes, and they both instantly assessed their options. All bad. Stopping and surrendering was out of the question. There wasn't room or time to skid into a reverse. A small ridge ran to the left, bumpy ground to the right.

"Right, right," yelled Rivers.

Murat slammed the accelerator back down and wrenched the SUV to the right, where there seemed to be a hope of relatively flat ground, but they didn't clear a gully cleanly, back tires hitting a lip that sent them airborne like an unguided missile. They landed with a bone-crunching thud, still at speed but with the back axle broken and digging into the hard-packed ground. The SUV spun fast and then more slowly. They came to rest one hundred yards off the road, along a deep, dry ravine.

The music in the SUV played on.

Rivers felt pain in his back and right leg and shook his head to clear his senses. He looked over at Murat, who was unconscious after being thrown into his door. Seat belts had saved their lives; but the airbags hadn't deployed, probably because they'd been stolen and sold.

In an instant, Murat's head jerked forward from a shot and then, amid splatter, the remaining part flipped back. Rivers felt wetness on his left arm and face.

Rivers slumped down and tried his door, which somehow came open, and he slid to the ground, landing shoulder-first. He rolled behind the engine, which ticked in its death throes. There was no flurry of shots to finish him.

Stunned, injured, he still had enough of his senses to take inventory. His SIG Sauer and sat phone were still on his belt. Not that either would help in this moment.

His training kicked in: *Get off the X.*

The *X* was this attack site.

Move.

He skittered into the ravine near the SUV as he heard voices approaching. It was deep and he could stand, although his injured back and leg were buckling him over.

One way was back toward Al-Hol, perhaps fifteen miles. The other, toward the secure airport, over one hundred.

Once they found the ravine, they would expect he'd take the short route.

He moved the far way for now, into the growing darkness. There were shadows in the bends of the ravine. He hugged the walls as he limped along.

Rivers heard the men at the wreck. And heard some men drop into the ravine. They seemed to be moving away, toward Al-Hol. Then he heard, in the near distance, movement coming toward him.

A swoosh and flames leaped from the wrecked SUV.

As Rivers moved, he hit the emergency alert button on his sat phone, which had a tracker. Help would be on the way.

He was hurt, with no water and only a vague notion of where he was. He moved as fast as he could, but then pulled himself from a shadow up atop the edge of the ravine. He could not prevent being overtaken by his pursuers. His only play now was to ambush them. His hand on the SIG Sauer trembled.

Rivers was sure of three things: He had seen a white truck at Al-Hol like the one that blocked the road. These thugs wanted to capture him rather than kill him, which they easily could have done already. They would kill him after torturing him for information.

Well, a fourth thing too: He would not allow himself to be taken alive.

14

H is hand was now steady gripping the SIG Sauer.

A figure came toward him in the ravine while he hid flat on an upper edge, hearing one person stumble in the dusk and shadows of the ravine, his path lit with a pencil flashlight. Noisy and lit. Definitely not a well-trained soldier. The faint light bounced slightly with each footstep coming closer.

His heart beat rapidly and he was mindful to keep his breathing quiet. He was an able shot but had never fired at a live target, much less with his own life in the balance. *Stay calm, calm, breathe.* The man was now about five feet below him in the ravine, and Rivers extended his weapon and fired three times.

He slid off the top of the ravine and hunched over the dead figure. He picked up the pencil flashlight and, before extinguishing it, ran it over the body. It was a kid, a teenager. Rivers was too busy picking him over—taking the AK-47 and an ID card—to feel anything. The shots would have been heard.

Rivers had planned his next step while tracking the pencil

flashlight's approach. He could stay and fight here but doubted he'd survive. He could keep going down the ravine, but he would be overtaken. He could climb up the other side of the ravine and work his way along the road, but his attackers could box him in between the ravine and the road.

So, he pulled himself up on the ravine lip where he had been and headed at a diagonal angle away from the scene. Into the unknown. He was hunched over, pain shooting from his hip down his right leg, but he found he could move at a decent clip. He picked a star as his beacon and limped away.

How much time was he ahead of his attackers?

Fear. He had to push it away to think. He breathed deeply as he limped. The fear was dampened yet still there—a small headache behind his eyes, a tightening of his chest, his stomach acidy. The pain in his back and leg actually helped him focus.

There would be hours of darkness, but once the attackers discovered his trail, they could come quick. And he guessed the way Murat had been slaughtered in the dusk and dust by one shot, an attacker was an able marksman with a long gun. Maybe with a nightscope.

Would his suspicion be confirmed when a bullet smashed into his back before he even heard its sound? Would he hear the angry wasp of a near miss?

He kept moving.

He was no match in a gunfight. Exposed in the open with a short-range AK and a close-contact handgun.

He kept moving.

He had no water in a parched land. An unknown star to guide him to an unknown destination.

He kept moving.

It was good that the high desert night was cooling, and the

dust had settled, and his beacon star was shining. There was still-ness, and it was calming.

Rivers remembered the note in his pocket, and his hand brushed the pocket with the paper. *Don't be a stranger.*

No, he wouldn't be a stranger if he could help it.

He kept moving.

Rivers knew he couldn't outdistance any pursuers for very long. At the same time, they weren't trained soldiers, if the kid in the ravine was an example. After stumbling along for about fifteen minutes, he still saw no tracking light, so he stopped and awkwardly sat on the hard-packed ground, his right hip and leg throbbing.

He took off his jacket and spread it over his head and bent down over his sat phone, trying to keep any possible light from escaping and broadcasting his position.

Quickly, he sent a message to the CIA control center for Angelos and Cowen. It was written staccato, the best his blurry vision and shaking fingers could manage:

ambush/gunmen follo
chechen dogu matsoy/woman umm isis leader left ah
nhatami/un translator in danger ah
un sykes probably dirty

Rivers hit Send and struggled to rise. All he had to do now was stay in the game.

15

The emergency alert from Rivers's phone flashed urgent red squares onto computers at security control centers at CIA headquarters, the Pentagon, and the nearest U.S. military command in Erbil. No one had to be told what to do. There were procedures.

Immediately, the CIA controllers messaged back to Rivers's phone so it would vibrate in a call for confirmation. Vibrate, because sound in certain situations could be deadly. It was rare that the stiff inset button of the phone alert could be triggered accidentally, but it could happen.

Rivers answered the vibrations with three presses on the recessed emergency button. Now his phone would continue to pulse his location and help would be rushed his way.

That wouldn't reach him in the next hours, though. He was in the middle of nowhere.

Angelos was poker-faced as he walked into the CIA control center with Cowen at his side in response to the emergency alert. Angelos was an almost thirty-year veteran who had cut his teeth in the chaos of the Global War on Terror: Afghanistan, Iraq, Syria, the Philippines, Africa, Congress. A field man turned bureaucrat after a bombing in the field left him with occasional bouts of vertigo.

Damn, he liked Rivers. He was particularly fond of the few—like Cowen and, once upon a time, Raz—who were what he called, in a nod to his beloved baseball, "closers." Give them difficult, dangerous, thankless missions and they'd pull it off. Maybe he was wrong about Rivers; maybe he wasn't one of the few. He was about to find out.

One thing was certain: Rivers was in real trouble to send up a flare for help.

Action proceeded quickly. The CIA redirected two drones toward the scene. Two CIA paramilitary teams were on the move, the one at the airport closest. Special Forces were streaming toward the area. Helicopters were readying.

Soon enough, Angelos and Cowen were given the message from Rivers sent via the control center:

ambush/gunmen follo
chechen dogu matsoy/woman umm isis left ah
nhatami/un translator in danger ah
un sykes probably dirty

Angelos looked relieved; Rivers had delivered. He turned to Cowen. "Now we have something to work with."

Hours passed. Rivers's lips were cracked and caked with dust. He was dragging his right leg. He kept telling himself, *Go straight, go*, so he wouldn't drift off and, God forbid, circle back into his pursuers. He had started walking toward one bright star and after a few hours changed to another, just a wrinkle to maybe slow down his pursuers.

How close were his pursuers?

He peeked back and saw faint light from his pursuers tracking the drag marks of his damaged leg in the dirt. He knew his flight had to soon turn to fight.

Rivers almost fell into a ravine. He saw it at the last moment, and a wave of fear hit him: If he was so inattentive, how could he put up a real fight? But the fear gave him a boost of energy and refocused his mind.

This is where I'll make my stand.

He slid into the shallow ravine, which was only as high as his elbows. Soon he could make out four lights, all small beams tracking his scuffs in the dirt.

Poor odds: four to one, and a long gun among them.

All the physical hardships and mental challenges of his Army and CIA training gave him some small measure of confidence: *Just do your job now, as you've been trained.*

Rivers moved quietly to his right in the ravine, finding a spot where he could rest the AK-47 that he had taken from the kid in the ravine on the ravine edge and, after firing, move around a slight bend to another shooting position.

His only chance was to keep his nerve and surprise them at close range.

Four shapes were now distinct, the pencil lights brighter and tilted to the ground.

Wait, wait, wait.

16

The helicopter touched with a bump, and Jack Rojas and his CIA paramilitary team jumped to the ground hidden in a cloud of whirling dust. They darted hunched to clear positions facing out in a clock pattern. In an instant, their ride was gone, low and quiet and running dark.

A mile separated them from a spot where the team could intercept Rivers. A surveillance drone had been marking his trek in the high desert and that of four pursuers. A voice told him over his headset that the drone showed Rivers had slid into a ravine and looked to be setting up an ambush. Move quick.

As if Rojas had to be told.

Angelos had rallied Rojas's team from their airport duty station, set them on the helicopter, and flung them out into the high desert to rescue Rivers. Another CIA paramilitary team was moving to the Al-Hol detention camp to protect two women: a UN translator and Nadia Hatami. Special Forces were directed to the scene of the attack on Rivers's vehicle, although a drone showed no activity there: just a smoldering wreck and a white truck nearby that appeared to be abandoned.

Ticktock. Tasks given, armed men on the move, and lives in the balance in a race against time. Not an unusual mission for Rojas's team.

Rojas and his men hadn't spoken a word on the ground. Their night vision goggles were down, and they were moving, quietly and rapidly as a well-practiced team.

Then, the deep bark of an AK-47 cut through the night. Followed in a moment by the sharp snap of a rifle. Then silence.

Damn, it's started, thought Rojas.

Trying to rescue someone during a gunfight is how that person gets killed.

They were moving quickly in the ravine, Rojas at the front, ready to stop and shout, *"Rivers!"* upon sighting anyone. Whoever it was had better answer quickly.

The team's sniper, Maxwell, set up, aiming out onto the open ground where the bad guys supposedly were. He was guessing the rifle shot came from a prone position that for the moment was hidden from him. He was ready to fire upon any flash of rifle fire.

Rojas guessed they were close. Sweat dripped down his back in the cool, black night.

Rivers had slunk down and moved after he fired his AK-47. He knew from a grunt and a howl that at least one of the four pursuers was wounded. But damn, the return fire from a high-powered rifle had whizzed close. He was dealing with a trained marksman.

He could guess their game plan: The marksman would keep watch to target him if he poked up his head. His pals would split right and left, move out perhaps fifty yards each, and slip into the ravine, and then work their way toward him.

His best bet, slim as it was, was to move deeper into the ravine and hunt for a pursuer. So, he did, as rapidly as he could to his right. But he was stumbling in the dark and dragging his bum leg and making too much noise. He stopped.

Let a noisemaker come to him.

Rivers lay flat on the bottom of the ravine, his handgun at the ready, selecting it over the AK-47 with its hard kick. He was betting the incoming killer would be scanning for an upright figure and might initially overlook him.

He heard faint footfalls. Someone trying to be careful, but still a disturbance of the stillness.

There. Maybe twenty-five feet away. A silhouette in the darkness. A muted crunch of shoes on rocky ground.

Fifteen feet.

Rivers leveled his handgun.

In that moment, the figure stopped, perhaps either seeing Rivers or sensing the small movement.

Rivers fired three times.

Rojas heard three shots—so close—and heard a body fall.

"Rivers," he called out.

A voice came in reply: "About fuckin' time."

17

Rivers was alive; his pursuers weren't.

Another gunman in the ravine had tried to shoot it out with the CIA team, an ill-advised decision. The marksman had run. Rojas's men pursued and called for him to surrender. But after a mile or so, he flung himself to the ground and shakily took aim. Maxwell, the CIA sniper, fired twice before the marksman got off a shot. Once to kill, a second to be certain.

Team members took photos of the dead men and collected their phones, wallets and pocket litter in individual plastic bags. Three of them appeared to be locals; the marksman had ID as the deputy security officer at Al-Hol. A driver's license had him as a Brit. Another ID had him as retired British Army, military police.

Their bodies were left in the high desert to be picked up later. The animals could have at them until then.

It was a rough neighborhood.

The argument came right away: Angelos wanted Rivers transported by helicopter directly to an Army medical facility in Erbil, about an hour away. Rivers said no. He wanted to go back to Al-Hol.

"We've got a team at Al-Hol," said Angelos. "You're not needed there. You need to get some medical attention."

"Does the team have Sykes and Nadia and the translator?" asked Rivers.

"Sykes fled and we've got drones and roadblocks up," said Angelos. He realized that Rivers felt responsible for Nadia Hatami and the UN translator. "There's nothing positive to be gained by your return to the detention camp."

Rivers noted the avoidance in the answer. He took a deep breath and calmly said, "They're dead, aren't they?"

Angelos no longer hedged. "Yes, they are."

"More reason for me to be back at Al-Hol," said Rivers. "I need to talk to Nadia's sister. I need to review Sykes's file, and the files on this Dogu and Umm. I know what I'm looking for. I can do it fastest."

Angelos mulled it over. Rivers was making a good argument.

"Let me talk to the medic first," he said. And Rivers passed him the sat phone.

"What's Rivers's condition?" asked Angelos.

The medic had examined Rivers and pumped a saline solution into the dehydrated and exhausted man. He had checked his injuries: a badly bruised hip and back, a swollen knee. He quickly explained all that to Angelos. Along with the information that Rivers's blood pressure was OK, and he had passed a cognitive test for head injuries.

"One question," said Angelos. "Is he good to go?"

The medic looked at Rivers and saw one of those guys who was driven.

"He's good to go, sir."

Rivers felt tired to the bone.

An accumulation of physical battery, mental stress, and now —it was hard to say exactly what to call it—a moral injury? His interview at Al-Hol had put Nadia Hatami and the UN translator in harm's way, and they were murdered. This day and night, with its frightful events, had happened so quickly. It left him sad and angry, but highly motivated.

He looked only half human when the helicopter landed. When he arrived at Al-Hol the day before, he had the look of a U.S. government inspector in the field, his cover job. He wore a polo shirt, khaki pants, a blue windbreaker affixed with the State Department seal, and Keen hiking boots. Now he was a filthy, bent man, smelling of dried sweat and Murat's blood, covered in ground-in dirt, his hair disheveled, and clothes ripped. And he still had the black eye from Paris.

"Maybe we get you a hot shower and clean clothes," said Rojas, who had stayed with him. But Rivers wouldn't be delayed from what he wanted to do.

He was steered into the UN administration building to a small office, and he asked to see the head of the UN contingent. While he waited, he called his Kurdish benefactor.

"Sad news, Mr. Nuri, but your man Murat was killed in an attack," said Rivers.

"I heard a few hours ago," said Nuri. "At least you survived.

My Peshmerga colleagues were following the intel chatter during the night and kept me informed. Those damn ISIS dogs.

"Murat worked for me for many years. A man to be trusted, no small thing," said Nuri. "I know his family. I will provide for them."

"Nadia also was murdered," said Rivers.

Nuri was silent for a moment.

"Yes," he said, his voice heavy with sadness, "Another good one taken."

18

David Talbot, the UN administrator, walked into the office and was shocked by the battered look of Rivers.

"We have a medical facility," he began, about to offer aid.

"We have work to do first," said Rivers. "To what extent do you know what happened?"

Talbot was a too-thin man who looked worn down by his year's work for a mission of unrelenting turmoil. The UN provided food, water, medicine, a school, and some internet access in the camp to the 55,000 women and children and a few straggler men. Always too little. Always a violent few.

He once had looked at the children occasionally staring at him from behind the barbed wire and felt angry and energized. Now he walked by their stares. Which told him it was time to go.

"Your security guy Sykes and his deputy attacked me and have now killed three people. What did you know about them?" said Rivers.

"I inherited them when I arrived a year ago," said Talbot.

"They were in charge of protecting the UN mission. They seemed to do their job. The Syrian Democratic Forces are in charge of the guards ringing the camp."

Rivers decided the only reason Sykes and his deputy would take the enormous step of attacking him on the way out of Al-Hol was fear of what Nadia Hatami had told him. Something criminal, something big. It was a calculated risk to kill him and blame his death on ISIS or smugglers. But the attack had gone sideways.

"Complaints of theft?"

"Nothing," said Talbot. "I've been doing this type of work for two decades; there's always some theft of food and medicine along the way. But it wasn't a major issue here. I credited Sykes and the Syrian guard commander. If a small portion of the supplies were lifted when they watched it carted into the camp, it wasn't much. By any metric, Sykes was doing a good job."

"What about smuggling people out?" After all, Nadia had told him that this Dogu and Umm had left the camp.

Talbot sat back and looked out the office window, to a great view of barbed wire and white tents. At least no children were staring back at him just then.

"There were no reports of that."

"No reports from Sykes, right," said Rivers, making it a statement rather than a question.

No answer, which was an answer.

Rivers had been sizing up Talbot. He didn't think he was lying or hiding anything. He was a bureaucrat keeping the UN supplies and services moving, unable to see the rot in his organization. Or not looking for it. After all, wasn't there always a little rot in these hellholes?

He sighed. He was being too hard on Talbot. The guy had

been living in this high-desert dust and unrelenting stress, trying to keep these people alive. More than he had been doing. Talbot might be on the outside of the barbed wire, but his life was still ensnared by it.

"I need to see Sykes's files, and his deputy's," said Rivers. "And files on a man named Dogu something and a woman Umm. And I'd like Nadia's sister and children brought here. I want to interview her."

Talbot got up to make it happen, but Rivers spoke again as he reached the door.

"What was the name of your translator who was murdered?" asked Rivers.

"April Tafesh," said Talbot. "She was twenty-four, and an American of Syrian descent, an administrative aide. Quite a lovely young woman. She would go to the camp school and read to the little ones in her off-hours."

Talbot smiled at the thought of her, then stopped and stared blankly at Rivers.

He had no more words.

The personnel files on security chief Brian Sykes and his now deceased deputy were what Rivers expected because they had been under Sykes's watchful eyes. Both men were hired after serving with the British Army in Iraq as military police helping to secure a base. Sykes was a lieutenant, the other a sergeant. The files had dates for them leaving the army and being hired at Al-Hol, but no vetting review or interviews, no references.

It smelled of an old-boys network. These guys knew or paid

off someone, probably both. These were good paying jobs. Especially with opportunities for some larceny on the side.

Talbot had dug out files on Dogu Matsoy and an Umm al-Nasr and dropped them off on the desk before Rivers as if they were radioactive.

There were about two dozen pages in Dogu's file.

The identification page had scanty data and a photo of a young man with hard eyes and a thick beard. Most answer spaces were left blank: parents' names, parents' nationality, place of birth, date of birth, entry date to Al-Hol. All blank.

Accepting signature: Brian Sykes.

The next page was a form entitled, *Circumstances of Capture.* Also blank.

Rivers thumbed through the rest.

There was a photocopy of his camp ID card and a medical exam form. At least someone had looked at him: Dogu was listed at five foot nine and 150 pounds. Brown and brown. A jagged shrapnel scar on his right forearm. No sign of malnutrition or physical defect.

Under Summary was one word: hostile. No signature on the medical exam.

Next were pages of violent incident reports, with Dogu as a rumored suspect, though each was marked "no witnesses."

Gossip was one thing, but there was no line to rat at the ISIS camp. Silence was the rule, enforced with a knife.

Now here was something: a page with an exemption allowing Dogu to remain at Al-Hol instead of being shipped to a nearby prison for ISIS men at age eighteen, as was customary. The reason: blank. The exemption was approved by Sykes.

There was a form allowing Dogu to work unloading food and supply trucks.

And that was it.

Nadia had said Dogu was long gone from the camp. And Talbot reported back that, while guards were trying to hunt him down in camp, no one had seen him for a long time.

Quite the mystery man.

Umm al-Nasr was even more of a mystery.

Her file was empty.

19

Hanaa was Nadia's younger sister, but she looked older. Kidnapped by ISIS, forced to be the wife of two ISIS fighters—both now dead—the mother of three children, survivor of a violent refugee camp, all of which would definitely account for her worn look. As a Yazidis captive of ISIS, she could have walked out of the Al-Hol detention camp at any time. But her children were branded as ISIS and could not leave. So, she stayed.

She was sitting in a chair in an office as Talbot directed, a small figure in her black burka, her eyes to the floor, seemingly compliant as her life had taught her to be, as a way to survive. Talbot was in the room to translate. Her children were playing in the next room, rumbling with an overtaxed, leaking air conditioner.

Rivers introduced himself, staying with his State Department cover, but then Hanaa interrupted him, her eyes on him. "Nadia is dead."

A statement, not a question. She had certainly observed all the armed men arriving and the oddity of being called with her children to the UN building, but Rivers wondered if anyone had already told her of Nadia's murder. He looked at Talbot, who simply shrugged.

For Hanaa, it wasn't hard to figure out. Her sister would be with her now if she could.

"Yes. I'm sorry to tell you that your sister has been killed, along with the young UN woman who sometimes helped at the school," said Rivers. He paused to give Hanaa time to absorb this, but she quickly said, "What do you want from me?"

"We're looking for information on a Dogu Matsoy, Umm al-Nasr, and the security man Sykes."

"I told her things here as sister's gossip. She always was trying to help her sister, help others," said Hanaa. "Nadia didn't understand that the fence here did not contain Dogu's reach."

"Tell me more about Dogu," said Rivers.

Hanaa searched Rivers's face, as if her gaze could penetrate flesh and bone and find the center of his being. He couldn't imagine what her life had been like—her family and its Yazidis village destroyed, the violent sexual assaults by ISIS fighters, and the struggle to keep her children alive. It wasn't new to Rivers, who had spent time in this sandbox with the Army. But it was a fresh reminder of what he tried to forget—a harsh, ugly world populated by murderers and thieves, and people just trying to survive.

"I have things to tell you," said Hanaa. "But only if you get me and my children out of here. We are not a threat. Most of the women and children here just want to go home. They are not threats. The few that are, you can see. They do not hide it."

Rivers had anticipated moving Hanaa, especially after last

night's murders. She'd be a target. He had talked to Talbot, who had parole power under certain conditions, and, with Rivers's intervention, Daryan Nuri had agreed to take Hanaa and her children to Erbil.

"You and your children will be in the care of Nadia's organization in Erbil," said Rivers. "You'll leave right after this conversation."

Hanaa nodded. No thanks given. This was a transaction, after all.

"Dogu?" prompted Rivers.

"A young man to whom the mean ones listened. He liked to sleep with the pretty girls; some consented hoping for favors, others he raped," said Hanaa. "He wasn't a regular fighter. It was said he helped supply the fighters and worked with those…" She pointed to a laptop computer sitting on the office desk and at the sat phone that Rivers had resting on the table before them. "He had those in camp, and he worked with the guards to steal medicine and food."

"Did Dogu rape you?" asked Rivers.

"I was not pretty enough."

"Why did he leave you alone since he knew that you talked regularly to your sister?"

Hanaa nodded. "He left me and my children alone because he knew I'd report back to him everything Nadia told me, and that I would tell her nothing useful. Though I did a little."

"And this Umm al-Nasr?"

"I kept away from her. She was pure evil," said Hanaa. "It was said that she had trained girls to wear suicide bombs. She had a group of girls in the camp. She and Dogu seemed to work together. She would point to people who defied her, and Dogu would use his knife."

"Where are Dogu and Umm?"

"Dogu left many months ago, Umm and the girls within the last few weeks. Dogu worked with the security man, and they all walked out. Where they are now…" Hanaa shrugged.

Rivers nodded. The conversation was at a natural end.

Dogu, Umm, and Sykes in the wind.

But Hanaa was not done.

"There was a rumor in camp that Dogu warned me never to tell Nadia, and I never did," said Hanaa. "He put a knife to my throat to help me remember."

"What rumor?"

"That Dogu's father was Omar al-Shishani," said Hanaa.

"Damn" was all Rivers could say to that.

Rojas was smoking against the administration building when Rivers exited. "Thought I'd see how you're doing and walk you over to the med station."

Rivers was sure Angelos had put him up to it.

Rojas offered a cigarette, which Rivers accepted, saying, "I only smoked these when I was in the sandbox. So here I am again."

They walked. Silent. Rojas didn't ask, and Rivers certainly didn't say anything about the interview and the files.

About a dozen kids, prompted by the excitement of helicopters and soldiers, watched them from behind the barbed wire. At least they looked fed and were wearing clean clothes. Yet their gaze seemed older than their years.

"I'd better finish this before I enter the med station," said

Rivers, puffing on the cigarette. "They'd probably tell me it's a danger to my health."

Rojas smiled at his droll humor.

It was a pleasure to see that while Rivers was beaten up, he wasn't beaten.

20

R ivers pulled up his sat phone and gestured to Rojas that he needed space. His visit to the med station would have to wait a few minutes. He got Angelos in short order.

"Nadia's sister told me an interesting rumor that Dogu threatened to kill her for if she repeated it," said Rivers. "The rumor was that Dogu's father was Omar al-Shishani."

"Fuck me," said Angelos.

"Yes, if true, Dogu is ISIS royalty."

They both knew of Omar. Who in their line of work didn't?

Omar the Chechen. Famous ISIS battle commander. So effective that the U.S. government named him a Specially Designated Global Terrorist and put out a $5 million reward for information leading to his capture.

There was no payout, however, because Omar was reportedly killed by a U.S. air strike in 2017. U.S. intelligence had confirmed his death.

Rivers told Angelos about the missing information in the

files, and the little he had learned about Dogu, Umm, and Sykes. There were leads: Dogu's father and computer access, Umm as a teacher of girls to be suicide bombers, Sykes running a dirty gateway in and out of the camp.

"Well, back to Paris for you," said Angelos. "Good work."

Rivers could hear a background conversation on the other end of the line, and then Angelos piped up. "I had Cowen listening in, and he just pulled something up on my screen. Something he remembered. There were two intel mentions in recent weeks about women getting smuggled out of Al-Hol. Didn't raise much of a stir...

"But considering the group of women in Paris now ...

"It came through Interpol, probably based on their monitoring of human trafficking. The intel reported that young women were being sold and smuggled out of the camp to be married, so to speak, to the remnants of ISIS supporters around the world. Someone gave them a catchy name..."

"ISIS brides."

———

Rivers left the medical unit with a diagnosis—his death was not imminent—and proceeded to a long shower at UN housing. He pulled on decently fitting clean clothes that had been rounded up.

His handgun and sat phone had gone to Rojas. Now he just had his ID, his wallet and his keys to shove into his pockets. Then it hit him: it was missing.

'Where's my dirty clothes? I left something in a pocket," Rivers said to Rojas.

"Oh, man, they were ratty, Rivers. They threw those things right into the burner."

Gone was Raz's scrawled note, *Don't be smitten, but don't be a stranger.*

During his desert ordeal, his hand had rubbed against it in his pants pocket; it felt like a talisman, with some magical power to keep him going and keep his hope alive.

Rivers sighed, then smiled.

He would not be a stranger.

PART TWO

21

The pretty young woman in the passport photos recovered at Baseyev's murder scene snuggled under the blanket, pretending she was back in familiar surroundings, as bad as they had been. She remembered her sister's warmth under the blanket with her at Al-Hol. She remembered rubbing shoulders and feeling safe while sitting with her sister and the other young women, listening to Umm. Her real sister and her new family—the girls devoted to and protected by Umm.

It was best to remember the good things; it helped you survive. A heady insight for a sixteen-year-old.

She did not think of Aslan, who was killed before her eyes, or the woman who took her here at gunpoint.

There were bars on the room's window, and the small space held just a bed and a prayer rug. Several times a day her keeper —a woman wearing a niqab that partially hid her face—allowed her to use the bathroom. Twice a day she brought a simple meal.

The keeper knew the young woman had scoured the room for

a makeshift weapon and found nothing. Her meal also offered nothing—a paper cup and plate, and a plastic spoon, which was accounted for when she was finished.

"What is your name?" the keeper would say in Arabic at every interaction.

She refused to answer, as Umm trained her at Al-Hol.

"When you talk to me, I will talk with you," said the keeper.

The young woman was glad that at least the person with the handgun who had murdered Aslan didn't seem to be around.

───────

The keeper Ayelet was a retired interrogator for Mossad, a woman who only left her home in a small town on coastal Spain for an occasional job that met her criteria: no torture, no guarantee of results, lucrative pay. This private work was mostly to pry apart bank executives and the sons-in-law of the wealthy to learn where the embezzled money could be found. She was known for producing results.

On the third day, the young woman gave her name: Fadwa Bashar. True or false, thought the interrogator, it was a start. A few things were known or suspected about this young woman. She had been part of the heist in Paris. She may have beheaded the driver. She had run off with a young man who was then murdered. And she was suspected of being Syrian and part of an ISIS terror gang.

"Thank you for your name, Fadwa," said Ayelet. "After a few questions, I can have a meal served to you. Perhaps you'll also tell me your favorite foods, which I can provide for you tomorrow." Such information could also narrow down where she was raised.

The interrogator started with a few questions, looking for subtle reactions or nonresponses to questions that could signal emotional ticks. She didn't expect much. Her work with ISIS believers—and this girl being part of a group pulling a bloody heist in Paris fit that bill—was that they had a hard shell. Battle-tested, so to speak.

But what the interrogator also knew was that a girl like Fadwa hadn't always been ISIS, and that there might be a speck of humanity underneath, a memory of a family's love that even ISIS could not destroy.

"Do you miss your boyfriend Aslan?"

No response. *No flick of an eye down or a tightening showing sadness for poor Aslan.*

"Why did you behead the driver?"

A slight frown on the lips. *She didn't do it,* thought the interrogator.

"Where in Syria did you come from for your trip to France?"

No reaction.

"Are you happy that you ran away from your ISIS group?"

No reaction.

"Are you sad that you left the group?"

A fleeting coldness. *There it was: a whisper of anger. At the group? At its leader?*

"Enough for now," said the interrogator. "Now, do you want to ask me a question?"

A pause, and then the girl said, "What do I need to do to get out of here?"

Ah, a transaction. This girl had been thinking ahead.

The interrogator spoke to the tall man who had pitched her this job. He had come to her home in Spain—something only a few knew how to do—and agreed to her conditions but had one of his own: her employer would remain anonymous. Which she did not see as a problem. Soon she was on a plane and then on her way to this farmhouse somewhere in France.

"Guard this one well," she warned the tall man. "I'll write today's summary so you can give it to your boss shortly."

She had interrogated countless hundreds, and this girl reminded her of a small number, thank God. They were the cool, calculating killers. Yet her initial assessment was that this girl's strongest loyalty was to herself, not ISIS, which she had left in Paris, after all. There was something about the group or its leader that angered her. And she doubted it was the beheading, for this girl had been soaked in ISIS brutality.

She sat back to write her memo on the laptop—just the facts —but she already was pondering what could account for any anger toward the ISIS group or its leader.

It was probably the leader.

This was the emotional crack to exploit.

22

"I thought I should come to see you before someone else beat you up or tried to kill you," said Raz Jackson, who made a show of looking Rivers up and down before delivering her verdict. "I think you need some time in a repair shop."

Rivers knew this to be true. When he had finished shaving and splashing cold water on his face an hour earlier, he looked at the black eye and swollen cheek that had replaced the sleek lines of his face. Bruises swept his back, right hip, and leg like a Jackson Pollack painting. And he felt worse than he looked.

Angelos had told him in a phone call to take some time off, and he had responded, "No."

"What did you just say?"

"Respectfully, hell no, sir."

"Then just don't die on me." And his boss hung up.

It was after the shower and phone call that Raz sat down at his breakfast table at the hotel and looked him over. She was aware of his adventure in the desert. It was less than twenty-four hours since his fight in the desert, the time spent at Al-Hol and then the Army hospital in Erbil for X-rays and then limping onto a flight that Angelos arranged back to Paris.

"It's good to see you," said Rivers. "I was thinking sometimes during my trek through the desert that I had to make it back to Paris to see you again."

"Only sometimes?"

"I was a little busy, after all," said Rivers.

Such a bland conversation, but they both seemed content that they were having it.

"Maybe we can have dinner?" said Rivers. "I have a catch-up meeting with the station this morning."

"Dinner would be good," she said.

She noticed something a little different about Rivers beyond his injuries. An edginess. "How rough was it?"

She saw Rivers's jaw clench, and he answered in a crisp, cold voice: "Rough, but I came out great compared to others."

The roster at the meeting caught him by surprise. Seated around the conference table in a U.S. Embassy secure room were a few he knew, others not. Harry Dalton, of course. French intel's Martin Lyons, who Rivers immediately thanked for speeding his entry through customs. Interpol's Adam Barnes. Then there was a guy who looked like a college linebacker plus thirty pounds who introduced himself as Mike Cowen, Angelos's aide. Last was the FBI's buttoned-up liaison to all things France.

Rivers gingerly sat down and was glad the chair wasn't one of the backbreakers common to U.S. facilities.

He knew they had been burning through data files and trading phone calls since Al-Hol was first mentioned. Now, thanks to his trip to the desert, they had a focus: Who was this Umm al-Nasr, who apparently was leading some sort of ISIS bride gang? Who was Dogu Matsoy, and was he the son of the fabled Omar the Chechen? And, along with the fleeing Brian Sykes, where in the hell were these people?

The meeting moved quickly—these weren't people to waste time or effort—and Rivers, in a bit of a haze, was thankful that he could just listen. Interpol's Barnes had put together some big pieces.

"A known name is Matsoy," said Barnes. "This is a Chechen family gang out of Odesa in Ukraine that is involved in smuggling: food, medicine, weapons, and drugs. And they're involved in moving the Syrian Captagon amphetamine into Europe and Russia. Dogu probably has links to them."

"The smuggling lines that Interpol monitors and tries to intercept would explain how Dogu, Sykes, and this Umm have been able to move about."

"What I don't understand," said Lyons, "is why Dogu Matsoy would have stayed for some time at Al-Hol when presumably he had a smuggling family that could buy his way out earlier?"

"Could be that he couldn't at first, that he was a prisoner out of contact with his Ukraine clan," said Dalton. "Maybe he needed to convince someone like Sykes to help him and reach out to them. And Sykes would do it for money, of course."

"So, does anybody have a read on this Umm?" asked Lyons.

"There were reports a few years back of a Western woman who converted to ISIS and had taken to teaching girls how to be suicide bombers," said Cowen. "But there was intel that she was killed in the same air strike that killed Omar the Chechen."

"That guy is confirmed dead, right?" asked Lyons.

"Army and intelligence reports confirmed he's dead," said Cowen. "Plus, there's been no sightings of Omar since 2017. He wasn't the type of guy to hide."

"Have we found any of these ISIS brides?" asked Rivers.

"No," said the FBI special agent, and others at the table nodded. "Woe to any young woman trying to enter the United States on a French passport. Each is getting special attention," said the FBI agent.

"We have adequate safeguards in place."

Famous last words thought Rivers.

"This Umm is on the loose," said Dalton. "But we have some leads on the others, thanks to our combined work. It looks like Sykes may be in Marseille and Dogu Matsoy in Odesa."

Dogu's location was logical, with the family connection, but Rivers said, "How did we track Sykes to Marseille?"

"Remember, the phone of Sykes's deputy who tried to kill you in the desert was recovered. On it were a few photos from both of them vacationing," said Cowen. "We were able to identify some boozy vacation photos as being taken in Marseille, which makes sense, because it's part of smugglers' routes. Checking there, we found Sykes came in on a fake passport."

"Interpol and the French police will scoop him up."

They were up and ready to leave when Rivers asked, "Who's leading the pursuit of Dogu?"

Cowen nodded to him. He wanted Rivers to stay behind as the group cleared the conference room.

"When do I leave?" said Rivers.

"In the morning. Get some rest; you need it," said Cowen. "We have our CIA station in Kyiv pulling together what info and contacts they have. It will be ready on your arrival. I'll have someone take you to the airport in the morning, with the documents you'll need. … At least this time there isn't a desert you can be chased across."

"True, nothing to worry about," said Rivers. "Just a meet-and-greet with a Mafia family in a war zone."

23

Raz didn't know what to make of Rivers or, more honestly, her infatuation with him. It was very unlike her, and unsettling.

She was in a catch-and-release stage in her relationships, for a young, single CEO like herself had her pick of rich, handsome men. She would hit the upscale restaurants and party with whoever caught her eye, and sometimes she went to bed with him. But not often.

Raz just wasn't one to meet a man and then quickly jump between the sheets. It wasn't prudishness or a disinterest in pleasures of the flesh. She just didn't find most men that interesting and worth the effort. They were—young or older—generally absorbed in their toys and their business success or, for too many, their grievances. But none of that seemed to apply to Rivers. Probably she didn't know him well enough.

He was good-looking in a rough way but not handsome.

Physically fit for sure. Had a sly sense of humor but wasn't a brilliant conversationalist. Nothing exceptional there. So maybe it was that in some ways Rivers was an echo of herself. A CIA operations officer who was a bit chewed on around the edges from his time in the Middle East. Raz knew she had never put her own past completely behind her. Perhaps it was Rivers telling her how he was haunted by the children's faces from Syria, a simple humanity that time and mission had not yet sanded down.

She could weigh all the pluses and minuses to this infatuation and Rivers himself, and Raz was still faced with a simple, unexplainable fact: she wanted to be with him. Which she knew under the circumstances was not wise. Rivers was CIA, and Raz had baggage from her past in the agency.

She snapped out of her musing when the driver pulled to the front of Rivers's hotel, where he was supposed to be waiting for their trip to dinner. He wasn't there. She sighed and went inside to find him. Scratch the lobby and the small bar; he was in neither. So, she went to his room. It was an old hotel of twenty rooms, all locked by keys. An easy door for her to toggle open. The lights were off.

Raz used her phone flashlight and quietly moved forward. There, sprawled on the bed, was Rivers. Apparently, he had returned from his station meetings in the late afternoon and laid down for a few minutes, hours ago.

She had to smile. She wanted to get Rivers in bed but had been thinking of something more romantic. She decided to leave the exhausted man alone, and she spread a light cover over him. He did not stir. Raz paused and then gently curled up beside him atop the cover.

The next morning Rivers woke with a start and smelled a bit

of lavender on the pillow next to him, and his hand reached out but found only an empty space. He had a thought of Raz snuggled close. A dream? His imagination surely.

He called Raz to apologize for missing dinner. There was no answer.

24

Rivers looked out at the patchwork of land at 30,000 feet below, three-plus hours from Paris to Kyiv, and wondered how his second war zone in a week would treat him. He'd been troubled since his return from Syria. Troubled by a sound or wisp of breeze that for a split second—a terrible one— would send him back to that desert wondering if a thumb-size AK bullet would rip into him. In a blink the worst of the fear would pass, but an unsettled feeling remained.

And then there was Raz, a woman who'd captured his longing for the first time in forever, but who was elusive.

Angelos had Rivers on a State Department flight into Kyiv because there were no commercial flights into war-torn Ukraine. A discreet Gulfstream. Comfortably padded seats. No open bar, or bar of any kind. He guessed he couldn't have everything.

A Diplomatic Security official and a U.S. Army colonel had been aboard when the plane left Brussels where NATO was head-quartered, and their curiosity was piqued with the stop in Paris for Rivers, especially when they got a look at his battered condition.

"You look like you should be coming out of Ukraine, not going in," said Colonel Kyle Marler when Rivers boarded the flight. "What bar fight did you lose?"

"I had a little dustup in Syria," said Rivers.

"Oh, you're the guy. You've certainly gotten everybody spun up over a possible terror threat," the colonel said. "I heard whispers of 'ISIS brides.' That's all we need now. Little girls in suicide vests."

He smiled. "And I remember names. Yours. You're the Army captain who trashed those SEALs in Mosul. You certainly have a knack for finding trouble, don't you?"

Rivers simply nodded. *Yeah, I am that guy.*

"You were the object of a tremendous amount of conversation at the time—you know, institutional pride, an Army intel guy beats up two SEALs. I'm surprised West Point didn't have you as a guest of honor at the Army-Navy Game."

"Well, to be honest, the SEALs were drunk, and a sergeant had them at gunpoint," said Rivers. "Hardly the stuff of legend.

"When it comes to trouble, I always seem to be at the wrong place at the wrong time."

"Do you know where the two are now?" said the colonel.

"In prison, of course."

"No, they're not. They were both pardoned in 2020, right before the election, with a bunch of bad actors."

"What?" said Rivers. "Damn, those guys should never be out."

He leaned against the window and a few minutes later was in a light but fitful sleep, from which at some point he awoke with a start. The colonel glanced at him.

"Tough dreams?" he said. "I get them too."

Ten minutes later, when they waited at the door to disembark, the colonel had some advice.

"Find out where those guys are," he warned. "They hate your guts. You not only sent them to prison, but you beat them up, which is an embarrassment within their lowlife clique. Don't wind up in a dark alley with them."

So, his dreams weren't his only trouble.

They took the stairs down from the exit door and looked around the airport, now used for incoming cargo and approved flights of passenger aircraft. A breeze blew from the west.

"This is where Ukraine made its stand," said the colonel. "Seizing this airport was the Russian's first target on the first day of its planned three-day victory over Ukraine. Their elite troops would seize it, move ten klicks to Kyiv and kill the president or send him fleeing."

"They didn't make it to Kyiv, and the president refused to leave."

The colonel stepped close to Rivers, looked him in the eyes and said quietly, "You said that when it came to trouble, you always are in the wrong place at the wrong time."

"You're wrong, Rivers. For the kids that night in Syria, you were the right man at the right place at the right time."

When Rivers got to Odesa a few hours later via helicopter, Russell, the CIA officer there, was less than thrilled to meet him.

"You know, there's a fucking war going on," he said. "And headquarters wants constant updates: real casualty figures, morale assessment, how Commander X or Political Leader Y is viewed, what Russian captives are saying. Oh, and can I find Suzie Q, a distant cousin of a Chicago alderman who's buddies with a congressman on the appropriations subcommittee, a girl from some village now in ruins."

"They have trouble understanding we're in a fluid situation here with a lot of rumors and little verifiable information. So, I just feed the beast with the best information I have and wait for the 'That's all?' and the next task.

"And now you."

Rivers let him vent. He knew well the frustrations of the guy in the field, his last taste of it in Paris.

"I need to see this police inspector," said Rivers, showing him a name from the paperwork that had been passed to him by Kyiv Station.

"Fat chance," said Russell. "I told Kyiv he was unavailable from stepping on a land mine.

"But one of his fellow inspectors was able to produce his police file on the Matsoys after we played *The Price Is Right,*" said Russell. "Rather thin pickings. You can thumb through yourself, but one lead I saw was an informant. I tracked down the guy."

Russell produced the file and a piece of paper on which he had scrawled *Isa Khasanov, Mykolaiv City. Medic Training Facility.*

"This guy Khasanov was a medic wounded at the front. He trains medics now," said Russell. "His wife is a Matsoy. He used to give the police captain information – for money, of course."

He gave Rivers a map, a handgun, and an envelope of cash, then pointed to a beat-looking sedan and to the east, "He's forty clicks that way."

Rivers leaned against the scarred sedan and dialed Raz on his phone. He wanted to apologize for missing dinner, but really just wanted to hear her voice. Maybe say something to make her laugh. She had a great laugh.

Rivers could usually sense the end of things from the start with a girlfriend. As the women probably could. As an Army officer with tours in the war zone, and then in the CIA, his was a rootless way to live. It had never bothered him before.

This seemed different. He wanted it to be different.

There was no answer to his call.

Rivers texted, *Smitten.*

25

P lywood.

     Huge stacks were being off-loaded from trucks visible from the bridge that Rivers was crossing into Mykolaiv. It was used, he knew, to board up blown-out windows and doors. There was a need for a lot of it here.

The horizon was dotted with crumbled buildings and rubble.

If Russian hopes and expectations of a quick end to Ukraine was strangled near the airport outside Kyiv, this river city also played its part. Once the Russians pushed up from Crimea, all they had to do was cross the one bridge at Mykolaiv to roll into Odesa, the prize on the Black Sea.

They never crossed the bridge.

Now Rivers was crossing it and wondering if his mission would also flame out here.

He was going to interview the medic Isa Khasanov about Dogu Matsoy, and he couldn't think of a single reason this guy would talk to him.

Rivers sometimes was used as a troubleshooter while part of Army intel in Iraq and Syria. He would talk with Sunni tribal chiefs or Shia militia leaders, or sometimes even with Iranian officers at prearranged sites, all to draw or enforce red lines to avoid unnecessary carnage or exchange prisoners. But he always had leverage in those talks: the U.S. military close by. Here he was on his own.

He'd just have to play it by ear, which maybe was one of his talents that Angelos valued.

Isa Khasanov sat on a bench outside the hospital, his face raised to the waning, but still warm sun. As Rivers approached, with a translator provided by the admin office, Khasanov stared at him and said, "I heard some American policeman was looking for me."

"I'm Tom Rivers and I'm not a police officer," he said. "I'm with the U.S. State Department."

Khasanov looked him over and shrugged. "Then not a policeman. Officially."

His face had that tight, drawn look of too much combat. Even after months away from the front in his recent role as a medic trainer.

"Were you one of the defenders who kept the Russians from moving across the bridge?" asked Rivers. He had decided to first engage Khasanov as the soldier he was.

"I fought the Russians all over and—finally—this bridge," said Khasanov. "But I have been fighting the Russians since 2014, when they first invaded my country.

"A long time," Khasanov said with a rueful grin.

Rivers was ready with another question—about how he'd become a medic—but Khasanov spoke first.

"Ask me what you came to ask me."

"Dogu Matsoy," said Rivers.

"Ah, Dogu," he said.

"Do you know him?" asked Rivers.

"I met him over the years because my wife is a Matsoy. I'm a decade older and we were never friends," said Khasanov. "But everyone knows of Dogu."

"Why is that?"

"Dogu was the wild one. Fast cars, faster women. Fast with a knife," said Khasanov. "Then suddenly—hard to figure—he's off to fight in Syria. I think the violence attracted him, the chance to make a name for himself."

"Have you seen him recently?"

"I thought he was dead. But you're here, so I guess not."

"Who among the Matsoys would have contact with him?"

"That is easy. That would be Raglan, the elder who runs the Matsoy business. He raised Dogu."

"How do I find him?"

"You don't. He finds you."

"Would any other Matsoy be able to talk to me about Dogu?"

"Only with Raglan's permission."

That prompted Rivers to pause.

"So why are you talking to me?

"I have Raglan's permission."

"Don't look surprised," said Khasanov. "Your presence and why you are here was known to Raglan as soon as your CIA man paid the Odesa policeman for that file. A good payday for him, collecting from your man and Raglan too."

Rivers nodded. *Of course.*

"The file says that you provided information to the police captain," said Rivers. "That was with Raglan's approval too?"

"Yes," said Khasanov. "I gave the police captain information on rival smugglers. It made him look good, and he looked the other way at Matsoy business."

"So why are you here and not living the good life?"

"My Muslim family was driven out of Chechnya by the Russians, and now Ukraine is my home. I grew up here; my family is here," said Khasanov. "I will not be driven out again by the Russians.

"Slava Ukraini!" he said. *Glory to Ukraine.*

Khasanov's eyes focused over Rivers's shoulder.

Rivers got up from the bench and saw a stout man with a loose jacket and a collapsible weapon under it approaching. He knew if there was one, there were more.

"You're in luck, Mr. CIA. Raglan will see you," said Khasanov. "Go with them. Don't resist."

Last time someone told him not to resist, Rivers wound up slugged to the Paris pavement. He wondered if he'd be so fortunate as to escape with just bruises this time.

26

At the farmhouse outside Paris, the hard shell of the ISIS girl was showing cracks.

Slowly, she opened up with some answers. She had traveled from Al-Hol in Syria to Paris via car to Beirut, by air to Marseille, and then by car again. In a group of six women—five girls like her and their leader.

Yes, they were all believers in ISIS and had been schooled to make bomb vests and wear them to targets, their aim to spark the resurrection of the caliphate.

Their targets? Only the leader knew. But considering the passport hijacking, obviously in America.

Why did she leave the group? No answer, but it certainly wasn't to run off to a love nest with the ill-fated Baseyev.

Did the beheading of the van driver offend her? This produced an intriguing answer.

"It was reckless." Cold, clinical.

She seemed a mixture of a girl pumped with ideology by a

group that kept her alive and a young woman skilled as a manipulator, thought Ayelet. But her sense was that this girl wasn't the type to push a trigger and perish for a cause. Instead, she was a survivor who had played a role to get out of Al-Hol.

This girl would be thinking she could manipulate her way to freedom with information. Ayelet could tell she was holding much back.

Her slow revelation of some answers came as it became clear to her that she could not escape. The bedroom where she spent almost all her time was secure. She was moved to talk with Ayelet in the company of two guards, and the interrogation room was scrubbed of all possible weapons. She wore an ankle monitor, even in the shower. And always, that tall man who ran the guards watched and watched.

She had tried to entice the tall man with sex when he checked on her at nightfall, spreading out naked on her bed.

The tall man smiled and said, "At least you tried."

He made sure, though, to remind his rotating pairs of guards that the penalty for falling prey to her would be a bullet from him, if she didn't kill them first.

"A chance for a few moments of pleasure for a lifetime in a grave," as he put it.

Today would be different, the slow probing about to catch some fire.

The tall man had given Ayelet the names of three people, new information that had been developed by her unknown employer: Umm al-Nasr, Dogu Matsoy, and Brian Sykes, all part of her Al-Hol escape.

In her hands, Ayelet thought it could work like a can opener on this girl. But should she lead with Umm al-Nasr, obviously the leader of the ISIS girls? Or lead with the others and then move to the most sensitive name?

Go with Umm. For once any name was unveiled, the girl would guess she was on the list.

Fadwa was brought into the interview room, a windowless space that worked to set the mood of a barren existence unless she cooperated. The girl nodded as she sat down, an acknowledgment as wooden as the table.

"And what will we talk about today?" said Fadwa, trying to take some control over the morning session.

Ayelet remained silent and stared at her for a full minute. And then, as if she was turning a page, she sat back in her chair and said, "Today let's talk about Umm al-Nasr."

The girl smiled—she had never smiled before—and said, "I was wondering when you would know of Umm."

Ayelet could see, however, that it was a defensive answer. There was a tightening of her eyes, a short catch of her breath, hard to detect but there, signaling the girl's composure was but a mask.

Ayelet leaned forward now, a more open, engaging posture. *Set the hook*, she thought.

"Why did you say Umm was reckless?" she asked, playing back the girl's earlier description of the beheading and pinning it on Umm.

Moments ticked by in silence.

The girl studied her hands, which had been trained to pack a vest with explosives and nails and to tightly strap it on with the detonator plunger ready to be thumbed. Umm had picked her team of pretty war-zone girls, soaking them in the belief of sacrifice for a holy cause, training them to follow her carefully laid plan. She got the group out of Al-Hol and to Paris, and the next step was to America.

But then came the beheading.

Fadwa remembered the terrified driver saying a prayer on the side of the highway. Aslan Baseyev yelling, "Stop," and Fadwa seeing Umm's blue eyes wide and crazy, her body shaking in rage; Umm sawing through the man's neck in a frenzy.

She did not know that out-of-control woman. She did not know why Umm would turn a simple heist into a bloody mess, but she knew it would bring unnecessary trouble. Her faith in Umm's competence was badly shaken.

Later that day, a terrified Baseyev asked her to run away with him. When she told Umm, at least she was her old self. *Do it*, she had said, *then kill him and return to me.*

How to explain all this to this interrogator?

"Was the beheading why you ran away with Baseyev?" prompted Ayelet to the still mute girl. It wouldn't be that by itself, for this ISIS girl would have seen violence and destruction on an epic scale. But there was something about it that had disturbed her.

"No, I went with Baseyev because Umm ordered me to go with him and kill him. I would have done it, but that woman came and killed him first and brought me here."

Ayelet didn't show surprise at the girl's emotionless description of murder. She had interrogated countless terrorists for the Mossad and this was typical.

"Describe Umm for me," she said.

"A warrior for Islam," said the girl. "A woman in her thirties, strong, with a voice that captures you."

"Where in Syria is she from?"

The girl hesitated just a beat before saying, "Raqqa," which had been the ISIS caliphate capital.

The answer did not ring true.

The girl was looking tired, and the session had borne some answers, given and hidden.

So Ayelet decided to wrap it up with the other two names.

"Who is Dogu Matsoy?"

"He arranged with Umm to get us out of the camp," said the girl. "It was said he was the son of the great ISIS commander Omar."

The girl paused, then said, "He was cruel. Dogu raped many of the girls. Umm kept him from raping us."

"And Brian Sykes?"

She shrugged. She didn't know the name.

Ayelet called for the guards, but as Fadwa stood, she thought of a last question.

"Do you miss the other girls?"

To Ayelet's surprise, the girl's body quivered once, and her stern eyes took on a watery sheen.

The girl said nothing. Her reaction said much.

27

Laughter and the chatter of conversations echoed down this old street of Marseille, and Brian Sykes grabbed the almost empty bottle of Maker's Mark Top Shelf Limited Edition from a table and took a swig, then looked outside his window.

He scowled. While the night held promise with a newly bought unopened bottle at the ready, he would have been far, far happier to be sharing it with a woman.

Sykes was staying on the second floor of a building off Cours Julian, an area rich in relaxed cafés and shops and graffiti he couldn't understand. Two small cafés, often loud with boisterous young people, livened up the new night. Earlier he had hunted for young women without success, for a bleary-eyed, cigar-smelling, middle-aged guy didn't seem to have curb appeal, even with biceps and a fat wallet to die for. He bought a new bottle of his favorite Kentucky bourbon on his way back to the apartment.

He had loads of cash, a head start with his Al-Hol escape, and no reason to think anyone knew where he was. Plus, job prospects: the drug smugglers from Syria to Europe always needed replacement manpower, as many of its workforce shot each other, overdosed, or were shot by management for dipping into the proceeds. Sykes always was a worker.

Maybe Dogu's smuggling family would even hire him. But only if everything else failed, for Sykes was wary of Dogu. He was smart, handsome, great command of English, Arabic and who knew what else; a young man who he had heard bought everything from ammo to pickup trucks to medicines on the black market for ISIS. But Dogu had a fast-twitch mean streak.

It had been a grand payday with Dogu and, after he left, still a steady flow of money to get people out of the camp and with the theft and resale of supplies. But then that State Department inspector showed up and talked to Nadia Hatami. Sykes's street smarts told him it was about Dogu and Umm—who else? —and that his name and misdeeds could be rolled up in any investigation.

He had sent his deputy, Arnold, and a few of his crew to intercept the U.S. inspector's car on the trip away from Al-Hol. The idea was to capture the guy, find out what he knew and, of course, kill him and the driver. Bury them in the desert. There'd only be a burned-out car and two missing people. Blame it on smugglers gone wild.

Fucking Arnold couldn't get it done. He should have known, for the man's best talent was as his drinking buddy.

He dozed off for a second, awakening with a start when his nearly empty bottle clattered to the floor.

The room was dark, but he suddenly could make out the small movement of a shadow in the gloom.

A police sniper was on the roof across from the apartment Sykes was renting. He saw no movement as his nightscope scanned the dark rooms, but some spaces were obscured from his sight.

Undercover police watched the building's entrance and rear exit and reported no movement. Interpol's Adam Barnes and French Intel's Paul Laurent listened from an unmarked van two blocks away. The raid commander was ready to go.

Sykes had been spotted as darkness fell at one of the few liquor stores that sold his favorite Maker's Mark Limited Edition, which was sold at only a few stores. There were many bottles of it when his quarters at Al-Hol were searched, and Laurent had suggested it could help locate him.

Police had been combing hotels and talking to managers of apartment rentals, checking ATM video, and checking on local Captagon gangs. But it was a police cadet who spotted Sykes. She saw a barrel-chested man enter a liquor store that she was assigned to watch, and she identified Sykes from a photo on her phone, and called it in. The cadet followed Sykes to this address.

Over the next hours, a surveillance net was thrown over the area. Shortly before dawn, with the street finally quiet and all lights turned off in the small building, the SWAT teams filed quietly through the front door and up the stairs to the target door. A dog barked, then two.

At the door, a police officer held a ballistic shield while another splintered the door open with a breaching ram. Flash-bangs followed.

No noise, no motion, besides their own.

Laurent and Barnes looked over the disappointing body of Brian Sykes, lying in a pool of blood with an empty bottle next to him. Disappointing in that he was not alive and, to be frank, his shirtless corpse was a testament to the ravages of hard drinking. Two bullet holes were centered in his chest.

In low voices to the side of the police and forensic cluster, they considered how Sykes had been murdered in the few hours between his sighting and the raid on his rental apartment. The police cadet had kept the front door under surveillance after following from the liquor store. But it had taken a few hours to close the net around the neighborhood and set up the raid. Unfortunately, for several hours, the back entrance was not fully secured. A mistake.

The back of Sykes's building led to a courtyard shared by other buildings, with courtyard entrances to two different streets. The police weren't immediately aware of this and originally only covered one of the streets. So, someone could enter unseen from an unmonitored door. A killer had.

The reality, Barnes and Laurent agreed, was that the killer knew the police had located Sykes and were slowly setting up a net around him. And had got to him first.

"We have a leak. In real time," said Barnes.

"… or our comms are compromised," said Laurent.

Possibly both.

Laurent looked over at the remaining untouched bottle of Maker's Mark and wished for a drink.

"It's the French police comms," he said.

"Consider this," he said to Barnes, "a man was murdered in Paris a few hours after the police identified him as a suspect in the passport heist. Now this: a murder right after the police identify Sykes's location. Both done quickly, under the police noses.

"Too much of a coincidence."

"And very professional," said Barnes.

Laurent pulled out his phone, then looked at it, realizing his encrypted call might not be secure. But he had to get the ball rolling. He called his boss, Martin Lyons in Paris, and told him what had happened and his suspicion.

A full-scale investigation of French police and intel communication systems was launched within the hour.

Lyons immediately asked Laurent the question he was still wrestling with. "Why?"

Answer that and it should lead to "Who?"

28

Tom Rivers looked at the man approaching with the collapsible weapon under his jacket and knew there were more. And he was right.

He could hear men coming from behind. Heavy steps, heavy men. What are called "muscle" for a reason.

They were, as things went, professional about it. Nodding to him to move toward the front of the hospital and then to two black Mercedes SUVs. The vehicles were highly polished; this smuggler kingpin Raglan Matsoy was clearly particular about his rides.

So, his conversation with the medic Isa Khasanov was leading to a meeting with Raglan. Only time would tell if that was good or bad.

Rivers sat in the back of an SUV with one of the bears next to him.

They moved at high-speed on the highway to Odesa, looped around it, and came into an area of increasingly expensive compounds, some old Ottoman-style mansions lovingly restored, others glass-fronted modern houses with views of the Black Sea.

It was an area never targeted by Russian missiles, for the invaders had enduring hopes of one day moving into these same seaside mansions.

The man next to Rivers removed a flask from a jacket pocket and took an unhealthy slug from it. He extended it to Rivers, who thought *why not?*, *a*llowing a biting, licorice-flavored liquor to roll down his throat. He nodded his thanks.

At least if this man killed him, it was nothing personal.

Rivers watched the driver thumb a remote on the dash, and the gates to a compound opened to a steep driveway and one of the glass houses.

He had always been at his best during frightful events, when for him it seemed either time slowed down or his mind sped faster. He had noted landmarks along the route to this compound and was now marking the number of guards and their placement and weapons. They parked, with the driver backing into a space and then putting the keys up on the visor. There were three more SUVs in the parking area. The house backed into a heavily wooded ridge.

Basically, he was hermetically sealed in a lion's den.

But Daniel, who emerged unscathed from his biblical den, didn't face the world's most murderous animal: man.

Maybe Raglan would tell him about Dogu and simply let him go.

Ha.

Rivers was nudged into a room with one wall a glass expanse looking out on the Black Sea, now marked in the dark by a few blinking lights, ships or buoys, he didn't know. His handgun and phone were put on a massive wood-carved desk. To its side was a workstation with three monitors and a laptop. Two sofas and two armchairs were to the side.

And there was Raglan Matsoy.

He probably was in his sixties but had not softened with age. He had a strong, square body with scarred, large hands that looked like they could squeeze the life out of someone and probably had. A trim beard and long, stylish hair were streaked with gray. He was talking on his phone and waved for Rivers to be seated.

The geography of the setup alarmed him.

He had been waved to a straight-backed wood chair. And behind it stood the type of man who you would not want to meet in a dark alley in a bad dream. A reptilian figure whose lean face held no expression, but his eyes burned into Rivers. He was a man who liked killing. Not just a job for him but an enjoyment.

Raglan put down his phone, moved to a nearby chair to face him and smiled at Rivers.

"Let us not play games, Mr. CIA," said Raglan. "I will tell you about Dogu and you will talk to me about your work."

"Thank you for taking the time to see me," said Rivers. "And thank you for speaking English, I don't speak Ukrainian or Russian."

"To be a successful businessman in the world, you need to know languages," said Raglan. "It is something that you Americans don't learn, to your detriment. So, you do not know languages, much less the people who speak them."

Rivers listened, his eyes focused on Raglan before him,

though a keen part of his hearing and awareness were attuned for any movement from the man behind him.

"Dogu Matsoy escaped from Al-Hol in Syria, and I'd like to speak to him about a woman at the camp," said Rivers. "Do you know where I can find him?"

Raglan looked curiously at Rivers, as if amazed at how little the CIA seemed to know.

"I am Dogu's uncle and his mentor," said Raglan who, in that moment, decided to tell his story, with evident pride. Rivers divined it was meant to be the last story he would ever hear.

"My dear brother-in-law Omar and I fought the Russians, who invaded our Chechnya, and when we lost, our capital obliterated, our men slaughtered by the Russians and the traitor Kadyrov, we fled first to relatives in Georgia's Pankisi Gorge and then elsewhere, including here."

"There were men who turned to vodka. There were those who turned to working. My talent is smuggling. And there were the imams preaching Jihad," he said. "Omar, bless him, joined the Jihadists and went to Syria, a man of faith who knew how to use his weapon.

"Dogu was his fourth son, and Omar asked me to watch over him until he called for him from Syria," said Raglan. "One by one, his three older sons were killed. By Russians and Shia and Americans. Omar never called for his last son. Dogu had become known as a Matsoy while here, but I knew he was always his father's son.

"Dogu went to his father when he was sixteen. Still, I was surprised by that. He was not a religious boy. He was smart and strong. Skilled in languages and business. He liked smuggling, fast cars, and a lot of women.

"But Dogu needed to shine in his father's eyes. He fought

beside his father for a while, but then they used him for his greater skills: to make deals and smuggle for ISIS."

"A wonderful story. Which doesn't tell me about now," said Rivers. It was an abrupt remark, and he could tell Raglan didn't like it.

He listened for movement behind him, for a shift of air. There was none. Yet.

Raglan brushed it off. But it was clear to him that this CIA man had nothing he needed to know.

"What does a young man like that do with his life after Syria and his father is dead?" said Raglan.

"What did you tell him, as his uncle and mentor, when you talked to him?"

Ragland nodded. "Dogu and I spoke after he left that camp in Syria. I thought he would come here, but he said no. He called instead.

"Dogu recited to me a bit of Chechen poetry that his father dearly loved:

> *'He ravaged anything that got in his path*
> *in order to make the land safe for his kind.'*

"Dogu hates Americans for killing his father, and he is his father's son.

"It is your country's turn to be ravaged."

Then: a whisper of fabric and the faintest swirl of air behind him.

Rivers launched up violently with his legs and twisted toward the man behind him. His only hope was to attack the attacker. He flung his left arm out to block any hand holding a gun or a knife.

His arm was caught in a wire garrote that the man was trying to slip over his head.

The wire slid down, but Rivers's forearm kept it from his neck. The wire cut into his forearm and along his jaw.

In his right hand, Rivers held a long sunglass ear stem that he had broken off while getting out of the Mercedes. Now he jammed it back into the killer's face. Once, then a second desperate stab slammed it into the killer's eye.

The man screamed; the garrote fell away.

Raglan was stunned and slow to react, but now he was up and moving to the weapons on his wooden desk. But Rivers—younger, quicker, and more motivated—rammed into him from behind, knocking him down.

Rivers stumbled to the desk and grabbed his handgun, spun and put two deadly shots into Raglan and one into the other man.

The piercing screams had sent the guards scrambling. Killing someone in Raglan's office to conclude an interrogation wasn't unusual, whether by gun or a wire. But it was done much more quietly.

Rivers scooped up his phone and Raglan's, which had skittered across the floor. He had spied a door to a balcony, from which he was able to drop ten feet to the ground and quickly moved to the driveway.

He ran as best he could, gun ready. The guards had rushed into the house, leaving the front clear.

Rivers ran to one of the Mercedes SUVs, found the key in the visor, started and gunned the engine. He worked the gate opener on the dashboard.

There was no gunfire.

Rivers figured he had a thirty-second head start.

Rivers slammed the accelerator and turned away from Odesa and the way he'd been driven to Raglan's compound. Rivers guessed his pursuers would assume he was going back the way he came. The road curved either way, which could help hide his lights.

After about two minutes, with no headlights to his rear, he turned onto a small road up and over the ridge. He was good with maps and had looked at one when he first landed. He believed there was a network of roads on the other side of the ridge that he could take back toward Odesa and the airport. The airport meant safety: it had a military base.

Rivers thumbed his phone and found Russell's number.

Two rings and the CIA officer answered.

"I'm on the run from Raglan Matsoy's gang," said Rivers. "About ten miles west of Odesa and driving to the airport. They'll kill me if they get me, and they might be coming for you too."

"You met with Raglan? Holy hell," said Russell.

"Yes, and I killed him."

There was a few seconds' pause. "Hmm, yes, you should drive fast to the airport," said Russell. "I'm going to hump up there myself. I'll call and tell them that we're coming and to look to clear a way for us. The gang would've guessed you're going to the airport. But maybe they're a bit disorganized right now."

Rivers zagged through some roads and found the highway toward Odesa, eventually followed highway signs to the airport and sped the entrance road. No ambush. He rolled up to the gate, identified himself and got out of the SUV slowly, hands up, handgun announced and left on the passenger seat. He was soon waved through.

His left forearm and hand were coated with blood, as was his shirt, from a nasty, six-inch gash along his jaw.

"God, Rivers, you look like shit," said Russell. "You really killed Raglan?"

"And a plus-one."

"Well, should we see a doctor here first or take a copter to Kyiv?"

"Kyiv, but maybe a medic while we wait," said Rivers, already dialing the number to Angelos's line.

Rivers confirmed Dogu was indeed the son of Omar the Chechen. And he said Dogu saw himself as his terrorist father's son and sought revenge on America.

What was that line in the poem Raglan had recited?

He ravaged anything that got in his path.

Rivers told Angelos that he had not learned Dogu's whereabouts, but he had retrieved his uncle's phone, which might provide clues.

He looked at his right hand, which held his phone as he talked with Angelos. It was shaking.

29

The interrogator, Ayelet, saw the girl's body language had changed. She moved lighter, her face unmasked and showing some emotion, smiling as she looked out a window at a tangle of leafy trees while being escorted to the interrogation room. She had accepted the reality of her situation: a prisoner, probably forever. But there was something she wanted, and she had something to say.

Ayelet decided to get right to it: "Do you miss the other girls?"

It was the question from the last interrogation session, which triggered a quiver in the girl's body, with her eyes fighting back tears.

"They are my sisters," said Fadwa. "We were always together during our lessons, sitting with shoulders touching, sometimes giggling behind Umm's back. When a day seemed bleak with a memory of family lost, a sister would hold your hand, and you knew that you had a new family.

"It was harder for me. The girls believed Umm, believed ISIS would sweep the world to purify it, but I did not have this belief. I don't know why."

"Didn't your attitude show to Umm?"

"I was her most able follower. Umm wanted to believe in all the girls, so it was easy for her to believe in me."

"Did Umm harm the girls you care about?"

"No, she took care that we were fed and protected, especially from Dogu," said the girl. "But training us to blow ourselves up, while an act for Allah in her eyes, isn't a holy one in mine."

"Umm told you to go with Aslan Baseyev after the robbery and kill him and then return," said Ayelet. "Were you going to kill him? Were you planning to return to Umm?"

"Yes. I had to return to Umm."

"Why? You could escape her."

"I had to return so we could escape," said the girl, emphasizing the word *we*.

"I needed to return and take from the group the one I love—my younger sister, Jomana."

At that, the trade was clear. Information for a pledge, however worthless, to try to save her sister.

"Tell me how to find Jomana," said Ayelet. "It helps me, and that helps you."

Fadwa looked resolute now. "I do not know where she is. But Umm was taking us to America. She said there were people there ready to help us."

"Specific targets?"

"I don't know. But you must try to save Jomana," said the girl. "She believes Umm, but she does not know better."

And then Fadwa said something that stunned Ayelet. It had to be the girl's greatest secret, and she was giving it up now in a desperate hope for her sister's salvation.

Ayelet immediately ended the interrogation.

She told the tall man as she moved to write her memo on her laptop, "We got it."

The tall man and guards took Fadwa back to the room with the barred windows.

Ayelet sat at her laptop and began a quick email that she would send to the tall man for his transmission to her anonymous employer—as she did after every session.

Today she dispensed with a description of the scene and the girl's litany of answers. She typed the key things she had learned from Fadwa today:

- Her sister Jomana was among the ISIS brides.
- Umm had unidentified targets and helpers in the United States.

She paused for a moment, reflecting that Fadwa, a young woman of such great potential, would never go to jail. The tall man, despite his denials, would surely see to that.

She typed the last and greatest revelation:

- Umm al-Nasr was also known to some in ISIS as Umm Ameriki.

The American.

PART THREE

30

Mary Greene scanned the passing crowd from her outdoor seat at the Northern Virginia restaurant, watching the young women with bare midriffs, couples pushing strollers, young men pretending not to be on the prowl, all dressed well and well fed. It reminded her of the scene from the *Hunger Games* when the district rubes see the fluffy citizens of the capital for the first time. It was Umm's second day as Mary Greene.

"This is what we will purify," said her companion, Rasheed Khadr.

Mary-Umm suppressed a smile at this young man's naivety. He was a dull tool, but useful. She had no expectation that her imminent acts would turn these people to the truth and purity of ISIS. Her intention was to have them ripping themselves apart. This rich, divided, materialistic America would become a land of dog-eat-dog, without law and order, like the world she knew.

Khadr looked at her and saw that she was once a highly

attractive woman but now had the drawn look of a spent marathoner. Still, there was crackling intensity in her blue eyes. People would think she exercised excessively—a middle-aged yoga freak perhaps. But what they actually saw was a devotion to ISIS terror and the ravages of surviving in the war zone. She made him feel that he wanted to be like her.

Blow the motherfuckers to pieces.

But Umm knew Khadr was simply a helper who probably would prove neither to be holy nor a warrior.

She knew all about Khadr and his hopes and weaknesses. He had been recruited through ISIS's social media outreach—hours upon hours of conversation with an attractive Muslim woman in Raqqa trained by a psychologist. *Empathize, praise, seduce.* Khadr was what they called a "halfling." His father was a Saudi national who married an American woman, and both were teachers: his father, engineering at George Washington University, and his mother, sixth grade at a Fairfax school. After 9/11, their child felt the sting of suspicion.

Khadr was an awkward teen, a good student with few friends at school. Instead, he had his bedroom laptop. A young woman named Amelia—a Brit who had joined ISIS in Syria—became his online companion. She made him feel special and, although he was far from the rough battlefield of ISIS against infidels in Syria, part of the struggle. A warrior.

Of course, Amelia and the ISIS caliphate were eventually buried by bullets and bombs. But a year back, Umm contacted Khadr, picking him from select files she secretly took to Al-Hol on a flash-drive. At first, he listened to Umm over the internet from curiosity and a desire to hear what had become of Amelia.

While poor Amelia was dead, Umm talked of bringing young women to America and needing help to do so. These young women would need Khadr's attention. He was older now, but emotionally stunted. Amelia had paved the way, and he was Umm's in no time.

She watched him sip his beer on this sunny day at a table in Tysons Corner. Umm knew Khadr would perish in a few days, either by carrying out her wishes or by her own hand if he refused.

She was at peace with that. She was the wife of Omar, the love of her life. Only one other had ever held her heart so dearly. She would avenge them both.

Mary Greene looked at the white wine she had ordered for show and decided to take a long sip. She certainly wasn't going to tell Khadr this, but her well-laid plans were DOA. Because only one of her five girls had arrived in America.

Her favorite and the most competent, Fadwa, disappeared in Paris, never returning from her mission to kill the weakling Aslan Baseyev. Three others had been scooped up trying to enter the United States on altered French passports. Umm had schooled them exhaustively but knew her desert girls were poor soil for gaming Western entry. She had expected some losses, but only one left?

And that was Jomana, the sister of Fadwa. Could it be that her fragile, twiglike presence, her perceived helplessness, had aided her entry?

She did have another, one with the potential to be her most lethal weapon now. Not Khadr, of course. It was Amanda, a young woman in Florida who had spent hours upon hours online with Umm. She was a recent convert to ISIS, and these often were the most fervent. None of her girls from Al-Hol knew of her, so she should still be invisible to the authorities.

Truth was, she could use Dogu's help right now. For beneath his mercurial personality was the sharp intellect and planning of a smuggler. He should be making contact shortly; they had promised each other that their separate plans would be coordinated. But Dogu did what Dogu wanted, and her cratered plans might not be useful to him now.

They had tolerated each other at the refugee camp, knowing they could help each other. But from the day Dogu arrived in Raqqa in Syria, they were at odds. Umm remembered the first meeting between Omar and his last son, who had arrived unexpectedly. Dogu had extended his arms to hug his father, a huge bear of a man with a long, bushy beard, and Omar stepped back and said, "Why have you come?"

It was as if Dogu had been slapped hard, his dream reconciliation shattered. Omar had then turned to Umm and took his wife's hand, a sign of public affection frowned upon by ISIS purists but ignored by the great battle commander. "See that he has a place to stay," Omar had told Umm. Dogu had just stared at them.

She had tried to explain Omar to Dogu—that he had lost three sons and didn't want to lose the last; that he was not a man to express much emotion. But the words rang hollow. Dogu had a talent for reading people, and he saw that in a glance his father had found him wanting. Omar saw a son who had grown up with money and clean sheets, fast women and cars. Omar had never known anything but hard ground and harder combat.

The coldness did not deter Dogu from idolizing his father; he just felt that it was his job to earn his respect. Which he eventually did. But Umm—the American wife who held the affection

Dogu did not have from Omar—would be the target of his anger. Dogu was the one who first called her Ameriki, a slur used by some in ISIS who never took to her. Omar heard and guessed its origin, another tear in the father-son relationship.

Still, after Omar was killed and Umm badly wounded by the American air strike, Dogu had Umm nursed back to health. And later, when both were captured by the Kurds and Americans, they settled into Al-Hol and worked together.

Umm wondered if Dogu's unknown plans to kill many Americans included her. Knowing him, it depended on how much value she had for him. *Was it enough?*

31

A*meriki.*

Angelos kept his poker face when he found out. It wasn't his worst nightmare; that would certainly overstate things, but it was bad news, nonetheless. As a successful operations director, he had contingency plans upon contingency plans. Since receiving the report on the audio from the van heist— "Now they will know I am here"—he had been working on this exact scenario. For one thing, he had dispatched Tom Rivers, hoping he could quietly confirm the identity of the terrorist who beheaded the van driver.

You had to place yourself in the unfolding days of the Islamic State to understand Ameriki. The fanatics were rolling out of Raqqa across Syria and moving into Iraq. Gunmen from ISIS—its new, catchy moniker—targeted young clubgoers in Paris, killing more than one hundred in one evening. A teacher outside Lyon was beheaded by a student newly wrapped up in ISIS, who felt the man had insulted the Prophet. A driver accelerated a U-Haul down a pedestrian walkway in New York City, killing nearly a dozen. In Bakersfield, California, a couple in black ISIS T-shirts attacked an annual meeting of an international company with many contracts supporting the U.S. presence in Iraq, mowing down nearly two dozen with automatic weapons' fire.

The tentacles of ISIS violence were reaching out.

And one of his assets—a woman used by the CIA to gather information about Islamic radicals—became a turncoat. She left a voice mail on her CIA handler's phone, which was then sent directly to Angelos: "Now you will know I am here." A personal warning of impending violence echoed later during that van heist in Paris.

Angelos had thought she was dead, killed along with her husband, Omar the Chechen, in a 2017 air strike. Now it seemed she was resurrected.

He knew critics—and, God forbid, congressional scalpers, if it got that far—would call into question his decisions back then to put his asset in harm's way. They would ignore the tenor of the time, the violence and fear hitting home. But that was life inside the Capital Beltway.

Angelos had received the intelligence of Umm's identity from a reliable source with a direct connection to Mossad. Now he had set a time to brief the CIA director, a retired senator who had not been aboard at the time. Built-in deniability. He envisioned that they'd quickly trek over to the director of National Intelligence—DNI for short—who oversaw eighteen intel agencies, including the CIA.

He would sell them on the obvious: contain Ameriki before she became public. It was what he had been pursuing from the start, when the audio file suggested she was possibly still alive.

Unsaid would be that his career was on the line. Perhaps even if he succeeded.

Angelos couldn't worry about that now. Ameriki was one of a thousand decisions he had made in a long career. Setbacks came with the territory; something to be managed.

With Kate Milano, the director of National Intelligence, it was important to come to the point quickly. And Angelos was her type of guy. Critics called him blunt, his disciples said "incisive."

Milano looked stylish in a navy-blue dress, no jewelry. A tall woman who was a CIA analyst back in the day, she had left after three years for the private sector. She founded a video game start-up that created fast-selling tactical, shoot-'em-up games and, more quietly, the strategic analysis software now used by the CIA and the FBI. With at least $100 million in the bank, Milano had returned to public service.

Sitting next to her in her office at Liberty Crossing, not far from the CIA, was Angelos's boss, Richard A. Harwell. A long-time senator who was unexpectedly defeated by a talk-radio host. His friends landed him the CIA directorship. After decades of being fawned over, Harwell couldn't hide the fact that he considered Angelos's bluntness a bit of disrespect.

"Why have you and the senator raced over to see me?" said Milano. Harwell preferred to be called Senator rather than his current title of Director, and Milano always stroked this minor vanity.

"There's a problem concerning NoE file 578," said Angelos.

That told her a lot: NoE files meant No Eyes, the most damaging ones buried deepest in the CIA archives.

"That file is for Susan Owens, a former asset for the CIA in the Middle East. She abandoned her mission of identifying leadership of ISIS in 2015 and instead joined ISIS. She was reported killed in a U.S. air strike in 2017."

Milano interrupted. "I take it if you're here that either she's not dead or her file has been leaked and the *Washington Post* is publishing an exposé."

"The first one," said Angelos. "For now. But one other thing. We are tracking an ISIS plot to attack the United States. Led by Susan Owens."

Milano absorbed that quietly for a moment, then said, "How close are you to preventing this attack?"

"Not close enough," said Angelos. "We have captured three young ISIS women trying to enter the country, but we believe that Owens and others are in the country. We do not yet have insight into their plot."

"FBI?"

"Alerted to a suspected ISIS plot in the homeland, but not to Owens's identity," said Angelos. "I didn't think it was a needed element for others to know immediately. At least until I talked with you both."

Milano and Harwell glanced at each other, and Milano said, "If Congress and the White House, much less the FBI, get wind of this woman before we tell them, well ..." She didn't have to finish.

"Time to raise the storm flag," she said. "I'm going to alert the FBI director and the National Security adviser. I would think that they'll want to keep Susan Owens's identity as a CIA asset a secret and wrap this up ASAP."

"One thing about Susan Owens," said Angelos. "She was first recruited and vetted and used by the FBI in college."

"Well, that is helpful," said Milano. "It should make the FBI a bit more eager to play ball."

She continued, "Was she one of yours, Mr. Angelos?"

"She was," said Angelos. "I'm sure some will say it was a mistake or an overreach. But it's not how I see it. This woman offered a unique hope that ISIS could be decapitated at a time when its international terror was in full fury.

"But, as every operations officer knows, shit happens."

Milano smiled at his bluntness. She was a realist who accepted that there were risks and unknowns. She would want to know more before deciding whether sending this woman into ISIS's orbit was a mistake or an overreach, and what that meant for Angelos's career.

Harwell was staring at him, his mind made up.

32

Rivers had barely limped off the plane from Kyiv to Paris when he was summoned by Harry Dalton, the CIA Paris Station chief. At least he offered coffee and croissants upon arrival.

"The boss wants to talk to us," said Dalton as they both settled before the video screen in a secure conference room at the U.S. Embassy.

"By the way, you looked like shit when you came out of Syria; now, you look like hell," said Dalton. Rivers's face featured fifteen stitches along the right jawline, and he had a well-wrapped forearm, all where the wire garrote had dug in. Purple bruising streaked his lower cheek.

Rivers only nodded; ibuprofen insufficient to restore his usual good cheer.

Angelos appeared on-screen with his aide, Cowen, who had traveled back from Paris. He appeared relaxed, smiling at something Cowen said, but Rivers noted his eyes looked tired and strained. Dalton glanced at Rivers; he saw it too.

"An hour or so ago I met with the DNI and the CIA director concerning new intelligence," said Angelos. "They are briefing the FBI director and National Security Council as a result. I'm pulling both of you inside the tent."

They had guessed when the sudden meeting was called that something was wrong. Now they knew for sure.

"The new intelligence is the identification of Umm al-Nasr," said Angelos. "She is an American. Real name Susan Owens, and she was a former CIA asset in the Middle East."

Rivers's breath caught, while he heard Dalton's stunned exhale.

"That's going to hurt," said Rivers without thinking.

Angelos nodded and said, "You can't imagine."

Rivers looked at Angelos's poker face and wondered how a man could so calmly handle the stress.

"I'll give you the lowdown on this woman's file and then we'll talk about how we can proceed," said Angelos. He had a thin folder in front of him, and Rivers could only wonder how deeply the real and lengthy file was buried.

Angelos began, "Susan Owens was recruited as a paid informant for the FBI in 2014 while a senior at the University of Kentucky, where she majored in Arabic and Islamic Studies. She was friendly with a group of Middle Eastern students. Most appeared nonpolitical, but one was identified by Owens as professing sympathy for ISIS in Syria. No actionable intel was gathered. As an aside, that one student she identified did in fact join ISIS in Syria. He was reported killed in 2016.

"Her FBI handler described her as an idealist looking for purpose in her life, which working for the U.S. government to defend America seemed to fulfill. Owens came from a fundamentalist Christian family who lived outside Nashville, Tennessee, and she seemed to be questioning her strict upbringing. Nothing unusual there. The retainer the FBI threw her way helped with her expenses. She was on scholarship but waitressing to pay her living expenses.

"After college, Owens decided to join friends met through her group for a stay in Egypt, and then began work for an aid organization in Cairo. Her Arabic proficiency was key to her job. We had tracked her, of course, and we were able to gain her as an asset. Her aid work was to provide health care to the poor, including some dissidents who had survived torture by Egyptian authorities. Owens began to hear anti-American rumblings and was open to reporting them to us. But a few months later, her CIA handler noted that she showed increasing sympathy for the dissidents.

"She was invited by an Egyptian dissident to visit Damascus in 2015 to meet with young people who supported the growing ISIS movement. We knew about the invitation and told her it sounded like a good idea. But we now know that while there, she met Omar al-Shishani, a charismatic leader who soon became known as Omar the Chechen, ISIS's best military commander. She didn't return to Egypt.

"Several weeks later, Owens relayed information to her CIA handler that ISIS aimed to kidnap a Western journalist at a certain time and place in Syria. CIA paramilitary forces moved to safeguard the journalist but were ambushed. Two were killed. Owens sent a voice message to her handler, "Now you will know I am here," and never was in contact with the CIA officer again.

"Our after-action assessment was that Owens came under the sway of this ISIS leader and became invested in a belief that ISIS was making a pure Islamic world. Reports surfaced that she married Omar. The worst, it was reported she became a trainer of female suicide bombers.

"Omar the Chechen was reported killed in an air strike on March 21, 2017, along with his wife, Umm al-Nasr—our Susan Owens.

"Along the way, it was decided to move all information concerning Susan Owens to a highly compartmentalized repository at the CIA.

"There you have it, gentlemen."

Rivers was ready to ask where Angelos had gotten the intel that Umm was Owens, but Angelos plowed right ahead, putting a photo of Susan Owens on the screen from her college days, and two computer-enhanced representations of what she might look like now.

Attractive but severe, thought Rivers.

"The FBI is putting out an intel flyer on her to law enforcement agencies around the country, identifying her as Susan Owens, an activist and former aid worker in Egypt," said Angelos. "Wanted for crimes committed as a member of ISIS."

"The press might catch wind of it, but ISIS isn't headline stuff anymore, so it might be inside-page news to them and a one-day story, if they deal with it at all."

"The CIA and FBI links will stay under wraps. There's no interest in exposing our mutual dirty laundry."

"The FBI has the investigation here and we have Dogu Matsoy, who may be in the Middle East or Europe. We might have a better idea once our techs dig into the phone Rivers retrieved from Raglan Matsoy in Odesa.

"And Tom," Angelos said as he dialed off, "very good work

in Syria and Ukraine. Ease up now. Harry has a lot of resources at his disposal to carry on."

"Thank you, sir," said Rivers, who relished the familiar "Tom" that his boss had used for the first time.

Dalton picked it up too and smiled, simply saying, "Perhaps you're less disposable."

Rivers felt even better when he retrieved his phone from the lockbox outside the secure room and saw the text from Raz: *Don't be a stranger.*

33

Raz ran her fingers lightly over Rivers's damaged face and saw him close his eyes and sigh in contentment. Jeez, he was a mess.

She had spied him in front of his hotel when her car arrived to pick him up for dinner. A tilted figure, face bruised and stitched. She'd heard that he collected important intel on Dogu in Odesa, but it had been a close call. You wouldn't guess that by the electric way he smiled at her when she got out of the car to hug him. And to touch his face.

"Forget dinner out, I'm taking you home," she said.

Who was he to argue?

They leaned into each other in the back seat of the Mercedes as the driver aimed toward the stately buildings of Le Marais, where Raz lived. Her hand cupped the back of his neck to pull him down a bit, so their heads touched. His hand rested on the thigh and knee that she draped over his leg. Nothing spoken. Everything said.

She lived in a three-story building that spoke of eloquence, its cream-colored limestone capturing the light of the waning day, modern windows crafted to a centuries-old look, a digital front door opening upon a tall carriage tunnel into an inner cobblestone courtyard.

"Pretty swanky place," Rivers said.

Raz simply said, "My home."

Rivers paused in the foyer, swept by sadness and fear that he was with a woman beyond his reach. Too pretty, too smart, too rich, too accomplished.

She could sense it. "I'm comfortable with you, Tom. Let yourself be comfortable with me," she said. "I feel I can just be myself with you."

He turned to her and took her in his arms. They kissed passionately and almost fell into the elevator when the door opened.

She giggled.

"Something special," she said.

It was a thought that came to her when she saw Rivers wince when they almost fell into the elevator. Raz lit some scented candles that flickered light and spread a smell of lavender. And she disappeared into a large bathroom, where he saw a huge, claw-foot bathtub to the side of a modern walk-in shower. She ran water into the deep tub, testing its warmth.

"Now take off your clothes and get in," she told Rivers, who had settled into a chair to watch this production.

Which he did. Awkwardly.

He had to balance on an edge of the tub to guide his injured leg up and over into the water, and then he sank in deep, marveling at the warmth.

"You move like an old man," she said.

"That I cannot deny," he said.

Raz pulled up a small table and delivered healthy pours of red wine into glasses.

And then she began to disrobe. Not some gaudy striptease but a simple, slow unveiling.

She slipped into the water opposite him, her long legs riding along his, the water rising above her pert breasts.

"Quite a seduction," said Rivers.

"I think you need some tender loving care," she said.

"We both do," he said.

34

Morning light arrived through sheer white curtains and settled on Rivers's face. He rolled over slowly, shifting through a tangle of covers, and came face-to-face with Raz, still asleep. There had been other mornings like this in his past, though often with a whisper of regret. A feeling that the woman beside him was but a temporary moment, however satisfying for both. Mornings brought honesty.

With Raz, he felt different. He felt he was where he was supposed to be.

They had chatted and laughed through the night when they weren't wrapped up in each other. They talked about interesting places and favorite cuisine and eventually relationships, avoiding any discussion of more worldly topics. They both loved Greek salad and Lebanese yogurt and swimming off coastal rocks, neither had current lovers and both were skeptical of long-term romance but wouldn't rule it out under the right circumstances. And they laughed.

Rivers had once been married; Raz, not.

"College romance," he said. "We were twenty-year-olds who confused loving sex for loving each other. I liked Laura one hell of a lot, but it simply wasn't going to work. She saw that first, way before I did. She was going to have a career; she's a lawyer now. But I was all about myself—a ROTC guy bound for the Army. Laura was never going to be an Army wife.

"I was a fool ever to think we could last. But I was crushed. How could she not love me enough?"

"Sounds like you still love her," said Raz.

"Always a little. It took me a while to realize the issue was me, not her," he said.

Raz smiled and said, "Many men don't get that far."

He listened to Raz's own recounting of love gained and lost, including one that had spun her around. Which she ended on her own terms. As she succeeded at Columbia, and the CIA, and then in business, a deep emotional life wasn't a priority for her. She even felt it could be a hindrance.

"I like men, a lot," she said. "Just not long relationships."

"Is that a warning?" he said.

"I hope not," she whispered, and hugged him closer.

They showered together and dressed. And Rivers had to shake his head in wonder that she had sent one of her bodyguards to break into his hotel room and gather some clean clothes. A benefit of being with the CEO of an intel company, he guessed.

This top-floor apartment had twenty-foot ceilings, and each room had a large fireplace befitting the wealthy who lived a luxurious life here in the 1800s. But Raz had made it comfortably livable, with contemporary sofas and wing chairs and large modernistic paintings—no originals, said Raz—strategically positioned. A wall of bookshelves in the den held small sculptures and several hundred romance novels, a weakness along with ice cream, she said. Every space was not filled; it left a lot for more, if more was so desired. Maybe that said a lot about her. Rivers liked it.

In the kitchen, the female bodyguard who was with Raz when they had dinner at the Paris restaurant had put out coffee and chocolate croissants from a local bakery. She looked like she'd be comfortable carrying in the mail or carrying out some thugs.

A chameleon. Top-end talent had that ability. Raz, for sure. She could dazzle at an elite cocktail party on a hotel rooftop in Paris or mingle as a CIA officer on the streets in the Middle East. Rivers? He felt he topped out as a street guy.

Raz took him down to the second floor of the building to show him the headquarters of her company, with a central command center filled with computer screens and three analysts. It struck Rivers immediately that this was a data mining operation, shifting through surveillance and any accompanying information fed from the hotels and businesses who hired her company.

"So, I see you're not just checking for credit card fraud," said Rivers.

"No, data is a commodity," she said. "It's a revenue stream when sorted and packaged."

"Who buys the information?"

"Depends ..." said Raz. "We are selective."

"And who are 'we'?" said Rivers, widening his arms to take in the whole visible operation.

"I have a partner. An Israeli, ex-Mossad," she said.

His eyes caught on a bank of digital clocks on a wall. He recognized the array: five clocks for the time zones of the global intelligence services comprising Five Eyes. It was the most secret intel-sharing group in the world led by the United States. Her customers for data?

"How did you fall in with your Israeli partner?" asked Rivers.

"We both worked in Cairo," she said.

Click: Cairo. Susan Owens. CIA handler. Raz.

Wasn't it always going to get to this? Hadn't Raz guided him here?

Raz saw it in his eyes, a momentary widening.

Do love affairs end with a click?

35

P aul Laurent thought Rivers could be one moody guy.

The French intel officer picked him up from what he knew was Raz Jackson's place. Why anyone would be in a sketchy mood after obviously spending the night with a beautiful woman was beyond him. It seemed to him Americans made things too difficult on themselves.

Laurent didn't hold himself as an expert on love; he was divorced and long married to his job, which was why he was divorced. He looked over at battered, cloudy Rivers, some twenty years his junior, and wondered if he would wind up like himself: alone. He hoped not.

"Remember Musa Gugaev, the old guy, two canes, at the Dudayev Centre? I got word that he wanted to see me," said Laurent. "It was suggested I bring you along, if you were still alive."

"I'm not going to get beat up on the sidewalk again, am I?" said Rivers.

"Even if we met the gang again, I doubt it," said Laurent. "You look so beat up already, they'd be ashamed if they added to it."

There was time to kill as they got hung up in morning traffic, and Laurent wanted to know more about Dogu from his Odesa visit than what he had seen in the report the CIA delivered to their French counterparts.

"How capable do you think this Dogu is at planning a terrorist strike?" he asked.

"High risk," said Rivers. "Think about it. He's only approaching his mid-twenties, and he's had experience smuggling out of Odesa, fighting on the front lines in Syria, running smuggling for ISIS, surviving the final battles, leveraging himself out of the Al-Hol camp, and now disappearing.

"He's described as highly intelligent, street smart, violent, a young man who wants to make his mark as Dogu the Chechen on a world stage, but not be a martyr.

"We need to think big regarding his targets," said Rivers.

Laurent nodded and said, "Yes, and remember that ISIS and Al Qaeda always want to use our own technology against us. Remember that plot to blow up thirteen airplanes flying to the United States? That sort of thing."

Silence settled in the car. Now Laurent felt moody.

It was eleven a.m. and Musa Gugaev sat in his musty chair, the two canes against the small table holding a bottle of bourbon and a few glasses.

"Ahh, I wanted to see if the CIA man said to have killed Raglan Matsoy was still alive," said Gugaev, making a show of looking Rivers up and down. "Maybe you're a little alive."

Word of Raglan's demise had traveled through the Chechen and Captagon smuggling circles. The old man offered drinks, which they declined. He put a few fingers' worth in his glass.

"Did you know Raglan Matsoy?" asked Rivers.

"Oh no. Just men like him," he said. "Hard-to-kill men. Probably Raglan underestimated you, as an American. He didn't see you are a hard-to-kill man too. His loss.

"But I did not send word to my friend Paul and you to congratulate you on your survival. Instead, perhaps to save your life."

He had Rivers's full attention.

"There are rumors, and I love rumors," said Gugaev. "What else is an old man to do?

"These damn ISIS have caused great concern in our community," he said. "Police attention, media attention. We Chechens are being looked at as a bunch of terrorists. We do not go about cutting people's heads off!"

Gugaev had grasped one of his canes and was striking it on the floor for emphasis.

Now he looked at Rivers.

"The rumor is that the Matsoys are looking to hire assassins to kill an American here in Paris," said Gugaev. "A local Chechen gang was approached but declined, and that's how I heard. You can be assured someone took the money."

"The name of the American?" asked Laurent.

"It was not spoken," said the old man. "But we know one American in Paris who has reason to fear."

A chill ran up Rivers's back.

"Thank you, my friend," said Laurent. "I will see you soon for a friendlier chat."

"I'm not finished," said Gugaev.

He pulled a piece of folded paper from his shirt pocket and gave it to Laurent. "The address of a man who fit this Dogu Matsoy's description. An Airbnb, one of those. He left a few days ago, but you may find something there. Also, the name of a pimp. This man got into an argument for abusing one of the prostitutes."

Maybe this was the scent of the ghost they were pursuing.

Laurent made a phone call to a vice detective and got a location for the pimp in Gugaev's note. Not far from the U.S. Embassy near some major hotels and Airbnbs popular with businessmen, some perhaps looking for a sexual adventure.

"I won't be long," Laurent said as he pulled up outside a café. "Try not to get assassinated while I'm gone."

"Funny, Paul."

He returned in five minutes.

"He identified Dogu from that picture we have of him from Al-Hol. The pimp said he paid extra for rough sex, but he almost killed the girl by strangling her. He wanted more money, and Dogu said he'd kill him. Which he thought he might do."

"Could Dogu still be at the Airbnb?" asked Rivers.

"No, the pimp said the girl saw an airline ticket to somewhere in the United States, she didn't quite remember because she was so in shock. Pimp says he's gone.

"I'll get a police detective to follow up, maybe get more."

While Laurent was away, Rivers checked his phone and saw a text from Raz: *smitten.*

He needed time to process the morning's revelation of Raz as case officer for Susan Owens in Cairo.

A lot to take in.

Rivers texted back: *smitten and confused.*

36

Their calls to Dalton at Paris Station and Laurent's boss, Martin Lyons, got the wheels rolling. Rivers was ordered to report back to the U.S. Embassy.

Laurent had checked his handgun before they exited the center after talking with Gugaev, although they both knew it would do little good if they were attacked. If the Matsoys wanted to kill a CIA officer in Paris, there'd be multiple gunmen with automatic weapons ... or poison in his wine ...

"... or a bomb under his car. Laurent hadn't thought of that last one until after he turned the ignition after talking to the pimp at the café.

"I have to say, Thomas, trouble follows you more than most."

Rivers smiled at the Gallic understatement.

"The bosses are going to kick me out of France," said Rivers.

"Certainly," said Laurent.

"Look," he continued, "tactically, it's the right move. Take you out of harm's way and give the police the chance to catch whoever it is. And politically, Dalton and Lyons don't want you to get killed on their turf."

"If I were you, I'd get lost for a while in South Beach in Miami, and see if your girlfriend will join you," said Laurent.

"A little sun and fun."

Laurent was allowed to pull into one of the Embassy's gates, and they walked to the secure room where they found Dalton and Lyons, with Angelos on the screen. Dalton debriefed them both, focusing on the old man's tip of a threat to assassinate an American.

"Since it's obviously directed at you, if true," said Dalton, nodding to Rivers, "we've already agreed that you're catching a flight out of here ASAP."

"We've had some luck with the phone you brought back from Odesa," said Dalton. "A call from Paris to Raglan came from a location that possibly corresponds to that mentioned Airbnb. That phone was promptly ditched, but we've been able to identify a new phone started up in the same proximity. Then we later lost track at Charles de Gaulle. There was such a tonnage of phones at the airport that we couldn't continue to track."

"So, it does appear to be Dogu," said Dalton.

Angelos could tell from Lyons's stoney expression that he was irked by this CIA work that intruded onto his French territory. He'd have to massage the situation later, maybe have a case of fine wine personally delivered to his French colleague.

"Assassinate an American," said Lyons. "We shouldn't have what you call 'tunnel vision.' Perhaps it's not Rivers. Maybe it's the ambassador or"—looking at Dalton— "the CIA station chief."

Dalton had put out a threat warning on the ambassador immediately after he received Rivers's call. But he hadn't considered himself in the line of fire. He didn't like that idea.

"This is an active threat," said Lyons. "My DGSE and Paris police are on full alert to find the assassins."

"So, Tom, looks like you'll be coming home," said Angelos. "Lucky for you, we've been able to round up a corporate jet to do the trick. You'll travel in style."

"Yes, sir," said Rivers.

But he wasn't going anywhere without seeing Raz.

Angelos and Dalton put up no fight. And within a half hour, two embassy SUVs were moving bumper to bumper to her apartment in Le Marais. Laurent and Rivers were in the first SUV, with the driver and a heavily armed security guard, called a "shooter." A second vehicle had another shooter riding with the driver.

"I'm going to miss you," said Laurent.

Rivers looked touched.

"It'll mean I'll be back behind my desk without having to drive you around," said Laurent with a twist of Gallic humor to ease the departure of a friend.

"It'll be a safer but less fun Paris."

37

"I was afraid you'd just text," said Raz.

He was standing in her apartment, the rumpled bedclothes from last night visible through a doorway.

"No way," said Rivers. "This morning threw me a curve, but you were open with me. Fact is, you've spun me all around."

He reached out to her and took Raz in his arms. "I don't know where we're going, but I want to be with you."

Raz smiled. She had heard more romantic lines in her day but none so welcome.

"Well," she said, "the good news is that the corporate jet you're taking is leased by my company. And I think I'll just tag along with you now."

She went into the bedroom and pulled a go bag from her closet. He followed and looked into the bathroom at the claw-foot tub. She followed his gaze. Who would ever imagine this ancient piece of cast-iron could hold such a wonderful memory?

At four p.m., with the first hint of shadows on the street, Rivers and Raz walked out the front door of her building and were ushered into the back seat of the second SUV. Rivers had seen Laurent smile from the front vehicle when he saw that Raz was taking the trip with him.

A few seconds later, as the SUVs eased forward, the street vibrated with a whoosh.

A rocket-propelled grenade fired from a rooftop barely flew over the roof of the black SUV in which Rivers rode and slammed into the front one, lifting the entire vehicle into the air, a flare of orange fire and black smoke engulfing it.

Their driver slammed their SUV in reverse, and a second RPG narrowly missed it. They were deafened by the blasts and saw an armor-piercing round slam through the windshield. The shooter in the passenger seat screamed.

Smoke followed them down the street, but it lessened just enough for Rivers to see the crippled hulk of the first SUV carrying Laurent lying in the road, licked by fire. Their driver had hit a red button on the dash, an alert for emergency help from the Embassy. He spun the car around at high speed in the inter- section.

He drove like a demon back toward the Embassy, at one point scraping past cars blocking him, wheels up over the curb. The engine groaned, the radio blaring cop talk of disaster. A police car fronted them in a block, and then another, sirens and lights clearing the way.

Rivers unbuckled his seatbelt, leaned forward and applied pressure to stop the heavy flow of blood from the unconscious shooter in the passenger seat. Raz steadied Rivers to keep him from being thrown about and reached out for the radio's microphone. She calmly gave their moving locations and the need for emergency medical aid.

The police cars sheared off at an Embassy gate while the SUV sped in and braked hard. The medical staff awaited the wounded shooter. Diplomatic Security officers quickly moved Raz and Rivers from the small courtyard through a door.

The late afternoon was full of sirens.

They were surrounded by guards and were guided down a delivery corridor, old overhead lights buzzing. The bodyguard was wheeled ahead.

Raz looked at Rivers, whose shirt was red and sticky with the shooter's blood and saw the agony on his face. He was in a dark place somewhere between shock and rage. Rivers kept repeating:

"Laurent."

PART FOUR

38

I t was morning in America, and Mary Greene's check of her phone didn't bring the news she desired.

She stepped into the shower and let the hot water run down her aching back. She looked over and saw the misting steam had erased her image in the large mirror. Funny how in all the time she'd spent in the high desert and in that godforsaken camp, she had never thought much about pain in her back, compliments of shrapnel. More pressing issues. Now, in these American moments, she had more time to think of herself. And her back hurt. Truly a First-World problem.

The former Umm al-Nasr and Susan Owens was staying at the Ritz at the Tysons Corner Galleria. She felt it was an excessively luxurious selection by Dogu, but also brilliant in that no one would expect to find a terrorist at the Ritz.

One of the hotel entrances was inside the Galleria, a three-level mall with treats like Cartier, Gucci, Dior, and Sassoon. She had had dinner at a place called the Lebanese Taverna, which tried to capture the ambience of a Middle Eastern restaurant. Good food, but it lacked the authentic feel of danger and chaos outside its doors.

It was time to wait.

Her helper, Khadr, had rented a town house a few miles away in McLean, and Umm knew he lusted after Jomana who was there with him. But the twiglike girl was not interested in sex, and the young man lacked the character for rape. She knew Jomana spent most of her time on her prayer rug. No doubt praying for her sister's arrival.

She had spoken with her American disciple Amanda briefly and in code over the phone. The supplies for the attacks were en route, she was told. She found it hard to wait.

Umm wondered what Dogu's own plans were, for he had refused to tell her.

"You want revenge," Dogu had said to her in rebuke. "I want to stun the world."

Umm long ago had buried Susan Owens, and Mary Greene was a convenient creation. She remained Umm al-Nasr in her heart.

She later sat with her treasured book open on her lap, half-watching the headline news. Pick a channel, and it was there now.

Terror attack in Paris in the elegant Le Marais neighborhood. At least two U.S. Embassy employees and a French officer killed. RPGs fired at a small caravan of cars. Sources say ISIS is behind the attack.

She felt a sense of fulfillment, the start of justice delivered. Dogu had arranged this attack on her former CIA handler Raz Jackson for her. Soon, her announcement giving ISIS credit for the attack—and promising more—would hit the internet and social media.

She so missed Omar, so missed the holy life of ISIS in Raqqa, creating a pure caliphate, the routine of the shrouded women buying fresh vegetables in the open market, the husbands brazen with their conquering passion. Only the unbelievers and unfaithful had to fear, as it should be. But American missiles had taken Omar and the shrapnel carved into her scars had sealed a burning hate.

Umm had been waiting for the attack in Paris, a signal from Dogu that their venture to kill their enemies—the enemies of ISIS—had begun.

She believed the CIA woman who had guided her in Cairo was now dead. Raz Jackson could leave the CIA, but she could never escape Umm's revenge.

She reached for her volume of *The Blaze of Truth*, which had sustained her for years, as she read and reread Ahlam al-Nasr's poetry celebrating mujahideen and the holy way of ISIS life. Ahlam was thought to be gone now, killed in the last battles. But her words lived for Umm, who long ago had adopted her last name in tribute.

Seemingly a million times, Umm had reread one of the lines of poetry, which Ahlam wrote after seeing Assad's murder of Syrian protestors, many mere children.

America was about to learn her favorite line: *"Their bullets shattered our brains like an earthquake."*

39

D ogu Matsoy liked playing tourist in New York City. What a great place for a young man with money, looks, an accent that made his English sound like it was spoken by an Italian. And he had that flair, a touch of arrogance and danger.

The young women in the high-end bars—lawyers, financial managers, dentists—couldn't imagine just how dangerous this attractive man, who billed himself as the managing partner of a global shipping concern, really was.

Of course, he kept his abuse on a leash with the very few of those he bedded. Instead, he unleashed his choking brutality on prostitutes. The best way to avoid the prying eyes of police. You just paid the pimp more for the damage.

Yet money couldn't buy everything. He had paid an Italian Captagon enforcer gang to kill that former CIA officer in Paris. They had fired two damn RPGs at a sitting target and still couldn't get the job done. He had set it up as the first strike in Umm's revenge tour: Kill the CIA officer who had run her in

Cairo and who had a hand in Omar's death, true or not. But the word on the street was the target escaped unharmed.

Umm would consider it a failure but killing U.S. Embassy and French personnel was a good announcement of ISIS's new muscle. Dogu also thought it could keep his pursuers focused on Paris and not the United States. Maybe there would be an opportunity later to take another crack at this Raz Jackson. As long as she didn't expect Dogu to pursue the task. His effort was a one and done.

He had tracked down this former CIA officer after he left Al-Hol and set up a small computer operation out of the remnants of ISIS at a property he leased on a remote Greek island. Everyone knew that if you wanted to know about U.S. government personnel, contact some of the Chinese who had hacked into its federal files and sold it on the side. It didn't come cheap.

After that, it was easy. The officer had left the CIA but turned up as a principal in a start-up business in Paris.

Dogu changed hotels in Manhattan every two days, using his pick of stolen identification and credit cards. He remembered his anger when Umm once described him to Omar as "Europeanized." Now he knew it was an asset. Uncle Raglan's guidance to learn languages and his underwriting of trips to Turkey, Greece, France, and Germany taught him how to blend in with the West.

And now, just the other day, he had learned about this singer Sinatra. Loved his voice. Dogu couldn't stop humming that song about New York.

He'd soon be *King of the Hill.*

40

Angelos appreciated that Kate Milano, the director of National Intelligence, had a mind faster and more incisive than his own. Able to juggle more things at once. Angelos knew he was pretty sharp himself, sly actually, and a master of contingency plans. But she was remarkable.

Milano was recounting, as they sat in her secure conference room, how she had parried Rep. Chad Pompano's unannounced visit to her office that morning. Milano, along with the FBI director, already were keeping the congressional leadership, called the Gang of Eight, in the loop. But Pompano and his loud House faction styled themselves as some sort of "new" leadership, as in masters of social media, and always wanted to promote contentious issues.

What was a better issue than CIA-FBI ineptitude in chasing down terrorists obviously bent on ravaging congressional districts like Pompano's in rural Arkansas.

"I have to say, Pompano has impressive hair," said Milano. "Must be all that shit-for-brains providing fertilizer."

"He marched in here quite rudely and demanded the Gang of Eight briefing. I asked him why his leadership didn't provide him with that information.

"He said, 'They say it's classified and need to know.'

"I told him that it still was, and that when he was in the Gang of Eight, I'll be happy to share such briefings with him."

"He got sulky, like his just showing up here would open the door for him."

"So, he went away mad," said Angelos.

"Not really," said Milano. "I sprinkled some sugar on him. Said I respected his coming to see me face-to-face, that he had a promising career, and that I would see what I could do to provide a briefing for him."

"Really?" said Angelos.

"Well, when he's in the Gang of Eight," she said.

Their conversation came without CIA Director Richard Harwell, who had first said he'd participate via secure video and then begged off. He cited an attack of gout, but the two seasoned professionals thought it was more about preserving as much deniability as possible. If news that a former FBI-CIA asset was now a terrorist at large became public, no spin—or facts—could prevent scorching public blowback. Especially from vultures like Pompano.

"Martin Lyons in Paris says it looks like it was an Italian drug smuggling gang that was hired for the hit," said Angelos. "He's thinking the target was Rivers for killing the Matsoy kingpin in Odesa, but he knows Raz Jackson is former CIA, so he's not ruling her out."

"And with this Susan Owens's link to Jackson, she easily could be the target," said Angelos.

"Revenge is the motivation for Susan Owens and Dogu," he continued. "Rivers reported that Dogu Matsoy wants to avenge his father by becoming a globally famous terrorist. Owens wants revenge too, but her targets could be more personal. Going after Raz would fit."

"So, their targets?" said Milano.

"The bin Laden targets for Dogu: New York City and D.C., more specifically the World Trade Center and the Capitol and Pentagon," said Angelos. "CIA and FBI for Owens."

"They'll come at us with some imagination," Milano said. "They had time in the desert to plan this out, and this Matsoy seems to have a lot of resources at his disposal."

"You know, I find this Susan Owens fascinating," said Milano. "I see the link that she was raised in a strict, fundamentalist family and then joined a new strict, fundamentalist family of sorts in ISIS. So many Cold War studies showed how hardcore Soviet communists who defected to the West often became hard-core Catholics. The strict creed could change, but not their personality as true believers in an authoritarian framework.

"What I don't understand is how Susan Owens in any incarnation came to train girls to become suicide bombers."

"Maybe teaching these girls to kill themselves was about Susan wanting to kill herself," said Angelos.

"Maybe, but I doubt it," said Milano. "I think it's just pure hatefulness. I wonder how she got that way."

41

Rivers had a small balcony befitting his small apartment in the Crystal City section of Arlington, Virginia. They were calling the neighborhood something else these days, he thought, with Amazon buying up a large chunk. But it was the same place, buffeted by jet noise from Reagan airport on its outskirts.

He leaned back in his lawn chair on the balcony, a bottle of Blue Moon cold and dripping in his hand and gazed inward at the big hole in his heart. *Laurent.* This was an echo of how he felt when Alex was killed near Mosul. A blackness.

Raz had wanted to stay with him, but this was something he thought he had to work out by himself.

Skyscrapers were the rule in Crystal City, and one blocked him from seeing the nearby Potomac River, wide and slow flowing, yet with a dangerous current below its apparent innocence. It was midday, only hours after the flight back from Paris landed, and he soon had to go see Angelos.

No doubt the operations director wanted to do his due diligence to see if his prized stalking horse still had some gallop in him.

He felt a slight breeze and some angle of the sun lit his face, and he felt an urge to talk to the only family he felt close to. Rivers searched his contact list and found the number for someone in a time zone several hours ahead: Daryan Nuri.

"I was thinking of you, Mr. Nuri, and thought I'd call to see how you and Hanaa were doing," said Rivers.

They chatted for a while, and Rivers relaxed a bit as he heard Hanaa had shown a knack as a seamstress of the colorful Yazidis clothes, and her children were settling into a school after their time at Al-Hol. Leila was doing well in college, and her father was frustrated, though forgiving, that she found ways to duck her bodyguard.

But then Nuri turned serious: "I can hear the struggle in your voice, Thomas."

Rivers broached the subject. "A colleague, a friend, was killed in that attack in Paris."

"No shame in being shaken up," said Nuri. "Consider it a tribute to your friend. Would you like to visit me and stay a while? The mountain air and quiet is healing."

"Just talking with you is helping me, though I do look forward to visiting you soon."

"We both know the blackness that comes with such a bitter death," said Nuri. "It comes in waves, and even now the thought of Alex chokes me. But the wave is less drowning each time, although I hope it never goes away."

"I spent so much time after my son's death asking, 'Why him?' but I came to realize it was also, 'Why me?'" Nuri continued. "Leila was the one who shocked me like a thunderbolt. I had spoken angrily to her about partying with friends, and she said, 'Father, I'm still alive.' It was six months after Alex's death, and I saw in that moment that I had put a shroud over my life and the lives of my children. There is so much to live for."

"Your friend in Paris, and our Alex, would want you to carry on. Live to your fullest. … Just some advice from an old man."

"Not so old, but very wise," said Rivers. "Hearing your voice has helped me a lot. Thank you."

"When you brought Alex's body home to me, you became a son, Thomas. Do not think you are ever alone. … Now, you must do what life expects of you."

Rivers's arrival created a stir in the CIA's Operations Center, the whispers of his near-death exploits in Syria and Odesa suddenly visible in the flesh, a limping man with a jagged rip along his jaw acknowledging them with a self-conscious smile.

Angelos watched him walk in and saw how he reacted—and chalked him up as walking wounded but good to go. Nothing hangdog or vacant about the young man.

He took a seat on the sofa in Angelos's office. Angelos sat across in an ergonomic office chair, and his aide, Cowen, was sitting down in another chair after juggling in three cups of coffee for them. Time for his next assignment.

"The investigation here at home is the FBI's juridiction," said Angelos. "We've got the international sphere and Harry Dalton is leading that from Paris."

"Which raises the question of what you want me to do here," said Rivers.

"Simple: You've been like a can opener on this whole thing.

With the clock ticking, why wouldn't I want one of my best weapons where the action is?"

Rivers could see where this was going and stayed quiet. A quick glance at Cowen detected a bit of unease.

"Susan Owens was an asset to our agency. Technically she never resigned, and we should be able to investigate our own," said Angelos.

Of course, there was the small matter of the CIA being barred from operating in the United States.

Angelos went to his desk and came back with a few items: a badge and identification for Thomas Rivers as a special agent for the Department of Homeland Security. A handgun. And a new phone.

"Is this …"

Angelos cut him off with a forceful, "Quiet."

Of course, Rivers's question was, *Is this legal?*

Rivers stared at Angelos, a spy of a thousand secrets. This man was invested in finding Susan Owens at all costs, and he'd sort through the bureaucratic wreckage later if it came to that. He explained that the credentials were to give Rivers an aura of official authority, if needed, in pursuing Dogu and Umm on the home turf barred to the CIA.

"Are you onboard?" asked Angelos.

Rivers simply nodded and reached for his new job identity and gear.

42

Rivers sat outside a Starbucks a few miles from CIA headquarters and awaited a contact who Angelos said would work with him.

Another Angelos secret production.

Exhaust and traffic noise rolled off the street like a heat wave, and Rivers realized looking back at the coffee shop's build and ample parking that it once was a gas station. It had progressed from one fill 'er up to another.

Rivers had cornered Cowen before he left the Operations Center, and the linebacker of a man simply had shrugged and said, "We're on thin ice on this one. Good luck."

Within minutes, a black Range Rover pulled up and a woman stepped out—and Raz greeted him with a megawatt smile and a touch of his cheek that sent an electric current up his spine.

"How are you doing, Tom?" she said. "I've been worried about you."

"I've missed you," he said quietly. "But what in the hell are you doing here?"

"Let's talk in the car as we drive," she said.

There was a driver and a bodyguard in the front, and Raz and Tom had the back behind a sound-dampening screen. No snuggling this time. All business.

"What's up with you and Angelos?" said Rivers.

Raz was expecting it.

"You've probably guessed most of it," she said. "When I was in Cairo, Susan was my asset. After it went bad, I left the agency. I was angry; I had recommended against sending her to the Damascus meeting where ISIS recruited her. I knew she was vulnerable. I was in despair about what happened. And I had a great opportunity available—my Israeli friend was talking about starting an IT security company.

"Fast forward now. Over time, I occasionally fed information to Angelos and Interpol's Barnes regarding drug and human smuggling that my company picked up.

"You can say I'm here now because I'm personally invested. I was there at Umm's creation, and I think she tried to have me killed in Paris. Or you, which I also would take personally.

"I think we have a chance at stopping her and this Dogu in time."

Rivers looked out the window at the traffic pileup as they creeped across the American Legion Bridge into Maryland. He remembered Laurent's advice to be careful around Raz, and her own advice, *Don't be smitten.*

Way too late for all that.

He reached over and took her hand.

Raz rang the doorbell and Rivers stood slightly behind, and a woman answered with a polite smile. She was on summer vacation from her job as a teacher at an elementary school. She looked like she could easily lay down the law to rambunctious fifth graders and, perhaps from that experience, quickly gave a wary look to the unknown two at her front door, as if she recognized a scam in progress.

"Hello, I'm Razanne Jackson and this is special agent Thomas Rivers"—here Rivers opened his jacket to show the badge attached to his belt— "and we are looking for the sister of Susan Owens."

Short and sweet.

Cowen had sent Rivers this address on his encrypted phone and some information on their target: Paula Daniels, a substitute teacher, mother of a two-year-old, and, most important, Susan's younger sister. He texted that Daniels was home this morning, on Facebook much of the time. She had been interviewed long ago when Susan Owens moved from being an FBI asset to a CIA one; a quick assessment, not a deep dive that an actual employee of the agency would endure.

Cowen had reviewed the brief writeup done by a government contractor at the Owens's home outside Nashville, and something caught his eye. It wasn't that the assessment ended, "No derogatory information." It was that, while Paula, the younger sister, was interviewed, the parents and neighbors had declined.

Odd. And Cowen, and Angelos when informed, disliked oddities. *Could it be something? Relevant to finding her? Who knows?*

The CIA managers knew it was the small print and footnotes of lives that often camouflaged important information.

"I'm Susan's sister," said the woman at the door. She looked perplexed, "Has something happened to her?"

"No," said Raz. "We're updating the paperwork of many federal employees. You've seen the news of all the leaks. So now everyone is being re-vetted." She was ready to explain that her sister was an asset overseas, but the woman didn't ask.

"Come in," said Paula, who still looked wary.

She lived with her accountant husband and daughter in a town house in Rockville, Maryland, in a subdivision of similar houses. Small patches of well-kept lawns, with plenty of trees and shrubs. A small park with a basketball court down the street, empty as they drove by. They smelled coffee as they sat in a sunroom off the kitchen, and Paula dropped the bomb.

"I'm surprised," she said. "I just had lunch with Susan yesterday after many years, and suddenly you're at my door. Susan did seem tired and tense. I know she's worked for the government for a long time overseas. Is she OK?"

Raz didn't blink, but her stomach fluttered. Rivers had sat down farthest from Paula and remained silent, seeing a potential rapport between the two women.

"We're not sure that she's OK," said Raz, mirroring some of Paula's wording and concern back to her.

"She's had a hard time overseas and didn't show up for an appointment at headquarters yesterday," said Raz. "We're concerned and trying to find her. She's very valued by the agency.

"Where did you have lunch with Susan?" she asked.

"A Silver Diner in Tysons," said Paula. "She said she'd just gotten back from Egypt and didn't have a car yet. So, I drove down there."

"Did Susan speak to you about her work overseas?"

"Just that she continues to work for one of those aid organizations that help people, a cover I would guess," said Paula. "But she said it was depressing; women and people of faith so mistreated."

She paused, then said, "Something was off with her. Look, I hadn't seen my sister for years, so we're not close, never were. But I deal with some kids and, good Lord, some parents, who need mental help, and she reminded me of the one or two who scare me. She had a cold anger just under the surface.

"I'm not quite sure why she bothered to see me," Paula continued. "I guess it's because I'm the only one left of our immediate family. Even with the awkwardness, I invited her to visit and meet my daughter, but she said she wasn't going to be around that long. She was always like that."

"Like what?"

"Susan always went her own way."

"What do you mean by that?" said Raz.

Paula paused, and Raz sensed it was the moment in an interview when a person was on the brink of opening up or shutting down. But it was nearly irresistible for people to talk about their past, particularly when there was something to talk about.

"We'd tell people we were from Nashville," said Paula. "But it was a crossroads outside. We were naïve girls growing up, sheltered in a community organized around our church. Susan was the oldest, then Mary a year younger, and me three years later."

Raz and Rivers glanced at each other. *Mary?*

"Both of us—Susan and me—wound up leaving," she said. "Because of Mary."

"Why was that?"

Paula took a deep breath.

"My father worked for the county highway department, a truck mechanic, and Mom stayed at home," she said. "Our family revolved around the local Christian church. Three times a week we were at the church, and there were always dinners with church families; we played only with church kids. My dad was a deacon, and our family time in the evening focused on reading the Bible, certainly not TV; we didn't have one."

"What happened?" Raz gently pressed.

"When Mary was fifteen, she accused the pastor's son of molesting her," said Paula. "Not directly. She was so scared, but she told Susan, and it was Susan who told Dad. He said Mary was making up a story and should repent, but then she turned up pregnant. Our dad wouldn't believe her about the pastor's boy, who wanted to study for the ministry himself. Susan argued with him, but Dad accused Mary of being a whore with nonbelieving boys.

"That night Mary took Dad's hunting rifle and shot herself," said Paula.

She was speaking without emotion, but her face showed her distress. She paused, then continued.

"Susan was studying at UK, already on the outs with our parents, who didn't want her to go to college. She had come home to help Mary, but after the night Mary died, she left and never came home again, not even for Mary's funeral."

Silence hung in the sunroom. Bees buzzed on a bush outside the window. Her daughter stirred from a nap and called for her Mommy.

Rivers texted some info to Cowen: *Paula had lunch with Susan at a Silver Diner in Tysons yesterday, perhaps video? Another sister Mary, look up Tenn suicide/info.*

He then held up his phone to Paula so she could see an AI-generated face of Susan Owens updated from her college identification photos.

"Yes, but maybe fifteen pounds lighter. She's rail thin," said Paula.

"Is Susan OK?" she asked, already knowing she wasn't.

"We'll see," said Raz. "We aim to see her soon."

43

Many of the women, and a few men, in the bar-restaurant had taken a peek at Steve Cohen, and wished he was on their menu.

He was long and lean, with wavy black hair, decked out in a loose white shirt and slim black denim. And damn, he had a smile. But he was anchored at a small table with an attractive woman and a man most notable for the long gash on his jaw.

Rivers quickly understood the dynamic: Raz was seated between lovers past and present.

"Steve is my partner in the company," said Raz, who had taken Rivers to the rooftop D.C. nightspot. "We met in Cairo when we were both working for our respective firms."

Mossad for Cohen, as Rivers recalled.

Cohen had invited Raz out tonight and said, "Bring the new guy along. It's work-related." But she knew he would not be able to help himself.

It had been more than an affair with Steve; a two-year bell

curve, with a heartbreaking last six months. He had never understood what soured the relationship, how she could turn him out of her bed but then was able to remain a friend and business partner.

But it was classic Raz. She had swum to the top of their romance and seen the limits of its possibilities. With that, she ended it. The problem was that Cohen was Cohen, a handsome man with a first-class mind for computers and intel but limited emotionally. He not only thought the sun rose with him each morning but that it should. His effortlessly successful life proved it. Raz saw she would never be more than a sparkling accessory to him.

Cohen had his arm around her chair and let it slip to her shoulders, and Rivers watched as Raz artfully made a slight turn that detached Steve's arm. The jujitsu of women.

Cohen didn't hide his long look sizing up Rivers and the badge peeking from his belt. He recognized the type. He'd be part of Israel's Sayeret Matkal, its fabled recon intelligence-gathering unit. Street smart, tough, sly. Maybe Raz preferred men with rough edges, he thought.

"While it's nice just getting together," said Cohen, "I wanted to give you some information I've come across. Your Dogu is quite the smart guy. He's reassembled the best of ISIS's surviving hacker crew. They're located somewhere in the Greek islands. Obviously, I've heard Mossad is looking to help U.S. intelligence to identify the location, and to pick up and tap into their internet traffic. This guy is emerging as a big-time threat."

Rivers remembered the computer room in Raz's office in Paris and its telltale clocks for Five Eyes.

"Who all has this information?" asked Rivers.

"Everyone who needs to know," said Cohen.

"OK, so my boss, then," said Rivers.

Cohen hesitated, then nodded.

So, Cohen knew Angelos. But then, who didn't Angelos know?

This time Cohen's hand came to rest on Raz's shoulder, and she didn't move away. It was so gentle, a touch of dear memory and friendship. Rivers recognized the moment, remembered his own wrenching breakup with his wife, who correctly saw their end before he even imagined it. It was challenging to feel sorry for a guy so pretty and rich, but Rivers did, at least in the moment.

"One more thing, just as important," said Cohen, back to business. "We've gotten some info that one of the Saudi princes soaked in that Wahhabi faith who used to underwrite ISIS put a pile of money into a bank in Cyprus that Dogu may be using as a bankroll. Another fishing net that might help you scoop up Dogu."

"Links to the Saudi government?" asked Rivers.

"Noooo," said Cohen. "An individual effort. The Saudi government always likes to see the United States squirm, but terrorism isn't their thing—against America, that is. No profit in it for them."

They finished the small plates—hummus, grape leaves, scallops, beef tenderloin and such—and Raz and Rivers moved to depart. Cohen looked like he would stay and troll the bar.

Raz reached up and kissed Cohen on the cheek, and he and Rivers shook hands.

"Take care of yourself, Raz," Cohen said. "See you back in Paris."

To Rivers, he simply said, "Luck."

44

Rivers exited under the helicopter's whirling blades and limped toward the man leaning against the dark blue sedan. The bird had sped him from CIA headquarters to Manhattan, and his back was screaming from the helicopter's shifts and bounces.

"John Xavier," said the man, sticking out his hand. "Lieutenant, NYPD Intelligence Bureau." He was in a pressed blue suit and polished brown shoes that Rivers noted had good tread for running, if necessary. Not always a desk man.

Angelos had called Rivers and Raz at two a.m. with the news that there was a lead on Dogu Matsoy. Police had been combing hotels in New York and Metro Washington for Dogu and Umm-Susan, all with no progress. But an item in Rivers's last report from Paris had produced a hit: Dogu was known to frequent prostitutes and was prone to violence against them.

"We've zeroed in on your Matsoy probably in one of the high-end hotels near Central Park," said Xavier. "He appears to be moving around, but that seems to be his nesting area. Vice found out about a guy who choked a call girl and Dogu's photo was IDed."

"These girls aren't streetwalkers. They're humping men and women in the city's better hotels who are mainly here on business. Good money," said Xavier. "They don't like to get bounced around that much."

"How did Vice pick up on it?" asked Rivers.

"A woman met one of our undercovers at a hotel bar and she made a mistake. Happens. She explicitly mentioned sex for money. The cop wanted information more than running her in, and she had something to trade. An encounter with a guy who choked her unconscious the night before, could have killed her."

"And she was going to keep that a secret?" said Rivers.

"The cost of business, so to speak. This girl is a grad student at Columbia working to make ends meet," said Xavier. "She doesn't need a mad pimp or a prostitution charge, so no cops. As it was, she said this wacko choked her out, asked her when she woke up if she's going to be a problem. She gives the right answer, no, and he stuffs two grand in 'forget money' between her breasts.

"Got to love it; she was so shaken up, she was working again the next night. This girl has absolutely no luck. She should just give up that life."

A call told Xavier that the police were still hunting for the hotel. "Our Critical Response Command is spun up and ready to pounce, once we locate this piece of shit," he told Rivers.

Xavier suddenly braked and pulled over toward a food cart on a sidewalk. "Hey, you want a pretzel? I want a pretzel. There's never a cart around HQ. I grew up on these things."

"Sure, why not," said Rivers. You had to eat when you could when you were on the roll.

Xavier grabbed his pretzel and moved away to lean against the hood of the car, leaving Rivers to get his. Rivers took a bite and found it surprisingly fresh and doughy.

The vender held out his hand for the five dollars each.

Rivers forked it over for both. Xavier had stiffed him.

A hotel's day security manager identified Dogu by his photo as a man who had arrived that morning. Standard room. Seventh floor. The NYPD's critical response undercover officers began to filter into the hotel, covering all exits.

"Think this guy will surrender?" said Xavier, who was listening with Rivers in the car over a command channel.

"His guys had RPGs in Paris," said Rivers, "so I don't think it's his style."

The undercover officers verified adjoining rooms were clear and, flashing badges, ordered a small group to sit down in a corner of the lobby to await evacuation. They had quite a show: Suddenly, black vans appeared at the front, with heavily armed, black-clad officers streaming in and right onto the two commandeered elevators. Others flowed to the two fire stairways.

Rivers got out of the car and stretched his sore back, looked up and down the lightly traveled side street. The honks and bustle from Columbus Circle seeped in from two blocks away.

Could they be so lucky as to capture Dogu Matsoy right now?

At 10:43 a.m., officers scanned a master card against the lock of Room 703 and flooded in behind a ballistic shield. Xavier yelled from the car, "They're in."

No sound of gunfire, much less RPGs.

And no Dogu.

By the time Rivers and Xavier reached the room, a bomb dog had swept through, and the command's intel and forensics team had taken up residence. Nothing in the safe. A few casual clothes, socks and underwear in a drawer. None of the high-value stuff —identification, receipts, laptop—was around.

"Hold it!" a police tech suddenly yelled.

He held a sweeper in his left hand, and it was now pointed at a small, circular object almost invisible against the upper window frame.

"It's live," said the tech.

Everyone froze. Rivers sucked in his breath—*live what?* He had been around IEDs and seen the results: limbs blown asunder. He shivered.

"It's a remote video feed," said the tech. "Someone is watching us."

At that, the tech put a piece of black electrical tape over the lens.

"Crafty bastard," said Xavier to Rivers.

Dogu was startled when his phone vibrated.

Then he saw on the screen that the video feed from the

remote he'd place atop the window was activated by motion. Armed, black-clad police flowed into his hotel room.

How had they found him? He had been so careful.

They were better than he imagined.

He sat down on a bench and watched the people moving around him, as well as police who were posted nearby, some scanning the crowd, some distracted in conversation. No one was looking at him. No one was noticing this clean-shaven young man dressed in khakis and a white polo shirt, a Yankees hat pulled low and sunglasses, with a small black knapsack.

Dogu breathed out. It was a minor irritation. He was carrying everything he needed: his passports, credit cards, IDs, various phone SIMS.

It was time, anyway, to leave the city that never slept. He had visited the shrine.

He had wandered the streets near the 9/11 Memorial and Museum, streets of old stone and brick buildings that had withstood the earthshaking disaster of that day. The World Trade Center had been rebuilt, and before him now were shiny prizewinning buildings to the sky, all rising west of the Wall Street financial district.

Dogu moved to the sound of the water. One of the two large reflecting pools, each with waterfalls dropping into chasms thirty feet deep. The large pools stood on the footprints of the Twin Towers that fell to bin Laden. The names of the 2,982 casualties of the terrorism were etched atop the walls.

Dogu stretched. He wondered how the Americans would memorialize this site after he turned it into a new cemetery.

His phone vibrated again—an encrypted message from his IT center in Greece that had received and analyzed the video feed from the hotel room. The message posted a photo of a man who had entered the room, with the words: *Recognition software IDs man at hotel as same man at hit in Paris.*

Dogu looked at the jagged rip along the jaw. He had heard from Odesa that Raglan's killer had arrived at the airport during his escape with such an injury.

CIA.

Dogu clicked off the phone. What to do about this CIA man was something to entertain during the next leg of his journey. Everything was a work in progress: He had been told some of Umm's weaponry had been delivered; some was delayed but would be available soon. His own final weapon was en route.

He stood and started walking to the nearby Staten Island ferry, which would put him in walking distance of the parking garage where the used Mercedes he had purchased was parked. A convertible. Should be fun to drive.

For now, he only had time to kill.

45

O ne morning Cowen by chance came through the front entrance at CIA headquarters with Angelos, and both men paused and stared at the inscription on the wall: *"and ye shall know the truth and the truth shall make you free – John 8:32."*

"Very aspirational," Angelos had muttered.

After all, the day-to-day work was deep in a gray zone of seducing people to betray their countries and elbowing through the fog and obstacles of bureaucracy to get the job done. Cowen admired his boss's razor-sharp operational mind and risk-taking – but lately had, as a trusted aide should, been voicing the need for more caution.

Cowen had warned Angelos that it was a mistake to give Rivers identification and a badge as a Homeland Security special agent— fakes created by the inhouse disguise and document gurus. Not as bad, but still inadvisable, was allowing an uncleared Raz Jackson into the Operations Center, despite her prior CIA employment.

But Angelos' long-lost asset Susan Owens had pushed his boss beyond risk-taking to recklessness in his opinion. He seemed bent on cleaning up his own mess. Commendable, but potentially messy too.

―――――

Cowen already had been in the office for three hours when he walked to the cafeteria, where he knew he would sin. He had the wide shoulders of a linebacker but now his waist was as broad. The two donuts he'd inescapably buy—Bavarian creams were his fix—would add to the bulge. Years back he'd gone to a dietician who told him that he was a stress eater. He thought, *No shit*.

At least he told himself he was limiting it to two donuts.

On his way out of the cafeteria, Cowen saw Marg Selby near the door, pausing as she scanned the room as people do when they look for an open seat at a table with co-workers. He was a bit surprised. She was an administrator of this or that on the top floor and was seldom to be seen with the proletariat.

There was something odd going on. Her scan swept right over Cowen, but he sensed that he was its target.

Marg had joined the agency decades ago when it ran as a boys' club and, pushed into paperwork, she became the discreet friend of the doers. Cowen once heard a rumor that Marg and Angelos had been an item, just a drop in the ocean of gossip that flowed through the place.

Cowen walked toward the doorway, and Marg stepped toward him. She smiled and reached up to straighten his askew tie. To anyone looking, it would seem a small moment between two old friends saying 'hello.' With that Marg moved past him.

Cowen continued through the exit, feeling a heavy weight descending upon his chest. As Marg had reached up to fix his tie, she had whispered: "The Inspector General is going to hang you cowboys over that badge."

Angelos had worked through the night and gone home for a shower and a few hours of shut-eye, and Cowen decided he'd wait for his return, for this required more than a groggy Angelos.

Only a select few knew of the fake badge and ID. Who had turned on Angelos?

Marg Selby helped manage much of the paperwork and calendars for the top brass, and Cowens could only conclude that she'd seen something that signaled the start of an IG investigation.

That was curious to Cowen. He knew enough about how the IG office operated to know it wouldn't go running to top management after receiving a complaint. The IG office prized its independence. The IG would privately examine the accusation and begin to assemble evidence. So, what was up?

He sat back and inhaled a donut and wondered how Selby would know. Maybe because someone had complained directly to upper management and then the accusation was referred to the IG from there. That could explain it.

Whatever the case, this was serious: He could see Angelos, himself, and Rivers in the crosshairs for violating regulations and, God forbid, for breaking criminal laws.

Cowen pulled out his cell phone and dialed his longtime

mentor, his boss way before Angelos: Harry Dalton, now the Paris Station chief, a man who always seemed to know more than most. His personal number.

Dalton picked up, spoke a few words and hung up.

Damn. The answer to the question of who Angelos's accuser was.

Richard Harwell, the CIA director.

46

"They're going to be coming for you."

Kate Milano was shocked. She had taken Harry Dalton's call because he was … well, Harry Dalton, not only the highly considered CIA chief of Paris Station but also a friend. Over the years, when she traveled as CEO of her IT company, she'd have lunch or dinner with this charming man in Athens, Paris, Jerusalem, wherever their paths crossed.

"You have my attention, Harry," she said.

"Have you heard about Angelos yet?" Dalton asked.

"No. What's going on?" she said.

"Harwell lodged an allegation against Angelos with the IG," said Dalton. "You can bet a campaign on the rumor mill will follow and look to shred him. The problem is it's more than a personal grudge. Angelos has been a key voice against his favorite project, and he wants to get his own guy in as operations director."

"How do you know all this?" asked Milano.

"Obtaining intelligence is what I do," said Dalton. "I've been smart enough not only to spy on our enemies and allies, but also on my own bureaucracy. Never wanted to wind up with me saying 'Et Tu' to a colleague shivving my career."

"What misstep did Angelos make?" she said.

"He dressed up Tom Rivers with fake Homeland Security credentials and a badge so he would seem to have some official cover for poking around in the United States." Dalton decided not to mention the handgun at this point.

"Lord, what the hell was he thinking?" Milano's tone ratcheted higher.

There were so many things wrong that Milano could see Angelos would be lucky to be allowed to retire. Creating fake credentials. Allowing the impersonation of a Homeland Security special agent. Using CIA personnel to investigate on U.S. soil, the domain of the FBI. She could count on Angelos to have explanations to mitigate the damage, but damage—perhaps career-killing damage—there was.

"Stupid, stupid," she muttered.

"On the bright side, Rivers obtained information while working with those credentials placing this Umm al-Nasr around Tysons," said Dalton. That would be a huge mitigating factor in Angelos's defense. Dalton had decided not to mention Raz Jackson's participation.

"So, now you can expect the CIA director to soon dust off his Saudi plan and work it along with his own guy as operations director and then, with his favorite congressmen, try to roll me over," said Milano, understanding Dalton's warning that they'd be coming for her.

It was a threat to be taken seriously: a powerful clique in Congress, lobbyists for oil and defense industries, and some members of the National Security Council in the White House, were on board with the CIA director.

The plan promoted by Harwell and his friends was to give a U.S. nod—and some technical assistance—to a group of Saudi princes who wanted to take back power from Crown Prince Mohammed bin Salman. Technical assistance, as in a temporary blackout of the capital Riyadh and the quiet provision of some tech wizardry to block internal communications. Some powerful Israeli diehards were prime promoters of the plan, incensed that MBS, as he was known, had renewed some diplomatic Saudi-Iranian relations after many decades.

"But first they have to sideline Angelos," said Dalton. "He's an obstacle to be feared by them—a respected voice on Mideast affairs who could be counted on to rally others against their plan and, worse, perhaps isn't above leaking its lack of merit to the media."

Milano saw that Harwell could easily also muddy her, pointing out that she had been meeting with Angelos without the CIA director's presence. *What did she know? What had she approved? Just asking*, he could say. A chipping away of her credibility could occur on social media and in anonymous stabs in the press.

"The old senator is pretty crafty," said Dalton. "He saw Angelos's vulnerability and he saw the intel that Dogu Matsoy might be bankrolled by a Saudi. His team will be off to the races on that, facts be dammed that it wasn't the Saudi government. They'll be talking in the halls of the White House and Pentagon, calling for action."

"Do they really think they can carry off their Saudi plan?" said Milano.

"Doubtful but possible, and also that win or lose, the United

States really loses," said Dalton. "If it works, the next step for these greedy bastards will be war with Iran. If it fails, MSB will cut our oil throat and plunge us into a recession."

"Well, Harry, time to walk and chew gum at the same time," said Milano. "We have to sidetrack Harwell while we stop some terrorists from attacking our country."

"All in a day's work," said Dalton.

47

Angelos could read the room, and he saw trouble.

Cowen and Rivers were sitting in stoney silence with the fake badge and credentials between them on the small conference table in his office,

"I suppose I should put that stuff in my safe," said Angelos.

"Yeah," said Cowen. "I've already logged the handgun back into the armory."

Angelos had gone home for a couple of hours and slept longer than planned. On the drive back to work, he got the scoop on the unsuccessful hunt for Dogu Matsoy in Manhattan. Now this.

Cowen spoke right up: "I received a tip that the Inspector General's office received a complaint that Rivers was pretending to be a Homeland Security special agent."

Angelos kept a poker face. "Well, the IG really won't like that."

Which seemed like an understatement to Rivers, who had

been thinking of the administrative, if not criminal, charges that may lie ahead.

"And you'll love this," said Cowen. "The complaint was lodged by Director Harwell."

Now Angelos looked surprised, and it took a lot to surprise him. His mind raced over who would have gone to the director. Angelos couldn't believe that the few who knew—old colleagues in arms— would dime him out.

He looked at Cowen but didn't ask the next question: Who told him about the complaint and the director's involvement? And Cowen didn't offer the information. Angelos guessed that Cowen didn't want Rivers to know. Perhaps even him.

"Well, an IG investigation is a problem," he said, "but it doesn't change much at the moment.

"Investigations take time," continued Angelos. "The IG office will want to interview Harwell, and maybe it already has. It'll work to check his information. They'll be thorough and that takes time. Then they'll interview others and finally us; Rivers first."

"All that buys me some time."

Rivers noted the *me* was not an *us*.

He was surprised that suddenly he felt—how to describe it— wary and a bit betrayed. He had long lost any innocence about the world, but he had come to put his trust in Angelos. And that trust was now shaken. Was that Angelos' fault, or his?

"Just remember, don't lie, don't be evasive when questioned by the IG office," said Angelos. "What's done is done, don't add to it."

The best case, thought Angelos, might be a quick retirement. So be it.

Cowen and Angelos huddled privately for a few minutes and then called Rivers back.

"Let's keep our eyes on the number one prize: finding those terrorists. I still consider Umm and everything she's involved with as the actions of the CIA asset Susan Owens. Not going to back off from that. This is not the CIA operating on American soil; it is the CIA conducting an internal investigation.

"You may not have the badge anymore," said Angelos to Rivers. "But a Joint Task Force led by the FBI was created this morning to coordinate efforts to catch the terrorists, and I've managed to get you and Raz Jackson listed as observers on the task force. So, you have some official status. Believe me, if I hadn't reminded them that Susan Owens was first recruited and vetted by the FBI, that wouldn't have happened. As it is, I'd say they complied grudgingly."

"If they got their act together quicker, I wouldn't have been tempted to go the fake badge route."

The words added to Rivers' simmering anger. He had been foolish to agree to use the fake ID and badge; that was on him. But he had trusted Angelos.

He stretched his stiff neck back and forth, knowing FBI agents out in the field would happily break his chops and make his presence uncomfortable, no matter what HQ-types decided about cooperation.

"So, Tom, we have a lead that the over-stretched FBI has low on their busy priority list. Which means you have to catch a flight to Tampa. Raz has a flight arranged, and you can meet her at Dulles."

Rivers walked out and thought the two would now discuss the real untouched question at this meeting: Who alerted Harwell?

48

Raz sat in the small lounge at the private jetway at Dulles Airport and picked at what bothered her: Was her infatuation with Rivers fated to be a brief affair?

It was that damn evening with Steve Cohen that nagged at her. Suddenly, with Cohen and Rivers side by side, she saw how they were alike and how different. The math wasn't clearly in Tom's favor.

Cohen was handsome, rich, an extrovert, a Mossad IT whiz turned entrepreneur. Tom was attractive when not beaten up, on a paltry GS pay-scale, an introvert, and—if Cohen was married to himself—Tom seemed married to his job.

Raz remembered exactly when her emotional math of Cohen finally went to zero. A morning in Cairo when she still struggled with Susan Owens's defection to ISIS. Cohen had simply dismissed her angst with a "Snap out of it. Grow up; that woman isn't worth it."

It was the belittling tone as much as the disregard for her feelings that did it, the last straw in their long decline.

Perhaps her feelings for Tom had as much to do with the adrenaline of this dangerous chase? She looked over at Rivers, who had arrived, kissed her gently, and sat down to paw through some email. She wondered if he too wondered, if he also had doubts. No, not the same way. He had a Zen quality: take life as it comes. She liked that, though she knew her preferred style was to make the life she wanted come to her.

"You weren't at this morning's meeting," said Rivers.

"Yes, Cowen called me and told me to get started on arranging this trip. Something was in his voice. When I asked, he said you'd fill me in."

"Angelos is jammed up over the badge he gave me and now has taken back. Seems the director has it in for him. He seemed calm about it, though."

"So, we're going in pursuit without even the pretense of authority with a badge?" said Raz. "How does that work?"

"The CIA is part of a joint task force headed by the FBI hunting the terrorists, and somehow Angelos has gotten us official status as 'observers,'" said Rivers. "So, we just play it straight. ID ourselves as CIA observers on the task force and press forward."

"Why didn't he just do that from the start?" said Raz.

"I think the joint task force just became official," said Rivers. "And Angelos couldn't wait."

She noted the annoyance in his voice.

Rivers had looked at the email Cowen sent to both of them. It was a brief for today's mission: Check out a woman named Amanda DeFeo in Tampa. The agency's Artificial Intelligence Unit had examined communications originating from Al-Hol and uncovered webcasts from Umm al-Nasr and the attached conversation boards. DeFeo had been mainlining the podcasts and communicating with Umm.

The woman was twenty-four, worked as a waitress when she worked, and had been arrested twice for crack possession and sent to rehab programs. Not a résumé for terrorist evil. But AI also dug up that she'd recently had internet contact with some criminal low-lifes. You are known by the company you keep.

Rivers felt naked as he was stripped of his weapon along with the badge. But he looked over at Raz's two well-armed bodyguards and felt better.

"I've booked us into a swanky hotel, Mr. Rivers," said Raz. "Nothing government rate on this trip."

"Private jet. Luxury hotel. Classy lady," said Rivers.

"What's not to like?" said Raz.

Rivers spent the first hour of the flight looking out the window at a patchwork of green and lines of roads along the Appalachian spine of the route. Zen? Deep in thought? Raz could tell he needed some solitude. His last few weeks would have put most people in a hospital bed, but he kept ticking.

Rivers had been nagged for some time by Laurent's advice to be wary of Raz, the leaks that resulted in Aslan's and Sykes's murders, the Five Eyes setup of her company, and Cohen's acknowledged link to Angelos. A mishmash of things.

His intuition had flashed that Cohen was the perfect tool that Angelos could have used if he had taken early action to try to find and silence any linkage of Umm to the CIA. Taking rash action was something Rivers now knew Angelos might take, considering the badge issue. Angelos could have given Cohen direct access to communications. Which could have led to scooping up the ISIS girl. But would Angelos have approved of the killing of Aslan Baseyev in Paris and Brian Skyes in Marseille? Would Cohen even do that?

He had no trouble thinking Angelos would use all means available for his own ends. But murder?

Rivers turned to Raz, looking solemn.

"Do you think Steve Cohen is working with Angelos?" he softly asked Raz.

She looked surprised, then irked by his question.

"Why do you care about Cohen?" asked Raz. Was his question jealousy or curiosity or simply business?

"I wonder what connection he has with Angelos," Rivers said. "He told us at the restaurant about a Dogu hideaway in Greece and about a Saudi prince privately funding Matsoy. That man is deeply involved in things."

A long pause, and then Raz said, "Of course, if you wonder about Cohen, you wonder about me."

"No, Raz, this is about him, not you."

"But aren't we a package deal?" she said. "We're connected by our past and by our business. You can't tell me that you haven't analyzed to what extent I work with Steve."

She knew that Tom had analyzed her early on, as she had him. Par for their training. But she was now a woman infatuated, well past any such calculation of agendas or motivations. To suspect Cohen was to have—not matter how briefly— suspected her anew. That hurt after their effortless, intimate time together.

"I'm not analyzing you," Rivers said with a wisp of irritation. Although he had, briefly.

Raz shrugged, feeling a tiny loss of innocence in their fledging affair that had made her feel like a girl again.

Yet, if she admitted it to herself, she too had been wondering about Steve Cohen.

Would their professional lives always intrude? Would it prove the end of them?

She turned away from Rivers.

The air between them felt frosty.

49

Mary Jones—yet another identity for Umm—was dressed casually in black jeans, a dark blue blouse, and a stylish gray jacket. The look of a single businesswoman going out to have a good time in Nashville, with friends or relatives or perhaps a pickup from a bar.

Good luck with that, thought Howell Larkin, the pilot of the prop Cessna picking her up at Dulles. He had looked her up and down and wondered if their overnight layover could produce some action. He noticed how the woman glared at his unwelcome once-over. No, not his type; too thin, too severe. The type to be going to Nashville to stake out a wayward husband en route to a big-dollar divorce.

"It's going to be a bumpy ride," said Larkin.

Umm ignored him.

Storms were running up from the Gulf, and he could safely hook around the worst, but still some wind and rain were unavoidable. The flight had been booked through a flight service bulletin board, a round-trip, one-night layover. It would take a few hours to reach Nashville, and Larkin settled in with the woman who was as mute as a mummy.

Her glacial face hid a burning question: *Where in the hell was Dogu?*

He was not in contact as promised. And, quite frankly, things were not going well.

Her ultimate plan was to have three teams—two girls in each team spreading terror, her five Al-Hol girls with the girl in Tampa. The capable Fadwa with Amanda in Florida for a key attack. Automatic weapons, bombs and suicide vests. Umm herself always had this target in Nashville, with an escape flight back to Northern Virginia.

But her chosen girls from Al-Hol had been winnowed from five to one, and that was Jomana, the weakest of the lot. Now Amanda, her follower in Tampa, had told her the automatic weapons had been delivered, but the C4 explosives had not.

The arms dealer arranged by Dogu said it would take more time. The thugs likely wanted to shake them down for more money. Dogu would have that money, or at least could convincingly threaten to murder them. But she did not have the money or his fast-twitch violence, and she could no longer control herself to wait.

As concerning, she had detected that Amanda seemed discouraged, and Umm worried her faithful American disciple was backsliding. At least Amanda fathomed her worry in the Skype call and tried to allay her fear, saying, "I'm still with you, my beloved teacher."

"Still." That bothered her.

She imagined that Dogu, who so opposed the timing of her Nashville targeting, had cut her loose. "It is too risky to begin your mission with this personal revenge," said Dogu. "If you are killed or captured, the others may not continue. Leave it to last."

She wanted it first. Of all the things she hated, she hated this target the most.

Umm decided to attack.

Umm picked up her dark gray Toyota SUV from the airport rental outlet and followed the directions on her cell phone, which took her on a ten-mile trek toward her hotel with a stop along the way.

As she approached her midway stop, she noticed the white van at the side of the 7-Eleven. Umm parked next to it, pressed to unlock the rear hatch and got out of her SUV. She tested that it was open. And then walked into the convenience store, picked out a Coke and waited in a short line and paid.

She returned and slid back into the driver's seat and started the SUV, seeing that there was no red warning for an open hatch. The white van was gone. It was done.

Later, in her hotel room, she opened the long tennis bag that had been left in the SUV and examined the Heckler & Koch MP5 submachine gun with its long, curved magazine and the Glock handgun and the extra mags for both. She would disassemble, clean and assemble both in the evening. Her hands were skilled at weapons and bombs.

She looked at a printout she had of a face—the one she would kill tomorrow, one among many hypocrites.

50

Raz wasn't going to be one of those women who took all the blame, but she realized as she simmered down that Rivers did have a reasonable concern about Cohen. And as the jet sliced through the clouds, she felt increasingly gentle toward him as she watched him sleeping.

His left hand twitched.

She had noted some bouts of irritation that seemed out of character and now this. *Shouldn't it have been expected that his savage fights for survival in Syria and Odesa didn't just leave him with physical injuries?*

After Cairo and the debacle with Susan's defection to ISIS and her breakup with Steve Cohen, Raz had seen a psychologist in London who was known on the rumor mill for discreetly treating MI6 personnel. She wasn't sleeping well and felt down, in a spiral of unhappiness.

"I feel like the sun doesn't rise on my mornings, just endless cloudy days," she said during the first session.

"Well, this is England and winter, and the sun's seldom to be seen," the psychologist said.

She laughed.

And he said, "That's more like you."

She had talked with him for several months and regained her balance, realizing joy and depression were flip sides of an all-natural coin. Raz liked the poster her psychologist had framed on his office wall: a guru in flowing robes on a surfboard with the words, *You can't stop the waves, but you can learn to surf.*

She would have to keep an eye on Rivers. He had made her angry, but she cared about him.

<hr />

An hour after landing in Tampa, they were at the last known address for Amanda DeFeo. It was her brother's condo, in a large building that curved around a swimming pool, at the moment empty of swimmers and sunbathers avoiding the oppressive heat. The two bodyguards had stayed back in the black SUV, and Rivers felt better that one gave him his spare handgun, which he tucked in his belt at his back.

Howard DeFeo answered his door and, after peering at Rivers's own CIA credentials and Raz behind him, heard, "Is Amanda around?"

"What has she gotten into now?" he replied.

"Just a few questions for her, if she's around," said Rivers, smiling and moving slowly over the threshold.

Howard turned and allowed Rivers and Raz to enter the living room, which had a collection of furniture that looked modern and more aesthetic than comfortable. A file sent along from HQ stated Howard was a computer programmer for a regional bank and was Amanda's older brother and the person who signed for her bail upon her two arrests involving drugs.

"Is Amanda OK?"

Howard was an old hand at talking to cops and lawyers about Amanda, and he hadn't detected the long face of a death notice on these two official visitors, but it never hurt to verify that she was alive.

"Why wouldn't she be OK?" said Rivers.

"Because she's Amanda," said Howard. "She's an addict. Recovering day by day, but I haven't seen her in two months. And that concerns me.

"Has she been arrested?" said Howard. You could see him puzzling why the CIA was at his door.

"Is she mixed up in something dangerous?"

"It would be best if we could find her and talk to her," said Raz.

"Amanda, Amanda," said Howard with a tone of affection but exasperation. "She is so delightful, but then she's also an ... addict."

"How long an addict?" asked Rivers.

"Oh, off and on, going on ten years. She was a good student, popular in high school, but started running with a fast crowd in her sophomore year and got pregnant. Miscarried. Our parents didn't throw her out, but ... well ... she liked the parties and the drugs."

"Do you know where she is?" said Raz.

"She went to live with a guy she met in rehab and then stopped answering my calls."

He went to his desk and scribbled out the address.

"God, I hope she's all right," said Howard. "I'd do anything to help her. I just have no idea what to do anymore."

Amanda's boyfriend, Darren Castro, sat on his couch, flexing his hands, nervous that two law enforcement types were grilling him. Well, maybe not grilling him, just asking questions, actually politely. But his history weighed on him: the police always had been at his door when he was doing something wrong. Maybe he just didn't know what it was this time. He'd been clean for nearly a year.

He answered a few questions about Amanda with *Don't know* —his standard answer to cops. As it was, he didn't know what Amanda was up to or where she was. And even if he knew, he didn't plan to jam her up.

"Look, Darren, we appreciate that you're being loyal to Amanda," said Rivers after a while. "But she seems to be mixing with some dangerous people, so she's at risk."

"I doubt that" said Castro.

"Why is that?" said Raz.

"Because if anything, she's gone off the edge hooked on religion."

Rivers gestured for Castro to continue. Which Castro thought it was safe to do and might mollify these two.

"Probably the last three months, Amanda would sit by herself with her earphones and her laptop. And she just got into this online woman preaching Islamic stuff. Some people were passing around these podcasts at our rehab center. I saw one and didn't like it. But Amanda …

"Well, at least it was better than being hooked on drugs. But she was mainlining it online.

"You really think she's in danger?" he asked.

"Do you know who this group is that Amanda was accessing online?" said Rivers.

Castro sighed and then thumbed through his phone to a link he had kept. It gave access to the Ahlam al-Nasr Society.

Raz and Rivers knew the name from the Umm chase: she was the female poet who wrote of the glories of the Islamic State, a woman thought killed in Syria in 2019. The inspiration for Umm's chosen last name.

"Where's Amanda?" said Raz.

Castro was past hiding anything now.

"She left this morning. I saw she took her laptop and had some big gym bag, so I was afraid she was leaving me. She never did that before. I didn't like all that religion stuff, but I like her a lot. I don't want to see her hurt."

He thumbed up an email that Amanda had sent after she left and showed it to them: "Stay clean, Darren. You're a good soul. Remember me as a girl who wanted to be good."

"Going to need your phone," said Raz, plucking it out of his hand. HQ would want its contents.

She quickly thumbed through it and asked, "What's this?" about an email to Castro marked "Alert re Amanda" from a few days back.

"Oh, there's a couple rehab buddies in this building, and we try to watch out for one another. One of the guys saw Amanda talking with two bad-looking dudes in the parking garage. So, he sent me this warning and their license plate number."

"Did you talk to Amanda about it?" said Raz.

"Yes, she just shrugged and said something like *sometimes you have to be bad to do good.* Whatever that means. You know, Amanda really is a wonderful girl. She's just looking for her missing pieces."

Within minutes of receiving the worrying information about Amanda DeFeo, Angelos warned security officials at nearby MacDill Air Force Base to its increased threat. It already had heightened security.

If Amanda and other wannabe terrorists were really going to launch an attack, MacDill was an inescapable target. There were jets brimming with fuel on the tarmac. And headquarters for the two commands that operate in the Middle East were located there. Special Forces was one, but the other was even more ripe for any Umm-inspired attack: Central Command, which had been in charge of the air strike that killed her beloved Omar the Chechen.

If Umm wanted revenge, there was a good target.

51

Running a license plate is Cop 101, but it was a full hour before the CIA analysis unit spat out real results after running the number for the sketchy guys in Amanda's garage through its pachinko-like maze of databases.

The BMW SUV was registered to an Eric Robinson in Tampa, but an ATF database flagged that as a known alias for a Travis Reeves. His name popped up as part of a current federal investigation into illicit drug and weapons sales along the East Coast. A guy who delivered weapons. A minnow in the whole scheme of things.

Rivers was debating on the phone with Angelos about whether to go to MacDill when the information was emailed to him and Raz. It was only when he clicked off his call that he opened the email … and froze.

An echo of something buried and brutal played in his mind. *Reeves… a lot of people are named Reeves … Superman was Reeves.* He read the email again.

Raz saw his expression. "Something wrong?"

"The car registration led to Travis Reeves," said Rivers. "Highly likely he's one of the Navy SEALs with the kids in Iraq who was pardoned by the president."

"Looks like he can't stay away from a life of crime," said Raz. "Maybe this time he'll be caught and stay in prison."

Rivers considered he was probably in the same city as such a guy, and a shiver went up his back.

They had stopped to check into their hotel while awaiting the reply for the registration from headquarters. Raz had reserved a top-floor suite that offered a panoramic view of Tampa Bay. The bathroom seemed larger than Rivers's small apartment.

The Tampa sky was hazy, a mix of late afternoon sun, trapped heat rising from the sidewalks, and the early rush hour belching car fumes. So much for a beach paradise.

They both felt the hiccup between them from the plane ride into Tampa. Like a musical note misplayed.

"I'm sorry I offended you, Raz," said Rivers.

"I can't stop trying to solve puzzles, that's just me," he said. "Cohen, Angelos—maybe there's something there, maybe not. But, yes, that meant wondering about you a bit."

He looked into her eyes and said, "I don't think it rises to the level of being unfaithful."

Raz liked that Rivers was acknowledging her feelings, and that he was honest in not apologizing for his questioning.

"I have my own reservations about Steve and Angelos," she said. "It was playing in the back of my mind until you brought it into the open.

"But Steve isn't the man I want on my mind."

They reached out and held hands.

"I think make-up sex would be nice," said Raz.

In the early evening, Angelos let them know the FBI had located an address for Travis Reeves and was assembling its SWAT team. Rivers and Raz could watch as task force observers and then assist to quickly identify anything helpful for preventing a MacDill attack.

Raz's SUV, with two bodyguards, was directed to park two blocks from a leased townhouse south of Tampa, the type of place where neighbors came and went, and people minded their own business. Lights were on in the townhouse, and Reeves's SUV sat in a rear driveway.

Two undercover cars staked out the exits.

A Ford F-150 went by without notice, with Reeves and his old SEAL buddy Billy Gavin at the wheel of his vehicle. They easily spotted an unmarked cop car as they returned from a beer and bourbon run.

Gavin drove several blocks and parked on a street with a view of the local middle school. They knew all the access and egress points in the area, and that this parking lot was a likely staging point for any raid. They popped beers and watched the assembled FBI: two vans, multiple cars. FBI and Tampa cops. They had a good overlook position, their vehicle just one of a long row of cars down the block.

"Looks like we'll be moving on," said Reeves.

They had well-established plans and contacts. Their next life would be a tour in Mexico until the heat wore down. Then perhaps Texas. It was hard to know exactly how hot the chase for them would be because they didn't know what had led to the raid. But they knew that when you run guns—their specialty—you wind up on the run at some point.

They looped toward the town house and parked within eyesight of the impending raid. Hanging around was a risk, but their experience was that cops got tunnel vision during these activities. *Enjoy the show.* They popped more beers.

All those years in Iraq, Afghanistan, and Africa had grinded them down to the men they always were: low-pulse killers. Able to watch without emotion another chapter in their lives close with police battering through their front door. The only thing to get a rise out of them would be the thought of prison doors closing on them again.

That'd never happen. Reeves and Gavin had a choice of weapons with them in the pickup truck.

At 12:05 a.m., the raid commenced.

Agents piled out of vans front and back. One raced to the front door, swung a battering ram and knocked it open. They raced in, their formations well-practiced.

"Clear, clear" continually came over the comms as agents swiftly moved through. Another van pulled up, and a handler led his bomb dog past the splintered front door.

"All clear. No one here," came the commander's call over the comm.

Another van pulled up: Forensic agents who would tear the place apart.

In Raz's SUV, Rivers had been twisting around uncomfortably in the back seat, and then he opened his rear door, saying, "Give me a minute. My back is tightening up. I have to stretch."

He got out and leaned against the SUV, loosening his still-damaged hip and back.

"Let's get out of here," he said when he got back in, "Let the FBI do their job. My back needs some rest."

And they drove off.

219

Rivers stared out the window. The truth was, he didn't want anything to do with Travis Reeves or his sidekick.

Reeves saw the police vans pull up and the cops go in, streaming out later with a disappointed walk.

Suddenly, Reeves said, "Fuck me."

His buddy, Gavin, looked over, alarmed. Maybe cops were sliding toward them.

"Here, here, here. Take a look at this, Billy," said Reeves, handing him the nightscope he had been using.

"Down on the right, a guy leaning on an SUV."

Gavin focused on the man and saw what Reeves saw.

"Glory days," he said. "It's that damn Army captain."

52

Raz's SUV moved from the suburbs to the city's waterfront, and Rivers watched the stream of residents and tourists packing in a long night. Unknowing of the threat at the door. The rhythm of American life seemed to make citizens oblivious to the real things that could kill them.

"We've got a tail. Ford pickup a half block back." It was the bodyguard driving who called it out.

No one needed to have the danger spelled out. They had just come from an unsuccessful raid on weapons dealers. The hunters could now be the hunted.

"Let's be ready, in case," said the bodyguard in the passenger seat. Rivers still had the handgun one of the bodyguards had given him earlier, so now the other bodyguard handed Raz his spare handgun. Larger weapons were in the back of the SUV.

The bodyguard sped their SUV into the underground hotel parking garage, stopping near an enclosed stairway up to the lobby.

They moved quickly, but not fast enough.

As Raz and Rivers slid out toward the stairway door and the bodyguard from the passenger seat went for the weapons bag, a barrage of bullets clipped the SUV and walls.

The bodyguard with the bag went down with a grunt.

Rivers and Raz flung themselves behind their SUV.

The concrete of the parking garage echoed with the blurt of automatic weapons' fire.

The ten feet from the SUV to the stairway door was a kill zone.

The bodyguard's body lay eyes open, but he had pushed the weapons bag toward them before he went still. Raz was closest and, as Rivers and the remaining bodyguard laid down cover fire, Raz darted to grab it and dove back.

Raz, Rivers, and the driver hunched behind the engine blocks of the SUV and another right next to them, the heavy bulk of metal a shield from the rounds tearing into the vehicles.

"We're pretty fucked here," said the bodyguard. "We move or we lose."

Rivers guessed their attackers were Reeves and his sidekick, and he didn't like their chances in a gunfight with two former SEALs who had cut their teeth on armed combat. Their best hope was to stay alive until SWAT arrived.

At least Raz's bodyguard was ex-SAS, the special forces of England. That evened the odds a bit.

He directed their shoot and scoot, saying, "Short bursts, short bursts." They had to conserve ammo. The bag Rivers was dragging was emptying of magazines fast.

The garage down ramp they were on turned into another down ramp, and they moved using vehicles as shields and slid through a steel railing to the next level below.

The noise was deafening, and the humidity and fearful movements wrung the energy out of them. And then things went from bad to worse.

One attacker followed them onto the next down ramp, but the other took the stairwell and came out behind them.

"Hide and seek isn't going to work much longer," said the bodyguard.

Reeves had been aiming for a quick kill and hadn't calculated that the SUV contained bodyguards and a weapons bag. And damn, this bodyguard he'd glimpsed was definitely special forces.

He heard police sirens in the distance.

He had already spotted a possible exit through a utility door, which should offer a way out. But he really *really* wanted to kill the captain.

"Try to keep cover here and good luck," said the bodyguard. He darted to outflank the attacker from the stairwell. And as that attacker popped up to return fire at Rivers, the bodyguard dropped him with two shots.

Reeves saw the bodyguard shoot his buddy and, even from half a ramp away and despite return fire, he had a momentary clean shot at the bodyguard and hit him.

Reeves then flung himself behind a car as Raz's shots peppered around him. He scuttled away, incoming sirens loud, toward that exit door.

At dawn's early light, Raz and Rivers were released from the questioning clutches of the FBI and local police, who were amazed at the gun battle. The carnage: two dead—a bodyguard and a weapons dealer—along with nearly fifty cars shot up with at least a thousand rounds fired. The wounded bodyguard would survive.

Local breaking news reports began to blanket a usually quiet Sunday morning news cycle, and the authorities peddled the story that two drug dealers on the run had tangled with FBI personnel. No CIA mention, much less of an intel CEO from Paris, or terrorists.

A weary Rivers and Raz sat silently by the huge glass window in their hotel room overlooking the water, sipping coffee from cardboard cups, a bitter brew from an overnight cop pot. Raz looked at Rivers, who stared hard at the emerging horizon, as if perhaps he could sail into it. And Rivers glanced and saw Raz trembling.

He leaned over and guided her up from her seat and onto his lap, where she tucked her head into the curve of his neck. A few minutes later they both were breathing gently.

53

Amanda's mind was racing, her commitment to Umm's mission caught in a whirlpool of children's laughter.

She was sitting in a coffee shop inside the MacDill commissary, ready to haul the automatic weapon out of a gym bag, when a mother and her two girls sat down at a nearby table.

Amanda had walked off a public bus with a group of base workers and flashed her stolen credentials to gain easy access. There were many guards, but a young woman in a group of commissary and cleaning workers only got a cursory glance. After that it was full steam ahead.

But now the girls' chatter stopped her cold.

There always were going to be children in the commissary, and Amanda had played through her rampage in her mind, walking the aisles through the grocery store and shooting the families of the infidels. But those dream children were faceless and, above all else, soundless.

These real girls were alive with laughter, chattering in their high-pitched way.

She smiled, and then almost cried at a long-lost memory: her own girlish laugh when she was perhaps eight years old, playing with her neighborhood girlfriends.

Maybe killing these girls would save them from what was to become of them?

Yet she really didn't believe that, despite all her twisted time as a drug addict and now as Umm's disciple.

Her commitment was wavering.

Umm had created a special place for Amanda DeFeo, a universe of sisters joined in birthing a world cleansed of the horrible people in their lives, a place where Amanda in her mind traded in her name Amanda for a new identity as Amara, something more poetic to her ear.

Amanda the oppressed; Amara the avenger.

Amanda the drug addict; Amara the warrior for Allah.

Amanda troubled; Amara at peace.

The dreamlike online meditations, with Umm's stern eyes and captivating voice, had driven away those demons of old that made a crack pipe her best friend. At this moment, though, Amanda suddenly felt a nerve-rending urge to flee into the smoky joy of the pipe.

What did Umm expect of her, with her plan gone to hell?!

Umm's plan was so simple when they discussed it over the last weeks. The target was the U.S. Central Command that had killed the holy warriors—and Umm's husband, Omar—and the commissary near it with the soldiers' families. A girl from Al-Hol named Fadwa was to attach C4 explosives to cars that always stopped at a coffee shop before heading to MacDill. She would follow on an e-bike and detonate them at the main gate.

Fadwa would then enter during the chaos and make her way to U.S. Central Command headquarters with weapons and a suicide vest, while Amanda attacked the commissary.

Dozens or hundreds might die. And the global headlines would feed the ISIS revival.

Or so Umm said.

But Fadwa and the explosives had not arrived as promised, yet Umm was hell-bent on proceeding.

If Amanda had Umm at her side, or even Fadwa, she might be able to be Amara the Avenger.

Alone, she was sliding into the grip of escaping into a crack pipe. *This is all too much*, she thought.

The voices of the girls ticked up.

Amanda got up from her seat and exited the coffee shop. Outside, she slightly opened the large gym bag and pulled out her laptop, tucking it under an arm. She tried to shove the bag into a trash container but the bag's rigid contents of a handgun and automatic weapon with its magazines caught on the hole for cups and trash. She zipped it wide open to rearrange the weapons to fit into the trash can.

"Stop. Don't move."

A weapon had slipped clear of the bag and was in her hands. She turned slightly, surprised, and glimpsed a uniformed guard with a weapon pointed at her.

With that movement, the soldier fired. Amanda DeFeo was dead before she hit the ground.

54

C IA Director Richard Harwell was well practiced at assuming credit for good news.

A terrorist shot dead at MacDill Air Force Base without casualties after a CIA officer uncovered the terrorist's identity and killed a weapons dealer was such a great story. Even if the Pentagon and FBI were taking credit for it. That only made the CIA look craftier.

He was having his usual Sunday brunch with an assortment of male and female members of Congress—*Oh, how he missed the days when it was just congressmen*—and a journalist on a leash. He'd mix this story in the bourbon, and there it'd be in the media. Anonymous sources, of course.

There was a minor downside: This was all due to Angelos's competence. Not enough to erase consequences for his reckless use of a fake credential, but possibly enough to allow his retirement in lieu of administrative charges. If the man's luck held, that is.

There was that other thing that he'd so gently slide into the brunch conversation. It'd seem like a slip of the tongue: *I just hope it's not really true that the Saudis are involved in this... again.*

It'd be aimed at the one bland face who broadcast on his favorite docile network. That one raw piece of unconfirmed intel that a Saudi prince was bankrolling the terrorist Dogu Matsoy wasn't something to waste.

He already was paving the way in Congress, the Pentagon, and the White House for a decision to oust the Saudi leader, Mohammed bin Salman.

The clock was ticking.

Cowen wondered how Angelos did it. He ate pizza and doughnuts and remained thin. Drank tankers of coffee and wasn't jittery. Mostly worked eighteen hours a day—sometimes more—and still kept ticking during emergencies, like now. He expected to see Angelos in a lighter mood after the attack on MacDill was a bust, but he sat at his desk, twirling a pen, and looking pensive.

"Don't you feel it?" said Angelos.

"Feel what, boss?" said Cowen.

"Like that chill before your ass is nailed by the flu. This is far from over."

"What do you think happened here?" asked Cowen.

A young woman killed probably throwing her weapon in the trash at MacDill was a sorry but welcome end to an attack.

"Well, let's play Twenty Questions," said Angelos. "Are Umm and Dogu incompetent?"

Cowen recognized that his boss was thinking out loud and didn't expect any replies.

"Dogu was a successful smuggler, so you can expect better than this. But Umm. A trainer of suicide girls. Maybe a weaker link in terms of planning.

"But why wouldn't Dogu be doing all the planning?"

Angelos began to see the outline: *Now they will see I am here* from the Paris execution. The *I*.

"Maybe because Umm is about revenge and isn't listening to Dogu.

"We got lucky. It isn't easy to beat our defenses to launch a terrorist attack from abroad. But we got lucky."

Angelos twirled his pen. "The only known known is that Umm and Dogu are not done. The worst is yet to come.

"I hope we remain lucky."

55

Umm knew it was the small things that could catch you, so she made sure to stay within a few miles of the speed limit. But if pulled over, she would act like just another single bleach blonde among the multitude visiting Nashville for its country music and dizzy promise of nightlife.

As she drove, she listened to Willie Nelson on some outlaw country station. She'd always liked Willie; there was an honesty about him.

She had arrived yesterday and would leave on the private plane in a few hours. All business, no shows. Music only on the car radio.

She had searched Google News on her phone for the latest. And—yes! —a flash of news from Tampa. But then, not what she wanted. Just a story about a big-bang gunfight in a hotel parking garage. Nothing from MacDill.

She was counting on her Amanda.

Her plans had gone sideways starting with the disappearance

in Paris of Fadwa, who was to be teamed with Amanda for the attack on the U.S. Central Command in Tampa. Then three of her Al-Hol girls were detained coming into the United States. Then the weapons dealers didn't provide the C4 explosives, saying the FBI had seized a cache of it somewhere.

A constant stream of setbacks.

If she were self-reflective, Umm would see that the unraveling began when she beheaded the van driver in the passport heist, which put a spotlight on the operations, reducing the chance of surprise.

Dogu from the start said that her focus on personal revenge could be her undoing. That was why he kept his distance.

Perhaps Amanda would come through. It was still early in the day. Umm had shown her a way out of her desolate life; now all she had to do was accept her martyrdom and the eternal praise of the oppressed. But she worried Amanda her disciple, now alone, could return to Amanda the drug addict.

Umm had printed a photo of Colby J. Hayes at the hotel. He was still sporting that nonchalant smile, even in this photo in the church bulletin, although his face was a bit thicker now that he was in his thirties.

Hayes was the communications director of a megachurch in a suburb of Nashville, and Umm could envision his life after scrolling through a series of online bulletins. There was Hayes standing beside his Porsche. There was Hayes on a golf course with the pastor and the big-dollar donors.

Let the flock see that the gospel of prosperity is real.

Such a long way from his father's small ministry in an old white church thirty miles outside Nashville, where there was so much gospel and so little prosperity.

She wondered what had happened that Colby had not become

a minister as planned. Perhaps he realized his reedy voice lacked the power to move an audience to rapture. He was the type to recognize his deficits early and slide to an alternate path to his earthly goal of financial salvation. So, he probably found what he was good at: public relations.

One of the bulletin articles was written by Hayes and was accompanied by a photo of him with his wife and three children on the lawn of their mansion. Umm had paused on that, wondering if he still recklessly bedded every woman or young girl he could. She thought it likely there were others who had been damaged, like her sister Mary.

Umm shuddered in that moment and remembered. Colby thrusting his tongue deep into her mouth, Colby's hands gliding up her thighs under her skirt. Colby laying upon her, grinding groin to groin. She'd had sex with Colby and liked it.

She had warned Colby to stay away from her younger sister when she went off to college. But Mary was pretty, so innocent, and Colby was Colby.

ISIS had taught Umm that killing was a tool of justice; their version of it, of course. Now Susan Owens was returning to deliver justice to Colby Hayes.

She was mesmerized for a moment by the Sunday service. There was a grip to the thunderous words, the heat of the packed crowd standing, the amens and scattered crying. Intensely shared emotion. Like a drug.

For a moment she was back at the little white church of her childhood, and there was an unexpected warmth to the memory.

The pastor was pacing on the stage, and the blue-gowned

choir behind him burst into song or amens at preordained moments. The pastor's voice was raised in denouncing the liberal alliance with Satan to corrupt their children with pornographic books in schools. As his tempo rose, his flock in the hundreds of seats, arced around the stage and in the balcony above, stood and swayed with arms reaching toward heaven amid shouts of *Amen*.

She stood by a side door near where the people in wheelchairs entered and were lined up watching the pastor. She had easily passed by a guard by helping a woman struggling with a complaining mother in a wheelchair. Umm wheeled in the woman, and the guard didn't even glance at the long bag on her shoulder.

Colby wasn't hard to find.

Second pew at the front on her side.

Umm walked up to the pew and confirmed it was Colby; no doubt about it. People were standing as the sermon heated up. No one paid attention to this woman with her shoulder bag. Then Hayes, probably with the sensation that someone was staring at him, turned and looked at her.

A quizzical look: *Did he know this woman?*

He turned away as no answer came to him.

Susan turned to the wall, shielding the bag, and drew the automatic weapon free, with its two extra magazines taped to it for quick reload.

Someone screamed.

Susan fired and began raking the crowd, with the dead and wounded falling as a heaving mass of panicked worshippers rushed to flee.

Susan walked into the pew, stepping over several bodies, to where Colby was hunched, trying to shield his wife and three children, who he'd shoved to the floor.

"This is for Mary Owens," said Susan.

She paused for a second, giving Colby time to comprehend, and then fired anew, killing them all. She didn't know if Colby had understood what she said. It really didn't matter to her. It was done.

Some guards or churchgoers were firing at her, but Susan dodged rapidly into the panicked stampede, dropping her weapon and wig in the chaos, moving to her car, parked on a side street for an easy getaway.

It was done, finally. For Mary.

But she knew it was mostly for herself.

PART FIVE

56

"Now you will do it my way," said Dogu.

A statement of fact or a command?

Umm had just closed the front door to the safe house leased by Rasheed Khadr in McLean, Virginia, upon her return on her private flight from Nashville.

There was Dogu, watching her from a chair, with an automatic weapon in his lap.

Had he heard the car pull up and taken this seat, striking a pose that was watchful, relaxed, and threatening all at once? Or had he sat this way for hours, knowing she'd eventually return? She'd been around Dogu for years and still couldn't predict him.

Umm was shocked to see him and alarmed.

"Where's Jomana?"

"She is in her room praying," said Dogu. "She was not happy to see me." Actually, *terrified* was more accurate.

"The boy is in a freezer in the floor below."

So that was that. At least Umm did not have to deal with naïve Rasheed.

"Omar would be disappointed in you," Dogu said.

A wave of anger flashed over Umm at the mention of her departed husband.

"You allowed yourself to be blinded by your personal hatred, and instead of an ISIS attack on the Tampa base as your priority, you failed there. You had to have your church first."

"You, Dogu, didn't succeed in getting me explosives," said Umm defiantly.

"I would have worked that out if you had waited," he said. "But even without them, your attacker at that airbase was weak. There could have been many dead if she had pulled the trigger."

Umm had heard the news, as Dogu had, that a woman with a weapon was killed by security at MacDill. It was a minor mention among the reports on the carnage in Nashville, now up to thirty-five churchgoers dead and many more wounded. No mention of ISIS yet.

She looked at Dogu anew, for she had not seen him since Al-Hol. He came across as a young but worldly man, dressed in black jeans and a white collared shirt that fitted his athletic frame. He had broad shoulders like his father, Omar, but not the barrel chest. A broad face, now clean-shaven. He was a hybrid of Europe and Chechen rebellion.

She now, for the first time, saw the resemblance to Omar—a beating heart of cold violence coupled with a charisma that would attract followers.

She already knew his intelligence and that menacing look that could appear like lightning.

Umm did not want to be at odds with Dogu.

"How can I be of service to your plans, Dogu?"

He nodded. "My men are sending out the internet message that the Nashville church was an attack by the ISIS faithful in retribution for defiling a Koran. With a promise that there will be more."

"I didn't know they defiled the holy book," she said.

"They didn't," said Dogu.

She saw *defiling a Koran* was an inspired touch.

Umm's plans had largely disappeared with her Al-Hol girls. She was eager to hear what Dogu had in the works. For her, without doubt, it would be a martyrdom mission. Because she had one to propose.

"Is she going to be of use to me?" said Dogu.

Umm was leaving the room to check Jomana and knew what the question meant: Was the girl capable of fulfilling a suicide mission? Or should she just join Khadr in the freezer?

Her mind spun. She really didn't know if the girl had the grit to press a plunger on a suicide vest, but Umm could always make a remote detonator.

"Leave her to me," she said. "The girl can help, and if she proves unable, I will kill her myself." Or leave her body in a public place, wired with an IED.

He nodded.

Umm did not like what she found: Jomana was in a fetal position and moaning under her blanket. She pulled it back and saw the blood between her thighs and the start of bruising on her neck. So, Dogu was up to the old ways he had practiced at Al-Hol: brutal rape and strangulation.

She had no issue with training girls to blow themselves up for the greater glory of ISIS, but she gritted her teeth at this bestiality.

Umm didn't know what fate was written for Dogu, but she thought it would be good if he died soon. If they were both alive after this mission in America, she'd try to take care of him herself.

They left a half hour later, with Dogu driving toward another safe house. He had leased several places in Metro Washington and in New York City with funds from an account with a Cyprus bank that had monies from his Saudi backer. Now he would drop them off at one house, before moving to his own hideout a mile or so away.

Another house outside D.C. contained former ISIS members who had fled Syria and were happy to be recruited for Dogu's operation to strike in the United States, especially because he did not expect them to be martyrs.

Then there were his stashes of weapons. At an area warehouse were two white vans—one with signage for a flower shop and another for a plumbing company—that would allow easy movement around the Washington area.

All he needed now was his special weapon, due to arrive imminently.

Dogu turned up the short driveway to Umm and Jomana's new digs: an old, one-story house toward the top of the ridge in woodsy Cabin John, Maryland. It was along the Potomac River, with the CIA headquarters, the U.S. Capitol, and the Pentagon within easy reach.

Dogu nodded with satisfaction.

57

Rivers limped into the CIA Operations Center at mid-afternoon and was aware of the eyes that lifted from computer screens or swiveled from conversations to pin him with stares, as if the sound of last night's gunfire drifted with him into the office.

He was the center of gossip this morning: *Damn, a gunfight...a good bet to be a short timer if he keeps this up.*

It didn't take close inspection to see Rivers had aged in the three weeks since he walked out with his new marching orders to Paris from Operations Director Angelos. He'd been in a car wreck and a gunfight in Syria, nearly murdered by garrote in Odesa, nearly killed by an RPG in Paris, and survived hundreds of rounds of gunfire in Tampa. He looked irritable.

Angelos waved him into his office.

"I supposed you heard the news. ISIS put out a statement taking credit for the carnage in Nashville," said Angelos. "There was a connection between Susan Owens and a casualty, Colby

Hayes. The sister you interviewed identified him as her sister's rapist. Seems our girl Umm is mixing the personal with business."

"Maybe she's coming after you?" said Rivers.

"She doesn't know me. She knows Raz."

"Which brings me to the topic at hand," said Angelos. "I directed you to get close to Raz to see what she and Steve Cohen were up to. What have you found out?"

It seemed odd to Rivers that with ISIS attacks underway, Angelos had energy to focus on this sideline concern of his. What worried him? Whatever it was, it mattered to him.

"I can sum up what I found in one word: nothing."

"Well, tell me the 'nothing' you found."

"Raz and Cohen are somewhat on the outs. And she is on the outs with you: Raz believes you're reckless, certainly in sending Susan Owens to within reach of ISIS to begin with, and perhaps in sending me into harm's way."

"Grow a pair, Rivers," said Angelos.

"Sounds to me like you've fallen for Raz's considerable charms," he continued. "You've certainly had time to at least clone her phone. Have you? Of course not."

"I saw the task as keeping my eyes open, not spying on Raz," said Rivers.

"Well, redeploy your dick so it understands your task is now to spy on her."

Rivers didn't need to consider: "No."

"What the fuck is 'no'?" said Angelos.

"You used the phrase 'mixing the personal with business,'" said Rivers. "Unless you explain how this is related to ISIS, I'm not spying on her."

Angelos gave Rivers a stare that was hard to read. Disappointed at his rebellion? Accepting this streak of independence? Worried at the anger rippling through Rivers?

"So, you've already decided to quit," Angelos said.

"After we nail Dogu and Umm, yes."

"Not many people tell the boss no," said Cowen.

"Were you listening?" said Rivers.

"No, but you both exited his office bruised."

"Why does he care about Raz and Cohen?"

"Oh, so that's what it was about," said Cowen. "I think he sees Raz in some ways as a daughter who rejected him. She was a star as an operations officer, his brightest star. As for Cohen, the guy is slippery and dangerous. Ex-Mossad, and light on the 'ex.' It's safe to say the boss sees some sort of game afoot with Cohen."

Cowen added, "You know, he's usually right about those things."

Angelos nodded to the large conference room, where staffers had streamed in for the daily meeting checking on their part in an interagency task force led by the FBI. Angelos at the head of the table, top managers around, and subordinates on chairs along the walls. Rivers took a seat at the table, where he normally wouldn't belong, and he saw Angelos stifle a smile at the bureaucratic aggression.

No one was going to claim a seat from the man with a jagged cut along his jaw and the gossipy reputation of surviving garottes and barrages of weapons' fire. It wasn't out of fear; it was respect. Many had served in hot zones; some knew colleagues who didn't make it. Here was a battered guy still in the fight. He had earned his damn seat at the big table.

There was a rustle of people shifting in their seats and wrestling with papers in their laps. So, Angelos waited, staring at all and no one. It quieted in seconds.

"We're behind the curve," Angelos started. "A mass casualty attack on U.S. soil. It was—is—our job to prevent that," he said. "And the terrorists are on the loose."

"What do we have?"

The managers began to tick off the knowns in a clipped, orderly manner:

- Analysis showed the American woman killed at MacDill Air Force Base was recruited via the internet, a method ISIS had refined. The armed woman did not attack a commissary with families. She left a coffee shop and possibly was throwing away her weapon when killed.
- Video showed a thin middle-aged woman as the terrorist at the Nashville church, probably Umm al-Nasr. The FBI was interviewing a private pilot who ferried a woman meeting that description from Dulles airport to Nashville and back.
- Analysis from a surveillance camera indicated a woman who may be Umm al-Nasr had lunch at a Tysons eatery with a young man as yet unidentified.
- A phone taken from a suspected weapons dealer who was killed in a gunfight in Tampa was being analyzed. Initial indication is that Waze was used

extensively for navigation, which would give a map of his automotive travels.

A web of law enforcement was closing in on the terrorist operation.

But Rivers only had one thought: *not fast enough.*

58

Rivers wondered what was behind the curtain.

Angelos again had planted the idea that Cohen—and perhaps even Raz—were working against the operations director in some way. His boss didn't explain his misgivings, leaving the idea less than an accusation but more than a worry. On the Angelos scale of things, Rivers would peg it as cloudy with a chance of a tornado. Otherwise, the boss wouldn't have mentioned it. Or demanded that he clone Raz's phone.

Rivers focus was on Cohen, not Raz.

At least at the end of the staff meeting Cowen had turned to him and said, "The boss says take a day off. You've earned it."

And, without a doubt, he had.

It was late afternoon, less than twenty-four hours since the gun battle in Tampa, and Rivers and Raz had only grabbed a fitful few hours of sleep. They clung to each other on her private jet back to D.C., shaky from the near-death attack and spent adrenaline. Every ache of Rivers's healing body was reawakened by the scuttling dodges and lunges on concrete to avoid the gunfire in the parking garage. Raz was bruised and scratched. They had thrown away their clothes, which stank of sweat, cigarette butts and leaked engine oil from the parking lot floor, and the blood of the bodyguard.

How could he feel at once numb yet angry?

Dogu, Umm, the rapist ex-SEALs, Raglan, and Sykes. A photo array in his mind of deadly faces and backstories. He wanted them gone, not to add to them. Now Angelos was throwing Cohen into some pile of suspicion, and Raz too.

Rivers returned to his one-bedroom apartment and let hot water in the shower pound his neck and back. He looked down at his right hip and thigh with its vast, yellowish bruising from the SUV rollover in Syria. He was feeling sorry for himself.

Moreover, he was feeling a deep darkness about Laurent. *God, how he missed that man's chuckle at the absurd, his joy in working the street.*

Rivers began to cry, and minutes went by in his spasms of grief, until his reservoir of tears ran dry. Then he thought again of Laurent, and this time he smiled. If he had learned anything from the man, it was to pursue joie de vivre, an inner joy that couldn't be erased. It would be a work in progress.

Of course, he wasn't going to spy on Raz, but he would keep his eyes open regarding Cohen. Didn't Cowen say Angelos was usually right about these things?

Raz was sprawled on the sofa in her Ritz suite in Tysons, sound asleep, a blanket pulled up over her head. A clutch of her brown hair peeked out, and a bare right foot was sticking out at the bottom. He sat in a wing chair and checked his watch: nearly four. And he sat back and enjoyed watching the slight rise and fall of the blanket with each of her breaths.

They'd been together about ten days in the past three weeks, what with his gallivanting around in search of the terrorists who beheaded the driver in Paris. He decided to let Raz sleep and calculated that they could get takeout from a nearby Lebanese restaurant, a late takeout unless she rallied.

Rivers sat back and breathed deeply and wondered what was in store for them. They were old enough to know infatuation would fade and demand an investment in shared time together. Mostly he wondered if a guy like him could have long-term appeal to a beautiful woman who was a rich CEO living in Paris.

He was sure Raz was having similar thoughts. All he could do was play the hand that was dealt him.

Raz sighed, and a second foot escaped the blanket, which Rivers repositioned. Warm feet, warm heart. Such small acts were the molecules of a relationship.

Rivers took out his encrypted phone to touch base with some of the people he had met along the way. First up: Harry Dalton in Paris.

He texted: *Mr. Dalton: Don't know how closely you're involved in events but available to pursue any leads you think need attention, if you have any. Rivers*

And then he texted John Xavier, the NYPD Intelligence lieutenant who had taken him under his wing in Manhattan: *Hey John: Any angles I can help you with? Tom Rivers*

They were smart men, and Rivers liked to pick the brains of smart people. Plus, perhaps Dalton could help save him from an IG-driven prosecution if it came to that, and Xavier might know of a job.

Raz stirred. Her head popped out and she sat up, her face still sleepy but beautiful to him. She yawned and muttered, "I must look a mess."

"I was thinking dinner in. Maybe the Lebanese from downstairs," he said.

She nodded agreement and added, "And a bottle of red wine. How was your meeting at work?"

When he hesitated, her look snapped awake and zeroed on his face with full attention.

"Something with Angelos, isn't it?" she said.

Surprised, he sat back. Was Raz that prescient? Was he so readable? Or did she have reason to be concerned?

"Angelos assigned me to meet you when he sent me to Paris," Rivers began.

She waved her hand dismissively. "Of course."

One plus one. Elementary. An operations officer and an ex-officer would scout each other. They both knew that, even if they had not acknowledged it.

He started again: "Angelos is concerned something is going on with Cohen, and you're linked to Cohen."

"… Which he wants you to find out about through me," Raz cut in. "What is it that Angelos wants to pry into my personal life about," she said angrily. "I share a business with Steve Cohen; why should he care?"

She yelled, "It's none of his fucking business."

Raz looked at her phone on the coffee table, reached out, and skidded it across to Rivers in his wing chair. "Here, I'm sure the mighty Angelos wants you to clone it. Why wait? Or did you already do it while I slept?"

"I told him no, Raz," said Rivers. He slid the phone gently back toward her.

"Well, for the record, Cohen is my business. Not yours, and not Angelos's," Raz said.

Rivers understood suddenly that Raz might love a new man, but some part of her still lingered with Cohen.

"It's your business except when he's the agency's business," Rivers said.

She stood up and stepped away. "No, that's not how I see it, Tom."

He remembered when he first saw her, the classy woman in a crowd of stale men in Paris. She had met his gaze, her marvelous blue eyes locking on his. And then, she looked away and suddenly the room felt colder to Rivers.

Like now.

59

Raz woke up the next morning, her hand checking the unused side of the bed.

She missed Tom, but maybe not that much. A few cups of coffee might help clarify whether their hearts separated would grow fonder. Doubts had been gnawing at her from the start. Not because she was a self-made CEO and he was a cog of a bureaucracy, or she was rich, and he was not. Well, in truth, those were factors. It was more that they were both bred and trained as CIA operations officers.

That meant their underlying personalities could be summed up as manipulative, paranoid, and mission oriented.

Even when you left the life, it didn't leave you—the scanning and wariness of others, the tendency to manipulate people and situations, the need for some risk and adrenaline in your life. Raz's managing the small intelligence company with Cohen largely checked those boxes. She couldn't see herself living with a man content to work within the confines of the CIA. Rivers showed signs of being larger than that, but would his streak of independence make him a star of the bureaucracy or drive him beyond its boundaries?

It probably wasn't good that the questions arose so early in their relationship, but maybe it was unavoidable, as this mission to find the terrorists compressed time itself and made their lives so vulnerable.

Amid all her doubts, though, she wasn't ready to throw away their relationship, for she clearly knew—and felt—something true.

She felt happy when she was with Tom.

Despite her defense of Cohen, Raz had misgivings about her business partner and former lover. Not that she would tell Rivers that, much less Angelos, for she felt strongly it was her personal business.

She would handle her suspicion in her usual style, by directly confronting Cohen.

One question for Cohen: Did he inform CIA Director Richard Harwell that Angelos had given Rivers the Homeland Security badge? Rivers had told Raz of the IG investigation and Harwell's complaint.

Raz remembered seeing Cohen scan Rivers's badge on his belt during their rooftop drinks in downtown Washington. Just a small tick in the evening, but there it was. Cohen would have marked its details and was cagey enough to figure out its probable illicit history. He already would know of Rivers's exploits in the field, if the ragged cut along his jaw didn't advertise it. Rivers was CIA, not Homeland Security.

She had remained fond of Steve. Once she was madly in love with him, and they were a couple, the handsome Mossad operative and the vibrant CIA officer in dusty Cairo. He was at heart a good man as far as she was concerned, despite his lofty self-esteem that eroded their affair.

Raz knew Cohen was quite capable of using the badge information against Angelos ... if his Mossad bosses so directed.

She suspected he already had.

But she would ask him and hope for a denial, and she would know if he lied.

Her intuition told her that Cohen had indeed dimed out Angelos to the CIA director.

But why?

60

Rivers awoke at the buzz of his phone and knew his twenty-four hours off from work were ending early. It was a sunny morning outside his window; apparently it hadn't gotten word of his stormy weather with Raz.

"Rasheed Khadr," said Cowen on the phone, as if that meant anything to Rivers.

"The FBI raided his apartment and his parents' home an hour ago. He's the young man in the video having lunch with Umm al-Nasr in Tysons."

"Great," said Rivers. He instantly figured the FBI hadn't found the young man or Cowen would have led with that milestone.

"What do you want me to do?"

"Khadr is in the wind," said Cowen. "I'm sending you some background already dug up on the guy. He seems a perfect mark for the ISIS social media machine. The FBI did turn up a lease in his apartment for a house in McLean. Its SWAT team is hustling over there. I'll send you the address.

"Maybe this is the whole enchilada; we'll find Umm and Dogu and stop the sons of bitches," said Cowen. "Get over there, but don't get shot if it becomes a war zone."

"Yeah, the paperwork would be awful," said Rivers.

"Your paperwork is already awful," Cowen said.

"Well, it'd be nice if it turned out to be one-stop shopping, and it could happen," said Rivers, "but my sense is Dogu wants his name up there in the neon lights with bin Laden. He's been ahead of us all this time."

Rivers gazed at the information sent him on Khadr—a student, a loner—and muttered, "Just another stupid kid." Although at twenty-three, no longer a kid.

The brick house was 1950s, from a time when middle-income people could afford to buy in McLean; a well-kept house, but the type that developers were tearing down to make way for mansions. You could pick one up for a cool $2.5 million unless you wanted more luxurious extras. The FBI cut off traffic and filtered in, moving neighbors to a community center two miles away.

A specialist studied Google maps and the terrain as scanned from a helicopter and calculated the blast direction and radius if a boatload of C4 blew—and the potential spray zone and carry of bullets from AK-47s and M4s. One house two blocks away stood in an unobstructed line of fire, right over the swing set in the back-yard. A nanny and girl were hustled away to the community center.

Teams readied to enter front and back, snipers perched on rooftops, and the incident commander got word from the helicopter that there were no heat signatures from occupants. Now all they had to worry about were IEDs left behind. ISIS in Syria were skilled at that sort of thing.

The bomb dog and handler moved through the front door after a battering ram splintered it open, accompanied by a small team with weapons ready.

By the time Rivers arrived twenty minutes later, the drama and adrenaline were gone, and the incident commander had time to question why a CIA officer was trying to tread on his scene.

"I'm on the task force," said Rivers. "I worked with the FBI crew down in Tampa two nights ago."

The commander looked at Rivers and then called his superiors to confirm it. And he stared at the ragged slice on Rivers's jaw. "Where'd you get that?"

"One of the terrorist's relatives objected to my being alive," said Rivers.

The commander received the OK and was satisfied—just part of an overall strange day—but he warned, "You're an observer only. Stay out of the way."

Rivers nodded.

Even though the bomb dog had swept the house without alerting to the presence of explosives, a bomb tech was taking his time opening a freezer in a utility room in the basement. The fear was that the interior cold and heavy metal might have masked a low-level explosive, perhaps just enough to decapitate an unwary person pulling the top open.

The tech slid a probe with a camera through the seal of the freezer top and declared, "Damn."

No IED, but there was Rasheed Khadr.

His body was partially frozen, and the blood from chest wounds—slender slices probably from a knife—was ice on the freezer's bottom. His legs were bent awkwardly, and it seemed likely someone had jumped on them to break them to fit him into the space.

Another soul to the body count, thought Rivers. The kid might have been a fool, but he didn't deserve this.

Forensics was busy throughout the house, collecting fingerprints and sheets from a rumpled bed.

Rivers sensed that Dogu had been here; the cool knifing and leg breaking were his sort of thing.

Cowen called and told Rivers a new piece of information: The lease for the house was signed by the kid Khadr, but the funds had been wired into his account from a bank in Cyprus, and the agency was ready to secretly access and identity the owner of the account.

"You might be going back to the Med before you know it," said Cowen.

Rivers had moved to a corner of the utility room to avoid the conversation disturbing the techs. That was when he saw it: a small black box with a tiny red light on a utility shelf hidden between paint cans.

"Guys, guys," Rivers shouted. "Check this *now*."

"Fuck," said the tech, looking at it. "Clear the house."

The rest of the bomb squad came in and soon identified it as a video camera that went live when the freezer was opened.

Dogu Matsoy had watched the proceedings at the freezer after his phone alerted him to the action there. If he had had some C4 with him at the time, he'd have set a welcome for them. Too bad.

As it was, he felt rewarded, for he had spotted anew a person of interest: the man with the jagged cut on his jaw. His uncle's killer. At a future time, they would have to meet.

61

The white van with the plumber's logo on its sides kept to the speed limit, and Dogu, in the passenger seat, watched this mystery CIA man with the jagged jaw on his phone.

His driver, Beslan, a fellow Chechen from Syria, turned right off busy Route 7 onto a two-lane road with old houses and mansions along its sides until, in a few miles, it ran to larger estates and a few horse farms.

"If they only knew what will happen," said the driver, glancing around at the quiet, tree-shaded homes. He looked over at Dogu with a toothy grin and said, "*Kaboom.*"

Yes, there would be some of that, thought Dogu. But the real menace was something much quieter, something that would set off a tidal wave of panic, something that would eat away the American arrogance.

Their destination was one of his two storage sites, an old stone building, once a general store at a crossroads, that a Dogu representative had leased as a spot for his new fictitious plumbing company. It had a huge storeroom with large rear doors that once allowed easy off-loading from wagons. That was how old it was. Trees and brush kept the rear invisible from the roads that bore only occasional traffic.

Dogu had learned as a smuggler to have multiple sites for storage, for hiding, and this was his second and last trip here to clear out this weapons cache and deliver its contents to those who'd use it.

"What are you going to do with the woman and the girl?" asked the driver. He didn't know if they had any value to Dogu's plan, and he didn't want to put a woman to waste. He had heard the grunts of Dogu with the mousy girl. He wouldn't mind taking a turn.

"Not them. They have a date with destiny," he said. "But you will be famous and have all the women you want. And you won't even have to be a martyr."

Sex and money. Dogu knew that was what motivated his men. Even the ones who still clung to their religious fervor. Faith felt weak compared to an erection.

Dogu had a use for Umm and the girl.

He always believed her plan to use ISIS brides to attack America was liable to fail. Even in Syria and Iraq, as ISIS swept like the wind to expand its caliphate, it was challenging to find martyrs to carry out suicide attacks. Spiteful, willful Umm calculated her red-hot hate and charisma would give her girls the necessary spine. Team them up, two by two, stronger with weaker. It might have worked, Dogu had to admit.

And it would have helped him. Her plan to attack the U.S.

Central Command in Tampa, CIA headquarters, and the Nashville church would have been a good opening act. His own plans could slide underneath unseen, unknown, unsought, as police and FBI and that damn CIA spun themselves around, responding to the surprise attacks.

However, in one moment, Umm threw away any chance of surprise. Her impulse to behead the van driver in Paris produced a glare of global attention and unleashed the dogs of the police and the spies. He couldn't believe how she had fouled it up. A simple mission he had set up: hijack the passports needed to get the girls into the United States. Quick and easy.

Beslan looked over at Dogu's tense face. "You always look like that when you're thinking of the madwoman," he said. "You should just kill her."

"Oh, she and the girl are very near dead," said Dogu. "But they'll be put to good use."

The van came around a blind bend and the stone building was ahead on the left, about a quarter mile away. Both men suddenly sat up rail straight, eyes wide and then scanning left, right, to the sky.

A black SUV was parked face out in the driveway. A long antenna on the back.

Police of some sort.

"Drive steady," said Dogu. But his driver needed no direction; he had grown up dodging police on foot and by car. The speedometer was nailed to the speed limit of 30.

Dogu pulled a handgun from under the seat and slid it under his jacket.

There was a man in the driveway, his jacket marked with the initials ATF. He turned around at the approaching van with a plumber's logo on its sides and saw the driver wave. He gave a nod in return.

The van halted at the stop sign at the crossroads, turned right and smoothly accelerated away, obeying the speed limit.

62

Reggie Hall was the last investigator left in the Tysons office of the Bureau of Alcohol, Tobacco, Firearms and Explosives when the call came in to check out a stone building about a dozen miles west. The rest of the crew had spilled out toward the ongoing scene in McLean, where the FBI raided a suspected ISIS safe house. He was the most recent hire, so he got to babysit the phones.

It was a higher-up from ATF headquarters in Washington who sounded peeved when he called and found only a lowly guy like Hall available. But he said to proceed to the scene of a possible weapons stash, and he'd send backup.

"Is this related to the terrorists?" asked Hall.

"Yes," the boss said, and then, realizing some context would help, added, "The FBI was able to access the WAZE on a phone taken from a slain terror suspect in that shoot-out in Tampa. Recently, there was a trip from Florida to the location I just gave you.

"These were weapons dealers."

Hall drove to the stone building, backed into the empty driveway of what really looked like an abandoned building. If there was a hint of anyone there, he'd have driven by and parked at an observable distance and waited for his backup. As it was, he was in the driveway, reaching in for his M4, when he heard the grind of a motor and saw a white van approach. Plumbing logo. A guy waved and turned at the intersection.

He began to circle the building, a front with large windows with a faded Coca-Cola sticker in one corner. Once a store. Old plywood backed the windows, which were intact. He saw an old lock on the front door but did not try it. He walked around on the driveway, seeing a side door with an old lock and didn't try it either.

The driveway was old gravel overrun with weeds, and Hall saw that a vehicle with wider than usual tires had mashed down a track. Which led to the back doors.

Large, wooden doors perhaps twelve feet across and ten high. A loading area and entrance from the past. There were no holes in the wood doors to peek through.

The lock stopped him cold. It was digital, the size of a large iPhone. He dared not touch it. Didn't want to breathe on it.

Hall had been an IED disarmer in the Army, and he had transitioned to investigation, away from the tech side, because he wanted to leave the possible bangs to someone else, certainly someone whose nerves were more intact.

He saw wires at the back of the digital lock running through a small hole drilled in the door. The edges of the hole showed it was newly drilled.

Hall already was on his radio calling in an alert for a rapid response team and bomb squad as he quickly made his way back to his SUV. He hoped he was right; a bad call on a day like this would be a very black mark for his career. But he felt certain about one thing: He would not touch, much less try to open, that lock.

His bet was it was wired to blow.

Three hours later, the ATF bomb squad was ready to go.

They had examined the lock and various ideas for entry and decided to gain access through the roof. A hoist took up three techs, and they quickly inserted an explorer camera through a small, drilled hole.

At first the media and law enforcement attention was pinned on the McLean house, which contained a dead body but no live terrorists. Word eventually got out that another operation was underway. At least law enforcement was ahead of the game and blocked roads up to a mile away from the stone building.

Minutes ticked by as the techs reported on their discoveries. The huge wooden door was wired with bricks of C4. The same with an interior door to the storeroom. In the middle were rectangular boxes, and the techs spelled out their contents:

- A large plastic container held perhaps two dozen bricks of C4 and detonators.
- Another box held AR-15s and magazines.
- A stack of three boxes took their breath away. They were marked AEROVIRONMENT, and the ATF techs knew what that meant. Worse, they reported marks on the dirty floor showing that there had been two more stacks of boxes right next to the remaining stack.

Back at the Operations Center, Angelos, Cowen, and Rivers were watching the feed on a video screen in the conference room.

"What's in those closed boxes?" asked Rivers.

"Something bad for sure," said Angelos.

———

Angelos called in a young staffer who was an expert in munitions and said, "AeroVironment?"

The guy knew right off the bat: "They're the manufacturer of the Switchblade drones, one of the most successful weapons we've sent to Ukraine."

The three stared at him, so he knew to continue. He was one of those who were masters of details.

"The drones are light, with fold-out wings that reach twenty-four inches across. Range twenty-five miles depending on the wind. They carry an explosive charge that they can drop or do a kamikaze thing. Very accurate."

"Defenses work well against them?" asked Angelos.

"Challenging. They'd be hard to track because of their small size, speed and silent electric motor."

"How big an explosive charge can each carry?"

"Bad news, good news here. If it was used to drop a cluster bomb of sorts on a group, it would shred them. But fly it into a building and it would have less effect—blast a hole, maybe start a fire. Unless it penetrated through a window, or the drones hit as a group.

"It's operated by a monitor like a tablet with a joystick or mouse or even your finger, tracing the screen on some setups.

You can enter the target coordinates, factor in wind and terrain and it'll follow via GPS."

"Easy to fly?"

"Very easy to fly. Challenging to set up with explosives, unless you're trained or have experience."

"Would some of those ISIS drone operators from a few years back be able to do it?"

"Oh, for sure; some of those guys were skilled operators. ISIS created the art of dropping bombs from drones during the battle for Mosul."

Angelos grimaced.

"Where would you launch them from if you wanted to hit the White House or Capitol?" asked Rivers.

"That's easy. I'd pick open parkland or a parking lot by the Potomac River, inside the Beltway, west of the Capitol. I'd run the drones low, right over the water, and turn left at the Mall. Targets ahead."

"Of course," said the staffer, "our building is along that route too."

63

Rivers looked at the text on his personal phone when he took it out of the secure lockbox outside the Operations Center and went for a Starbucks coffee on the CIA campus. A Raz text: *Going to Paris for a while.*

He wasn't surprised, but seeing the words hurt. He sipped his coffee and thought it was a little brackish, but maybe it was just his mood.

Rivers went back to the office and Cowen caught his unsettled look.

"You OK?"

"Fucking great," said Rivers.

That was a whole conversation on emotional turmoil for men. Rivers took a deep breath and compartmentalized to focus on the business at hand. *But how he missed her.*

Rivers sat and watched the video screen showing the large Joint Task Force meeting. The dangers of the Switchblade drones were laid bare, as well as the expected route moving east along the Potomac River toward CIA headquarters, the White House and the Capitol at the mall, and the Pentagon.

The AFT briefer outlined what was found—and not found— in the stone building's storeroom: eighteen bricks of C4; eight AF-15s rigged to auto fire, full mags; and three Switchblade drones. Scuffs on the dirty floor suggested two other stacks of drones had been there recently—an estimated six more drones.

An FBI spokesperson said several investigations were already underway to see how Switchblade drones were stolen from a cache bound for Ukraine.

Another FBI official identified the body at the McLean house as that of a Rasheed Khadr, and that the CIA and other agencies were tracking a financial record found at his apartment that involved a payment from an account at a Cyprus bank for the lease of the house.

All short and sweet.

With the video off and the staff rising from their seats, Rivers said, "We're missing something."

Angelos sat back down, and the others did the same.

"These Switchblade drones are giving us tunnel vision," said Rivers. "Dogu Matsoy wants to outdo Osama bin Laden. Switch- blade drones attacking Washington would shock America and the world, but the explosive power of drones with C4 would be small, the death toll limited.

"It wouldn't be big enough to make Dogu the baddest terrorist who ever lived."

64

"Our favorite CIA director has asked me to have coffee with him later this morning," said Harry Dalton, who at that moment was having coffee with DNI Kate Milano in her office.

An old friend and trusted colleague, the Paris Station chief had tipped her off to the CIA director's move to push Angelos out by reporting the badge misuse to the Inspector General, and that she might be next on a hit list for removal.

Dalton liked that she had forgone the usual wall-of-fame photos of her with the president, senators, and a long list of dignitaries. She had made a fortune with her private business outside of government; she didn't need a power wall to display her reach or boost her image.

"Well, I had my own interesting appointment when the day started," said Milano. "The deputy National Security adviser stopped by and said they were all revved up over the intel of a

Saudi bankrolling this Dogu Matsoy. A whole slew of powerful people wants a plan of action. He pronounced 'action' with emphasis."

"Of course, they already have a plan," said Dalton.

"Yes, that plan," she said. "He'd like me to endorse it. He knows CIA Director Harwell supports it. He'd just like Angelos to be shut down because he muddies the water with his resistance. If the media got wind that the higher-ups were rolling over the advice of the working men and women, there'd be hell to pay."

"Didn't this all happen before?" he said, partly in jest.

"Yes, how do we spell Iraq and Cheney?" she said.

"Well, the esteemed director thinks it's a good idea to support a renegade band of Saudi princes against Crown Prince Mohammed bin Salman," said Dalton. "In his mind, we can provide technical support and turn off the power grid in Riyad at the right time, so they can overthrow him.

"Take things back to where they were: our friends in power and the oil taps open whenever we want."

Dalton was on a roll now. "Of course, we'd be supporting the same princes who had their pants pulled down and their bank accounts raided when the crown prince took over," he said. "They couldn't beat him then and he's stronger now."

"A fever dream of a power clique in Washington," said Milano. "The idea of self-declared great men doing great things…"

"Making great money too," Dalton finished.

"So, what do you think the CIA director wants with you?" she asked with faux innocence.

"Well, no one ever asked me if I supported this idea because I wasn't in the chain of decision-making," said Dalton. "Now I'm sure the director is going to wave the open job of deputy CIA director before me if I pledge to support his Saudi plan. That would nullify any Angelos opposition because he'd now work for me. He'll still expect me to get rid of Angelos."

So, you would take the offered job and …," said Milano.

"Then I'd slow-walk the whole thing from my end, say I can't give my approval until there's a workable plan. I'd point out that if it went bad and it was shown there was lousy planning, it'd roll back on them," he said. "Of course, there's no real planning behind this scheme."

Milano nodded. She knew Dalton's reputation as a skilled bureaucratic operator and sly manipulator. She realized, however, the danger he presented, friend or not.

If Dalton got the job, he could do as he said and stall this Saudi misadventure. Or maybe he would decide to dress up some hustled planning and approve the Saudi scheme. He'd be well rewarded if it worked: forever money from consulting jobs and board directorships after an early retirement. Even if the plan was pursued and failed, he probably was smart enough to avoid blame and maneuver to take Harwell's job.

Maybe even hers.

Dalton could almost see the calculations in her mind.

"Look, let me put you at ease," he said. "Two things. First, the Saudi idea is stupid, and I can't put the agency I believe in and worked in for twenty-six years behind it. Second, I'm going to wind up as CIA director anyway."

He said it with certainty.

Which led to more calculations in her mind about what he had cooking against Harwell.

"So, you'll lie to your boss," said Milano.

"For the greater good," said Dalton. "And I'll enjoy every second of it."

None of this put her mind at ease.

65

Rivers headed home to his oversize closet of an apartment, looking to catch a shower and a few hours of sleep. He had found that his limp was minor now except when he was tired, and he was tired.

The Sirius news channel on his car radio had leaked information about the Nashville terrorists on the loose having Switchblade drones. There were instant demands from pundits and some congressional members for the president to take the podium, again.

The old man had taken to the presidential pulpit damning the Nashville killer and promising swift justice. Now Rivers imagined the furious debates in the White House to drum up a revised response. His advice, not that anyone asked, would be to let the FBI director handle it.

Angelos had remarked as Rivers was leaving, "Wait till someone leaks that there's a Saudi angle. The temperature to do something will be volcanic."

The professionals knew that you just had to keep doing your job, step by step, and tune out the noise. But more than anyone else, they heard the tick tick tick of the threat.

Rivers's phone buzzed as he drove, and he saw he had two texts. He pulled to the curb rather than try to drive and read at the same time.

The first was from John Xavier, the police lieutenant in New York, responding to Rivers's earlier text asking if he could help in any way: *On full alert up here but no sign of bad guys. No reports of more prostitute stranglings a la Matsoy. Keep the faith.*

The other was from Harry Dalton, who just hours before was named the CIA's deputy director: *We'll have coffee soon.*

Yeah, Rivers could tell Dalton then that he'd be pulling the plug on his CIA job, maybe try to enlist him to fend off any prosecution over the damn badge.

At least it was exciting while it lasted.

Dogu wondered why anyone would live this way if they didn't have to: a one-bedroom apartment above a noisy road. The purpose of life for a man was to make money, fuck women, have sons, and—especially for Dogu—gain global fame that would result in the melodious flow of Arabic poetry written of his exploits. T-shirts with his face like those for bin Laden would be a pleasure, as long as he was alive.

But this guy Thomas Rivers lived like a monk. He had learned Rivers's name from a darknet website that tracked the Paris RPG attack, and then paid a Chinese broker for his personal information, including this address. China hacked all the personal information for a vast number of U.S. government employees and, true to the mercantile spirit, would sell it for an outrageous sum. Dogu was happy to pay.

Now he was here in the man's apartment, ready to murder the CIA man who murdered Uncle Raglan.

Dogu hid in the living room, scanned the hallway leading from the front door, dim but visible in the last afternoon sun coming through the windows. The room had a TV, a sofa and chair, and there was a bedroom with a queen bed and a few plastic bins for clothes. A tight kitchen and a tighter bathroom. A few books here and there. No pictures of family. Nothing on the walls.

It added to the picture of the man for Dogu. This was a way station, not a home. Rivers was a soldier used to traveling with what he could carry on his back.

Dogu picked his spot, readied his handgun, relaxed and waited.

In a while, the front door opened and lightly closed, and Dogu heard the steps. Dogu was hidden around the corner, where the hall met the living room. The man was slower than he expected, limping or one step searching forward before the next. Had his presence been discovered?

The moment came: Dogu's handgun was level and he fired once, then again. And there was the thump of the body hitting the wall and falling to the floor. A handgun that was in the man's hand skittered across the floor.

Dogu looked down at the body jerking in its losing competition with life and saw the face was a gaping mess.

Job well done.

66

Dogu remembered his father, Omar, sitting in Raqqa with his closest friends, all transfixed by his gravelly voice and clear eyes that were harsh, kind, or with humor, as the times demanded. Omar the Chechen. Admired for his battle tactics, revered for his courage leading the attacks. He would tell his men, *We will teach the infidels tomorrow, inshallah.*

Inshallah. If Allah wills it.

It took an American missile falling from the sky to finally kill him. Umm was there. With him in life, and also on the edge of his circle of nightly friends. And with him at his death. Her body had been torn by the searing shrapnel, but Dogu saw something else had happened. Before Umm was coiled in a deep belief in Omar and the holiness of ISIS's cause, but afterward ...

He watched her now in the seat across from him in this Maryland suburb of the Capitol and saw it: a woman still coiled, but with a hate festering along with the remnants of metal that were gouged into her bones. With her pain came revenge.

He actually was happy to have her with him now, with her commitment to death that he could use, for his own motivation was revenge for his father, but mostly fame and definitely survival. He had learned from Omar the patient planning of tactics and how to produce waves of attacks. All that he was ready to apply.

After the murder of the CIA man, tonight was a time of rest. Tomorrow was devoted to getting all the weapons ready for the attacks and to review his plan and timing among the assembled. He had instructed and tested his people singly in what they would do. But for the first time, most would understand the whole picture of the killing to come.

The final ingredient had been picked up from the cargo depot at Dulles airport, hidden amid shipments of pharmaceutical drugs from the Ukraine. With care, his team would attach it to the explosives.

Then the day of attacks, when he could declare, *We will teach the infidels, inshallah.*

And become the world's most famous terrorist and a global hero to the billions who despised the West.

Dogu the Chechen

67

"Well, at least you aren't dead," said Angelos.

Rivers had opened his apartment door, saw the clump of a body, and stepped away. His heart racing as he ran down the hallway to the stairs. There he took a deep breath and called CIA security, all the time listening, listening … hearing nothing. He had no weapon.

He had only a glimpse of a man in slacks and a loose jacket on the hall floor, legs toward the door, an array of blood and brains on the white side wall. He couldn't tell who it was. Who could it be?

Then the grim realization hit: Someone gunned down this man thinking it was him.

He had just braved weeks of death-defying action, but this was profoundly more up close and personal. Raglan's attempt to kill him felt very personal, but it hadn't happened in Rivers's own home.

Local police were the first to arrive and, despite the CIA

alerting them that one of their officers was involved but unarmed, Rivers immediately raised his hands as he saw them enter the lobby. Soon uniforms and suits filled the building, police with long guns, FBI armed with questions.

That was when Angelos arrived, remarkably fast.

He scanned Rivers up and down, and saw he looked a bit ashen. "Remember to breathe, Tom," he said. "Know who the guy is?"

"No."

"You didn't shoot him, did you?"

"No."

"You don't have a weapon, do you?" said Angelos, worried that Rivers somehow had an agency firearm despite returning the handgun with the fake badge.

"No, none," said Rivers. "But it's lucky I didn't need one."

An FBI official came up to Rivers. "A few questions," he said. "Do you know who the dead man is in your apartment?"

"I can't answer that," said Rivers. "I didn't recognize the body from the glimpse I had of him on the hallway floor. And I haven't heard a name."

"His wallet says he's Travis Reeves."

"Well, then I know him," said Rivers. "He's one of the weapons dealers from the fight in Tampa, related to the shooting at MacDill."

"Why would he come all this way to try to kill you?"

"Well, he tried to kill me in Tampa and failed," said Rivers. "I think he wanted to finish the job.

"It's personal. Years back in the Army in Iraq, I took Reeves and his sidekick into custody for a crime—raping kids—and then testified against them.

"He hated my guts."

The FBI official nodded. He needed the answers for his field report and drifted away with a "thanks, good luck. We'll have to interview you later."

Angelos stared at him and said, "Never seen anything like this. A man comes to your apartment to murder you and he's murdered by a man who is there to murder you."

"Remarkable you're still alive."

"I'm just a popular guy," said Rivers, his quip hiding a queasy feeling.

His would-be killer was still out there.

Raz called upon hearing of his latest brush with disaster.

"Oh, thank God, you're all right," she said. "You are, aren't you? You didn't get shot or anything?"

"No, not a scratch."

Nothing like a near-death experience to, again, clarify a relationship.

"Are you in Paris?" asked Rivers.

"No, New York City," she said. "I learned Cohen was here, so I didn't go to Paris. I'm having lunch with him tomorrow. I have some questions for him.

"I still have the room at the Ritz if you need a place to stay," she said.

"I could use it," said Rivers. "My place isn't livable, pardon the pun.

"I've missed you," he said.

"And I've missed you," said Raz. "Look, I don't know if we'll work out, but we should have fun trying."

68

A shaken Rivers returned to the Operations Center with Angelos and settled into his boss's office with coffee and donuts for a review of the state of things.

"So, Dogu really wants you dead," said Angelos after a while. The Chechen was the obvious answer to the identity of the mystery killer. "You and Raz seem to be magnets for the type of terrorists who hold personal grudges."

Rivers had no snappy comeback.

"I think I'm just going to camp out at Raz's suite at the Ritz," said Rivers. "She's up in New York but should be back later tomorrow. I'm about done in."

"I'm assigning you some security," said Angelos. He expected a protest but got none.

Maybe Rivers had reached the end of the line.

Rivers was taking a sip of his coffee when a call was put through to him on one of Angelos's lines. It was from Russell, the CIA officer who had worked with him in Odesa.

"I'm typing the cable now, but I wanted to tell you direct, so you guys can begin to act on it," said Russell. "We have nuclear material on the loose. Confirmed. And our intel shows it's already been delivered to D.C."

Rivers sat straight up in a chair in Angelos's office, almost spilling his coffee.

"What sort of nuclear stuff are you talking about?" Rivers said, waving to Angelos to close his office door as he put the call on speaker.

We're talking eight small, shielded packages of something called cesium chloride. It's low-level radioactive, but you put it in a suicide vest or pipe bomb, and it'll get blasted over everything."

Rivers whispered to Angelos that it was Russell in Odesa, and the operations director nodded.

"How confirmed is this? What is your source of information?" said Angelos.

"A few hours ago, investigators working here from our Department of Energy responded to a call from police who had been called to check a sick crew on a trawler at the port. They found an extremely sick crew and a cigarette lighter–size thing on a table cracked and emitting a blue light."

"They backed off, and within the hour our DOE guys went aboard—all wearing protective gear, of course—and found what they said was a package of this cesium stuff.

"They interviewed the crew quickly and were told the trawler had picked up nine packages of this stuff in Crimea from a Russian black-marketer and delivered it to the Matsoy group a few days ago here in Odesa, but they were allowed to keep a dented package that they could sell as part of their payment. It leaked.

"There was a raid on the Matsoy gang, and DOE found paperwork showing the shielded packages had been mixed into a pharmaceutical shipment and sent via air to Dulles International Airport, delivered yesterday."

So that was it, thought Rivers, the big finish.

The thing that would make Dogu's attack even bigger than six Switchblade drones with C4 silently motoring down the Potomac River to take on all the defenses everyone presumed—and hoped—protected the Capitol.

He wondered just how bad this stuff was.

The answer came quickly.

Two hours later, Dr. Marie Espina, an expert from the DOE, told dozens of classified listeners on a video conference, "It's a weapon of terror rather than of mass destruction. No mushroom cloud. More people might die in the following panic—traffic accidents, crowd panic, falls and the like—than from the presence of cesium chloride.

"For example, attach it to pipe bombs in a backpack. Explode it and shrapnel will have a kill zone of perhaps one hundred feet. This radioactive material could kill those who survive in that radius within days. But there's a quick descending risk the farther you are away from the blast. It isn't lethal at the lower exposures that come as it disperses, although it can make you very sick from long-term exposure.

"The problem is that this talc-like power or dust will travel on the wind, attach to shoes and clothes, dogs, be tracked into buildings, vehicles, homes miles away. People will panic at the idea of breathing it in and getting radioactive sickness: vomiting, weakness, hair loss. It's not a deadly risk outside the blast zone and the nearest area, but who will listen to that? There will be panic.

"The potency of the dust degrades over a couple of months, but in the blocks around a blast, there will be higher-than-normal levels of background radiation for quite some time. Perhaps by multiples of five to eight. Again, long-term exposure in those affected areas is a real health concern.

"To reduce that risk in those areas, experts would need to remove soil and decontaminate buildings. Costly and time consuming. Even when it's safe by government standards, it'll be hard to get many people back into that section of a city.

"So, there'd be no mushroom cloud," she said again. "But there'd be a hurricane of chaos and fear.

"And violence," said Dr. Espina. "People aren't nice when they panic."

69

Dogu was keeping his white-hot temper in check as dawn approached, mainly by avoiding looking at Umm.

The evening before, they had sat and talked briefly when Dogu came back from murdering the CIA agent in his apartment, briefly because they were strangers to their own emotions beyond the edgy ones they used for survival. Still, they talked of a shared memory: of Omar telling stories with his circle of friends in the evenings. It was as close as either could get to a circle of friends, for both Dogu and Umm had none of their own.

Dogu had risen to leave the room when Umm said, "Don't go to her." A low but stern warning. He stopped in his tracks and turned to this woman who dared to command him.

"I will go to Jomana as I like," Dogu said in a rising voice.

"She stares at the wall and cries after you strangle and thrust into her," said Umm. "We need her for an important target. Leave her alone now and I can get her ready."

Dogu's lips curled in a snarl. This girl Jomana was so

much trouble, and now Umm was trying to halt her best use to him. But the girl was to wear a suicide vest to an important target, and already they had decided to rig it with a remote detonator because she could not be trusted to act. Still, the girl had to move to the location. Perhaps Umm was right.

Of course, Umm had a very personal concern. If Jomana couldn't perform, Umm would be next to take her place, and Umm wanted to murder a more personal target.

Dogu dug out his car keys and left to go to his own safe house. Later, he would turn to Pornhub for a less than satisfying experience and rise early.

Dogu looked out at the weapons of terror laid out on the warehouse floor and tables, and the six techs who were busy assembling them. They were all veterans of ISIS, with experience in making IEDs and operating drones, and they had eagerly joined Dogu's mission once they understood they were not to be martyrs.

They were in a small warehouse amid at least a dozen small shops in Bailey's Crossroads, Virginia, conveniently within the Capital Beltway. Work vans came and went in the area, and nobody paid attention.

Dogu tried not to look at Umm, for some of his ill-temper was a result of his lustless night, but it was mostly the text from Odesa, alerting him that U.S. officials knew about the radioactive dust and that it had made it to D.C.

Should he move up the attacks to today?

He was surprised agents had tracked him in Manhattan and

then had discovered the stone house with the remaining weapons cache. Now this. How close were they?

Beslan, his driver to the stone house, saw his boss was upset and guessed the reason. He sidled up and said, "I told you that you should just kill the bitch. She disrespects you. I'll be happy to do it."

Dogu looked at him blankly for a moment, deep in thought. He was half right.

Beslan was an able lieutenant, but Dogu wasn't going to tell him that the CIA now knew of the radioactive dust. He had seen men cave when they thought a missile might at any time drop onto their heads.

"She'll die soon enough," Dogu said to him. It took some effort for him to keep from looking up to where a missile might penetrate this warehouse roof.

This was a day to run through the timing and order of attacks for tomorrow, and for his techs to check and continue to practice the quick assembly of the Switchblade drones.

He recalled an American expression from when he was polishing his English: practice makes perfect. How could he forget it? It had been an American flight attendant in Athens who taught him that—and more—over a long weekend. She had introduced him to a choking sex game.

Even though some of the plans hadn't worked out, he had confidence in his ISIS followers and their craft.

A white van—plumbing logo removed—contained six assembled launch stands for the Switchblade drones, and racks for the drones themselves. They could be slid out, drones mounted, and wings spread, in a few minutes.

Four backpacks held pipe bombs with C4 and nails.

Bombs were assembled so they could easily be magnetically stuck to vehicles and detonated remotely.

A half-dozen hobbyist drones were fitted with C4.

The eight small steel containers of cesium chloride would be attached to several weapons at Dogu's direction. He was happy his attacks would create chaos and silently spread the killer dust and terror to everyday people. A bit distracted, he was playing with what he'd say in the video for social media announcing the attacks and ISIS's revenge.

A video starring Dogu the Chechen.

70

"You look marvelous," said Steve Cohen, sitting down at Raz's side at a table to the rear of the small Italian restaurant a few blocks north of Manhattan's Washington Square, a gem known to locals and fans coveting fresh pasta and crisp salads.

"I look tired," said Raz. "You look marvelous."

And he did: tanned, slim, wearing a Euro-lean suit and a white shirt tastefully open at the throat and that smile.

She found him attractive as always, which was why even as co-CEOs of their intel company in Paris, she rationed her time with him. She was not a saint, and it was easy to remember he was imaginative as her former lover.

In some ways, they were perfect together, and probably, for a week or two, could still be. But Raz always remembered the agony of the breakup and the irreparable reason for it: While Cohen loved her in his way, he loved himself immeasurably more. After two years together, she had found his self-absorption insufferable. Yet it amazed her that this über-talented, beautiful man had not totally replaced her in all the ways a man feels for a woman.

But today she felt frosty toward Cohen, especially after talking with her friend Adam Barnes, the Interpol inspector in Paris, who was skilled at divining the secret linkages among the intel agencies, businesses, and politics at play in Europe and along the Mediterranean. He told her that he had been looking into recent events with Harry Dalton, and they had uncovered discomforting information about Cohen.

Now Cohen stopped smiling, alert that Raz was all business, her mood announced by her frown. She had phoned to meet him, and he didn't think it was a social call, but he saw that she had come with her professional A-game. Her mind could be like a knife cutting to the core of things, and now he felt its sharp edge.

"You're playing a game and putting our company at risk," said Raz.

An accusation, though unspecific.

"I'm not putting our company at risk," Cohen said.

"You are if you're working for Mossad against the CIA," she said.

Cohen wondered how much she knew, and how.

"You know we both kept some allegiance to our agencies, passing along information as needed to stop bad things," he said. "But why are you thinking I'm working for Mossad against the CIA?"

Slippery.

"There's intelligence information that you used our company assets to kidnap an ISIS woman in Paris and kill her boyfriend, and then a man named Sykes," she said.

He was stunned by her level of knowledge but recovered in an instant.

"A harsh accusation. Who says?"

There were only a few who might even have a suspicion, and Cohen quickly came to think of her friend Barnes, though the unsinkable Rivers was a possibility.

Raz didn't answer.

"Anyone can have suspicions," said Cohen. "Isn't the intel business about planting them, creating a hall of mirrors?"

So, it was true. Raz could hear it in the slight pauses and the tone of his voice, a narrowing of his eyes that only someone who knew him intimately could detect.

"You murdered for your bosses," she hissed. "And used our company."

"Mere suspicions, Raz," said Cohen, but he knew his words sounded hollow to her.

"I'll expect you to buy me out of the company," she said. "I can't be associated with a company that is at risk of criminal charges and dissolution. I'll have a lawyer deliver my price tomorrow. If you need some cash, ask your damn Mossad friends."

Cohen noticed she was only concerned about the company, not him.

If it ever came to it, he was confident that whatever surfaced would be unprovable in any court of law; but this was the court of Raz, and she had found him guilty.

She stood abruptly, and a few people looked over at what seemed like a lovers' quarrel between two beautiful, rich people who shouldn't have a care in the world.

Raz began to walk away, then turned and spat out, "You betrayed me."

"I want you to consider one thing, Raz," said Cohen quietly. "Maybe I'm working with Mossad and the CIA together."

71

A distressed Cohen wasn't alert when he left the restaurant, and things went from bad to worse for him.

He was walking along the quiet street toward busy Sixth Avenue to catch a taxi when a man stepped out of a doorway, blocking him. At the same time someone jabbed something like a gun into his back and then slid a hood over his head. He heard a van and was thrown into it. He didn't struggle; what was the point?

A young man walking his dog saw it all and thought to call 911, then walked on. He thought the man who got hooded looked vaguely Middle Eastern, and those were probably federal agents, so good riddance.

The vehicle drove for perhaps twenty minutes before backing into an enclosed space that echoed like a garage. He was then walked inside to a room and put on a straight-backed chair. At least they hadn't sawed one leg short, which would have prompted the classic, wearying balancing act.

He heard someone behind him, an intentional "Ahem," and then he heard that person walk to his front and sit in a chair. His hood was removed.

Cohen blinked and then said, "Hello, Mr. Dalton. What can I do for you today?"

"How was lunch?" said Dalton.

"Cold," said Cohen.

"Well, I think we can have you out of here in time for a more satisfying early dinner."

"Did Raz set me up?" asked Cohen.

"No, I piggybacked on the lunch date without her knowledge.

"So, let's make this simple," said Dalton. "I just have a few questions and some career advice. And you'll answer me because I'm a good friend to have and a bad enemy to make."

"I don't think you're going to pull out my fingernails or disappear me, so I don't see what promise this meeting holds for you," said Cohen.

"Point well taken, but I do have leverage," said Dalton. "Your Mossad buddies will know that you've been rudely taken by the CIA's new deputy director. I've made sure they'll hear of it. So, you're burned to them, whether you speak to me or not. They won't trust you.

"And considering I've heard you had some people killed for them, they might decide secrets are best left with the dead," Dalton continued. "You're in danger unless I put my protective arms around you. Burned or dead to them, or working for me."

Dalton continued, "I've been working with Interpol's Adam Barnes and French intel's Martin Lyons, and our artful reconstruction of phone data, travel data from your company's vehicles, video searches and the like, puts you in the crosshairs for scooping up the ISIS girl and killing her boyfriend and then

Sykes. You and your company are implicated, particularly using the ex-Mossad woman on your staff as the shooter."

"Mere suspicions," said Cohen.

"No. But insufficient evidence, yes," said Dalton. "Yet a deeper investigation could be expected to find more evidence. As it is, there is a consensus to let it go if you cooperate."

"Crimes happened in France, so why would Lyons agree to that?" said Cohen.

"Martin Lyons has more wit than I knew," said Dalton. "He said, *When a man gets his dick caught in his zipper, all men wince in pain.* The CIA and Mossad are exposed here, but French intel also would face blowback if everything became public."

Cohen was a realist and knew Mossad would freak at his temporary rendition by the CIA's deputy director. He found the choice to disavow his homeland far easier than he would have expected. He'd been working with a faction of the old guard in Mossad that was running an unauthorized operation, which they'd deny. Knowing Mossad's ruthless track record of dealing with fallen officers eased the way to his decision.

"Go on," he said to Dalton.

"OK, question number one: Why did Mossad want to capture the young woman in Paris?"

"Well, grabbing the girl seemed the fastest way to confirm who the beheader was. Like your Angelos, we had a suspicion it was a resurrected Susan Owens. As it was, the ISIS girl confirmed it, which I passed on to Angelos, who had asked me to keep my eyes open. It was easy to grab her; we already were tapped into local Chechen snitches and the French police comms."

"Question number two: So why kill anyone?"

"It created an opportunity. Angelos and I communicated back

and forth. Unofficial channels. He had reason to hide that the terrorist leader was a former CIA asset, so who would believe his denials that he ordered killings to hide it? The thought by my bosses was to push him to stop resisting a plan to oust the Saudi crown prince, which my bosses support."

Ahh, that plan, thought Dalton; it all led back to the fever dream to oust the Saudi leader and restore the days of a rabid anti-Iran regime and a flexible partner in providing oil.

"Question number three: Where does CIA Director Harwell fit in all this?"

"Well, he's one of the originators of the Saudi plan. I told the director about Angelos and the fake badge, which I saw when I had drinks with Raz and Rivers. That set Angelos up for removal. Of course, now that you're the deputy director, that isn't urgent. Harwell doesn't know about the murders. But my bosses know, if needed, it could be used to provide leverage with him, same as with Angelos."

"Let me ask you a question," said Cohen. "Are you going to support the plan?"

"It's a stupid idea," said Dalton.

"Yes, but many powerful people are behind it," said Cohen. "Sometimes stupid ideas proceed; and sometimes they even work."

Dalton shrugged. "Last question. Why call in the murder and leave the passports in plain sight in Paris?"

"Breadcrumbs. The investigation into the beheading was slow, so we decided to help it along. To add pressure on Angelos."

"Well, we're done," said Dalton. "Of course, as you see, this was videotaped, and we'll have a statement for you to sign. I'll be in touch about our new arrangement."

"You'll let my former bosses know I'm now one of yours, right?" said Cohen.

"That's the deal."

Dalton was pleased. He had nailed down some answers. More important, he now had leverage against CIA Director Harwell. Just whispers of a secret relationship with Mossad, a possible tie to murders in France, would tarnish the prized reputation of the "senator." And Dalton would be happy to tell Harwell that he'd start such whispers, beginning with the *Washington Post*. He could see Harwell stepping down, clearing the way for him to serve as acting director with a splendid shot at becoming the director.

"Before I go, one more question," said Dalton. "Did you ever confront Angelos with the murders, and that he needed to stand down from his resistance to the Saudi plan?"

Cohen smiled. "Yes, a rather brief encounter. Your Mr. Angelos told me to fuck off."

Now Dalton smiled, for some things were still right with the world.

72

Rivers once was on an airliner caught by wind shear as it came in for a landing, the force suddenly yanking the plane to earth like a fast elevator. There was a tug of his safety belt as he was lifted from his seat. "Hail Mary, full ..." the woman next to him began to pray. And then the plane leveled with a jolt and powered to a smooth, if fast, landing. The skill of the pilots? Luck? Who knew?

He had that same feeling—waiting helplessly for doom or deliverance—as he sat in Angelos's office. He simply had nothing to do. He was along for the ride while the FBI, the ATF, and every police agency imaginable pursued leads. And while Operations Center analysts chewed on incoming cables and reports looking for a crack in the case.

Social media was ablaze with conjectures and armchair insights about the terrorist threat, but nothing about radioactive dust yet. That would make it worse for the CIA and the president, who already were being criticized as failing to keep the country safe. He assumed the cable news pundits were having a field day.

The aides in the While House were behind the curve in considering their responses, even as the official state of things already was clear for anyone to see. There were small white blimps with high-powered monitors tethered over the Capital area; and helicopters zigzagged, sniffing for radioactivity; and police and soldiers with weapons slung across their protective vests stood guard or combed through public places.

A lot of people were remembering 9/11 and rediscovering the feeling of frayed nerves mixed with cluelessness: *What is happening? Am I safe?*

It was morning and Rivers sat with Angelos in his office, the pile of empty coffee cups testimony to a long day fallen through a long night. They were two professionals who had turned all the evidence inside out, only to come up empty.

"I'm sorry you're in the IG's crosshairs," said Angelos. "It was a good bet gone sideways, although we did get some actionable information. If it's any consolation, you've done such valuable work that using a fake badge and credentials on my orders shouldn't cost you your job.

"Although you said you're quitting," continued Angelos. "I'd feel bad if it was on account of me. The agency can use your talents, needs them. Too many people have their asses and their brains parked in their chairs. And if you stay, there's a plus."

"What's the plus?" said Rivers.

"I won't be here. They should let me retire under the threat of charges, but I do worry that I could still get nailed to the wall," said Angelos.

"I'm leaving for me, not because of you," Rivers said. He'd

had ample time to weigh his future, and he would feel hand-cuffed by continuing to work in the CIA officialdom. As for Angelos, he was an effective boss but too secretive and Machi-avellian for his tastes, which, of course, might be what made him so effective as an operations director.

"What do think you'll do? Work for Raz's outfit? You, Raz, and Cohen—that'd be cozy."

That was the thing about Angelos: Was he actually interested in Rivers's future? Or had he started this conversation only to arrive at Cohen and Raz?

"No, not Raz's company," said Rivers. He was thinking of Daryan Nuri and his Kurdish commercial empire. If not that, something else in the Mediterranean area he knew.

Something nagged at Rivers: "What is it with Steve Cohen and you?"

"Let's just say there's a game underway, and I'm someone they'd like to take off the board," said Angelos.

"Cryptic," said Rivers.

"Intentionally," said Angelos.

"I'm guessing, then, Mossad," said Rivers.

Angelos shrugged. "At least you can forget my order to clone Raz's phone. Don't need it now, not that you were going to do it. I had a chance to clear the air with Mr. Cohen."

"Is he still alive?" asked Rivers.

"Of course," said Angelos. "Despite what you might think, I don't go around killing people."

Rivers sat back and began to ponder the rumors and gossip that swirled through the CIA and what had been written by some of the real journalists in Washington, who kept their ears to the ground.

Mossad, CIA, Congress, Saudi oil. Rivers had a faint outline of an idea, but Angelos interrupted his train of thought.

"Fuck us all," said Angelos. He spun his computer screen so Rivers could see it, and there was the *New York Post* with a screaming headline:

LOOSE NUKES

73

C haos.

    Exactly what a terrorist wants, but not what Dogu wanted at this precise moment. He was expecting it after the text from Odesa that alerted him that the United States knew of his radioactive weapon. A leak to the media, for that was what America does.

LOOSE NUKES screamed the *New York Post* on his news app.

But this early leak was inconvenient: He had planned to drive to New York City late in the day, but now roads would be clogged and he'd have to make an early start.

So Dogu quickly assembled his troops for a full run-through of tomorrow's attacks and the need to triple check the attachment of the radioactive containers to his selected weapons, and to continue to practice assembling the Switchblade drones on their launchers.

His lieutenant, Beslan, quietly asked, "Should we launch our attacks now?"

Dogu had considered it; it was still early, and they were primed, and the Loose Nukes news would take hold of the public over the next few hours.

"We'll keep to tomorrow," said Dogu.

Let the infidels sweat.

Now, hours earlier than he had planned, Dogu left in his leased BMW SUV with his duffel bag and headed toward New York City. He was north of Philadelphia before the roadways jammed with panicked drivers. Still, he pressed forward, hour after hour, and saw that most traffic was away from New York City as he got closer. Late in the afternoon he arrived.

He had left the warehouse in the capable hands of Beslan and had asked Umm to preach in the early evening, when his crew would sit for a communal meal at the warehouse and then sleep, if they could, on the floor on mats.

Umm's top talent was useful now: She had a captivating voice, melodious before rising in stern command, and would give a sermon on the holiness of their ISIS mission and the glory of their actions. Her passion was authentic, and surprising coming from a woman who, though still attractive, seemed so cold and was physically shrinking like a prune.

Dogu wondered if Osama bin Laden felt the low electricity of edgy nerves as his terror operation unfolded.

He wondered and worried: The U.S. agents had surprised him at the stone building and in discovering the existence of the radioactive dust.

How close were his enemies?

He considered as he drove: maybe Beslan was right; maybe he should have launched the attacks.

"I'm Gloria."

He would call her nothing.

Dogu had reached his apartment after parking his SUV in a rented garage, and then he felt his compulsion, inescapably powerful, an urge not to be denied. He needed, now more than ever, the release of a woman, a woman he could strangle during sex, her eyes at first accepting the violence as a prostitute highly paid for the abuse, but then the eyes panicking that this anonymous man would not stop.

He had called an escort service, and despite the unusually late hour, a woman was provided who fit his cited desires: young, dark hair, not fat, no piercings, no meth hags, no drugs at all, rough play accepted.

The man on the call laughed. "It's late, pal. You got to take what you can get."

Dogu mentioned what he'd pay—multiples of any expected price—and the man said, "I can get what you need, but you won't be her first of the night."

Now Gloria was here, and Dogu took his time to undress her, first with his eyes. More middle-aged than young, though her lifestyle could make that deceiving. A bit fuller in shape than he preferred; he should have specified *thin*. But he was in that hazy state of mind where his compulsion was outracing any thought.

At the right time for him, Gloria's eyes bulged in panic just as he liked, wondering if he would loosen the scarf around her neck. He didn't want to and held it tight seconds past when it should have come loose. Finally, he loosened it.

He kicked her out immediately.

Dogu felt like himself again. His was a good life, and he

wanted more: fame as the world's greatest holy warrior, with billions adoring him.

Soon, the dawn of attack.

He looked at watch … just a few hours now.

74

Raz felt liberated and sad at the same time.

Sad that Cohen had fallen to such sordid depths, yet free from old entanglements. Operating the private intel company together had been a step away from the love affair, but not a clean break. She would soon be even richer and have a sterling business reputation upon which to build a new enterprise.

And there was Tom.

The idea of spending time with him—perhaps a long time—felt appealing. He was good looking, pending healing, and had a sharp mind and wit. And he certainly showed resilience in this terrorist hunt. All good qualities. But it was his capacity to care and be human that held magnetic power over her, who had seen so much violence. At his best, Tom Rivers was the soldier who stood up for the brutalized children in Iraq. A lot of men had no best.

Her corporate jet trembled in choppy air en route back to D.C. and the Ritz. She hoped Tom would be there.

It looked like the jet was going to sneak into Dulles before its anticipated meltdown in this loose nuke scare. Which she knew was more than a scare.

———————

Raz and Tom fell into each other's arms when she came through the door at the Ritz, a long, luxurious touch of warmth with a hint of lust.

He thought she looked radiant, her blue eyes flashing, not at all worn by the recent angry day. Whatever had happened in Manhattan—and she would tell him—had washed over her like a healing balm. In his heart, he knew it was bad for Cohen and good for him.

And Raz thought … well, Tom looked bruised, bent, and scarred, but he had that smile and an easy grip on her. He had worked through the night with Angelos and then drove to the hotel, security following, and managed to get a few hours of sleep.

They sat with a glass of wine from a small stash of bottles he had procured, along with an outlay of Lebanese food.

"Well, what do you think about hanging out with a rich woman?" Raz said.

"How rich?" Tom countered.

She smirked at his reply.

"As long as you're that woman, I'm delighted," he said.

"The right answer," said Raz.

She filled him in on the details, and Tom said he increasingly understood some behind-the-scenes intrigue in the agency— things about Harwell, Cohen, Angelos, and Saudi Arabia—and she didn't care, and he didn't elaborate. It wasn't important at this moment.

"Do you remember that first night in the jazz club?" she asked.

"Of course," said Tom. "I remember how you took my breath away and the slow dances. And I remember you disappearing but leaving me that note: *Don't be smitten, don't be a stranger.*"

"Well, I won't disappear this time," she said. And then they were dancing to a slow, jazzy Diana Krall song that Tom had put on, and their bodies moved to the same rhythm.

"This is the way we should be," said Raz.

PART SIX

75

"How rude," muttered a sleepy Raz.

A phone was buzzing, and Rivers gently rolled to it and answered, as Raz immediately took possession of his warm spot in the bed. It was 1:32 a.m.

"Got a live tip, get here," said John Xavier.

In a flash, Rivers was up and dressing, adding a splash of water on his face. Angelos gave him the keys to an agency helicopter, so to speak, for a ninety-minute ride to a heliport in midtown Manhattan. As he settled in and watched the night lights flicker by, he finally got an update from the police lieutenant.

"Vice called me and said an escort service they were monitoring had a client who fits our alert on Dogu," said Xavier. "The pimp didn't immediately put two and two together, though while the guy said he wanted *rough play*, it wasn't until the woman finished and called that he understood she was almost strangled to death.

"We're rallying the SWAT team and already beginning to flood in observers around a condo building on the Lower East Side. Bomb squad too.

"Probably be ready to enter right before dawn."

"I'll be there by then," said Rivers.

He had come to admire Dogu's resourcefulness. Damn, the CIA had to tap dozens of people with access to the greatest technology, from recon satellites to drones, to undertake their operations. This guy dreamed this up behind the Al-Hol barbwire and was using the remnants of ISIS.

He had never underestimated Dogu. Could they be so lucky that his kinky sex urges spawned the break they needed?

Could they be so lucky that the damn condo building wouldn't blow up and spread radiation into lower Manhattans?

With the sky east of Manhattan turning lighter, a breeze off the East River drifting down the street, SWAT teams filed in and up the stairs to a second-floor condo. Amazingly quiet. A single dog barked. No lights were observed coming on. They were set to ram the door open and did after a quick check from a bomb tech.

The door splintered at its lock with a sound to wake the dead. The incident commander had elected not to rouse the other tenants in the six-condo building, a decision that weighed on her. The safety of citizens was paramount, but securing the possible radioactive material here demanded maximum surprise, speed, and lethality.

SWAT rumbled through the hall, living room, kitchen, bath, and bedroom. Rumpled sheets, but no one home. Xavier and Rivers walked through the condo looking for … anything. But there weren't papers or maps, much less a phone or laptop. It looked like a place for a one-night stand.

That bugged Rivers.

Dogu was slippery yet a planner: If he had this condo as a potential pleasure palace, he'd have a real war nest nearby.

"We need to talk to a tenant or two," said Rivers to Xavier. Which wouldn't be too hard because the tenants were opening their doors to see what was happening, only to find hallways flooded with heavily armed SWAT.

A woman who lived on the first floor told them that both units on the second floor had been sublet for several months by the owners, who were away in Europe. She didn't know who the temporary tenants were.

"People mind their own business here," she said.

Rivers climbed the stairs to check the other condo and saw Xavier had abandoned him. But he soon reappeared bearing the battering ram. "A man needs the right tools," he said. Three swings and the door gave.

No Dogu. But inside the living room, furniture had been moved aside. Nailed to a wall was the black flag of ISIS with its white Arabic script, *There is No God but God*. A camera stand was aimed at the space before it, where someone could be recorded.

There were some papers on the coffee table. Notes in perhaps Chechen or a Russian language. Maybe a script for a video session? Perhaps thoughts on the attack? Rivers quickly scanned the pages on his phone and sent it off to Angelos, Cowen, and the CIA Operations Center for immediate translation and analysis. Xavier sent it to his command.

A forensic team poured in, its commander expressing dissatisfaction with their handling of evidence.

Then Rivers's phone buzzed, and Angelos was telling him a Dogu video had hit social media. He watched it with Xavier on his phone.

In the video, Dogu wore black and stood before the flag of ISIS. The flag in this room.

Dogu was a young man with an interesting but hard face and a gravelly voice. He spoke with confidence.

"The Islamic State rises again to punish America, the great evil in the world. I am Dogu Matsoy, a servant of the faithful. And today, I pledge to continue the work of the holy warrior Osama bin Laden. He said in his last message to the evil West, 'How is it right for you to occupy our countries and kill our women and children and expect to live in peace and security? The equation is clear: you are killed as you kill.' Today, as it was on September 11, our sword of justice falls on America. I am a Chechen by birth, thrown from my homeland, a man who found a home in the embrace of my father, Omar Shishani, the great ISIS military commander in Syria. Today, I take vengeance for their deaths, and I raise the ISIS banner in a renewed war. Watch, America. First was Nashville. Today our dirty bombs will eat the life from your bones. Dogu Matsoy brings death to America, as you deserve."

Even though it was what he expected, Xavier said, "Fuck us all."

A good guess was that the rebuilt World Trade Center and Wall Street were the targets. High-alert security already protected the area. Dogu would know that.

So, what was his game?

76

Umm and Jomana were the first out of the warehouse door in Northern Virginia, steeled by the video from Dogu that had just flashed over the internet. At least Umm felt that way. Jomana looked as if she was sleepwalking, but Umm had her moving.

Over the last two nights, with Dogu out of her bed, Umm had sat with Jomana and spoke as she had so often at Al-Hol, talking of holy duty to the faithful, of the joy of martyrdom.

"Fadwa is dead, isn't she?" Jomana asked of her sister, who had disappeared in Paris.

"That is certain," Umm said. "I sent her on a task from which she should have returned, but she did not. The infidels certainly killed her. Now it is a blessing that you can kill infidels. And then join in the everlasting embrace of your sister.

"I know how you snuggled with your sister under the covers," said Umm, who saw a loving smile light Jomana's face. "That will be your reward, to again snuggle with your sister."

Still, in this morning light, Umm saw a blankness in Jomana's face and wondered if she would deliver to the target her suicide vest with its pipe bombs and radioactive dust.

One of Beslan's techs drove them carefully to their destination, over the 14th Street Bridge into Washington, D.C., a trip made long by the snarl of traffic. They had started early, at Dogu's instruction. Once he had wanted to start the first attack at 9:11 a.m., but now he just wanted them to launch as soon as possible.

Umm and Jomana got out of the car outside the L'Enfant Plaza Metro station, where several train lines converged. They both carried backpacks, and Umm wondered if there would be police checks and bomb dogs, but she also knew the variety and number of potential targets in the Capital would thin any resources for a place like this.

As it was, Jomana was bound to attract every police eye. Dogu had made sure she was wearing a yellow jacket, thinking that police would see and then dismiss her as a threat, for terrorists would want to move unseen, not in plain sight. A frail girl, no less.

They entered the station past a few police, used prepaid fare-cards through the turnstiles, and went down the elevator. A small number of people, befitting the scare.

When the Yellow Line train arrived, Umm saw Jomana aboard, a small push at the elbow to help her. Then, through the window, she saw the girl, so slight, take a seat. Umm walked away, sliding off her own backpack and tucking it by the side of the escalator as she stepped on it. It would detonate on a timer and foul the station and trains going to the Metro Center and elsewhere.

Jomana's train would reach its next stop in a few minutes: the station at the Pentagon.

The Marine major glanced over at the girl in the yellow jacket; so frail, but there was something beyond just her slight frame. She had tears in her eyes and was sniffling. Then a cold shudder ran through him as he saw the plunger in her hand.

All his senses went alert. He had served tours in Afghanistan and knew the horror of IEDs and suicide bombers. But he saw something else here: a girl struggling with the idea of being a martyr.

A woman saw him staring at the girl, and she looked. Her eyes went wide. She picked up her phone to call for help.

The Marine slowly and calmly moved toward the girl and knelt on one knee in the aisle beside her, his hands open. He spoke to her in a low, gentle voice. "I am here to help you, not to hurt you. Please don't hurt us." He repeated it again and again. Gently, calmly, *easy does it*.

The girl trembled and clearly didn't understand his words, but Jomana understood that he meant no harm to her. He sounded gentle. His eyes rested on hers. He meant no harm, that she could tell. "I am here to help, please don't hurt us," he continued. Her thumb was on the detonation plunger.

The train was braking to enter the Pentagon station, still in the tunnel but moments from arriving at the concourse for exiting and entering the train.

Jomana nodded to the Marine, her tears now heavy, her body

shaking. She removed her thumb from the plunger and let it fall from her hand, dangling from its wire.

The major opened his arms, signaling that he would hold her if she chose. She slid toward him for his human touch.

In that instant, at 7:40 a.m., Jomana's bomb vest was detonated remotely by Umm.

77

Dogu had a plan for delivering his dirty bombs to the most protected sites in New York City without even going there.

His targets were always Ground Zero, the site resurrected from the ashes of 9/11, now occupied by stunning silver skyscrapers and the 9/11 Memorial and Museum, and the financial district at Wall Street.

Could there be anything more shocking to Americans than to again make it a killing field?

It was early morning, and Dogu was walking casually over to Chinatown, where he had rented a garage to store the tools of today's trade. His years growing up in smuggling gave him an ability to blend in, and he slouched as he walked, a pace without purpose, just like a guy who worked from his apartment out on a coffee run.

An old man and woman were poking at fresh vegetables at a sidewalk display. A delivery bicyclist sped by with plastic bags from a bagel store in a front basket. Some people were hurrying to a subway station, and the sound of a train's screeching brakes could be heard from the sidewalk grates a block away. A police car cruised by—nothing amiss in sight.

His plans had been made unnecessarily complicated by Umm's recklessness, the beheading in Paris sparking a hunt for terrorists, as well as her ill-timed attacks in Nashville and Tampa. The Ground Zero site always was under tight security, but it had been made impenetrable with the new threat.

Or so authorities would think.

But Dogu had a plan, quite imaginative, he had to admit.

Umm. Reckless Umm. Dogu thought about killing her many times, but he knew he wouldn't. In her way she was the passionate author of all these attacks.

Dogu had been depressed first by his father's death, and then by ISIS's collapse and his Al-Hol detention. But he witnessed Umm, her body carved by shrapnel, emerge as if she'd been purified into hard steel by the fire of the missile. And it steeled him.

Umm the Avenger.

A half hour later he was in motion.

Dogu was collecting a dirty but reliable e-bike from the garage in Chinatown, where he had stashed the SUV the night before. He changed into this morning's work clothes: well-worn blue jeans, a faded McSorley's T-shirt, and a rumpled Mets cap. All thanks to the cheap, thrift clothing store near the apartment.

He pulled from a duffle bag two large white plastic bags and placed them into the basket attached to the e-bike handlebars. He placed atop them another two bags marked Chinatown Market and smelling of the spicey food he'd just picked up. The bottom two contained his dirty bombs.

He closed and locked the garage, its usefulness not done. He had read that there were 65,000 bicycle food deliverers in New York City. They were seen but unseen by the people who lived there. Now he was one of them.

Dogu's phone buzzed with an incoming text, and he nodded happily at the news: Explosions at two Metro stations in metro Washington, D.C., including at the Pentagon.

Dogu glided down Broadway, which was clogged with multiple police, National Guard, and alphabet agency officers and vehicles, mostly with lights flashing.

A cop pointed at his Mets cap and yelled, "The Mets suck!" And Dogu nodded agreement and waved as a couple of cops laughed. One man in a blue jacket gave him a long, professional look, but then glanced away.

The e-bike took Dogu steadily to within two blocks of where he wanted to be. He then turned left into a side street and went a block to an area vacant of police attention. He pulled out his phone and called 911.

"Smoke inside Trinity Church. Maybe a fire." Short and sweet.

The New York City Fire Department was always on the job. There might be an alert for terrorism, but they still were there to answer the call for a normal run to a historic church that had had small fires in the past, especially during a recent renovation. Engines and ladder trucks from two firehouses automatically responded to the old, iconic church on Broadway at Wall Street. One firehouse was located at the 9/11 Memorial, less than a quarter mile away, another a little more than a half a mile out.

Within a minute, sirens were in the air.

Now came the risky part.

———

Dogu rode back to Broadway and saw a fire engine arrive, with the farther one coming down Broadway. He slowly moved toward the church.

The fire engines angled in front of the church, with one ladder truck remaining on a side street and then the other pulling into the same side street, setting up so driver's windows faced each other for easy conversation. No smoke, probably a false alarm.

Most of the eyeballs—law enforcement and a few pedestrians —were on the geared-up firefighters entering the church and the engines loudly idling out front.

Dogu rolled into the side street. where the ladder trucks idled, stopping at the rear of a rig. He quickly pulled a pipe bomb with a magnetic plate from a white plastic bag and clicked it underneath the huge bumper. He almost tipped over his bike as he leaned but recovered and moved on.

His heart raced and sweat ran down his back.

But there were no yells to stop.

The next one was much riskier. The trucks were facing in opposite directions, so Dogu couldn't get to the back of the next truck without passing right in front of a windshield from which the driver or anyone else in the cab could see him.

He took a deep breath, passing along the truck's side, then into plain sight. He angled toward the back of the next rig. Just a delivery guy on a bike. He attached the next bomb.

As he leaned back on his bike, a firefighter appeared from the side of the truck: "What the fuck you doing?"

"Just looking, man, just looking," said Dogu.

"I don't buy that," said the firefighter.

He hadn't seen Dogu touch anything, but so many jerks were always trying to steal something as memorabilia off the trucks from the fabled 9/11 fire station. This guy wore a crushed Mets hat, and a faded McSorley's tee, and the firefighter sized him up as a guy moving rapidly into a faded life who'd be happy to grab something if he could.

Dogu bent his head like a dog submitting to a bad-dog rebuke, and a hand slid to his hip, near the handgun at his back.

"Get out of here," said the firefighter. "I've got my eye on you."

Dogu zoomed two blocks away to watch until the engines and ladder trucks cleared and moved toward their firehouses by the 9/11 Memorial and the edge of Wall Street.

Then there would be the explosions when he hit the remote detonators.

He had a change of clothes and a motorcycle in the garage and a short ride to a boat at City Island. It would take him to an outgoing cargo ship captained by a Chechen.

He and the captain would drink champagne that night.

78

Seconds counted.

The translation of the note found in Dogu's apartment streamed via text onto Rivers's phone, and he was glad in that moment that he had stayed here instead of rushing with Lt. Xavier toward Ground Zero.

The notes were sketchy, largely for the video speech that was up on the internet now. But there were other jottings, as apparently Dogu thought through how to maneuver his attacks through the chaos and defenses.

"Attach to fire trucks" was one snippet.

"CIA"

"D at Idylwood Park"

There was a last item that made Rivers cringe.

He turned to the leader of the forensics techs, showed her the text and asked, "This mean anything to you?"

The woman scrunched her face in concentration, recognizing the radioactive threat because her team had just hunted for a trace

328

in this apartment. Her FDNY radio murmured from where it was attached to her belt, information of fire alerts and firehouse responses and statuses that she understood as it played like background music.

She looked up, tense with understanding.

"We have engines and ladders out now near the 9/11 Memorial," she said.

Attach to fire trucks—nothing more needed to be said.

Rivers was on his phone to Xavier and then Angelos. The tech leader called dispatch.

Seconds counted.

The fire commander on scene took the urgent information in stride as his mind spun in calculations of time and distance and casualties.

A breeze floated from the Hudson, and he shivered under his heavy black fire coat, though not from the cooler wisp of air. He had responded on 9/11, a young man who was ready to enter a stairwell in the North Tower but was sent running to safety in a dense cloud of dust after the other tower fell first. So many funerals. He would like to avoid them on his watch.

Time was his enemy.

He guessed a bomb would be set, or be remotely triggered, for when the first rigs went the quarter mile back to its 9/11 fire station. Mere minutes. He had to buy some time.

He ordered the firefighters who had begun to stream out of the building after finding no smoke or fire to reenter the old church. He ordered the bomb squad to rush the heavy steel container that could swallow pipe bomb blasts to the side street.

It already was on a truck outside the 9/11 firehouse and could be here in minutes.

No one had been around the engines within plain sight on Broadway, so it was clear to him that the ladder trucks on the side street had been the target.

He spoke on a private radio channel to his ladder truck drivers and was told a firefighter with them had seen a delivery guy on a bike near the back of a rig.

Sneaky bastard, he thought.

He disregarded one thought: If he alerted the police that a bicycle deliverer was probably within eyesight, all hell would break loose. And the terrorist would detonate immediately.

The fire commander had the feeling he was out of time. Tick-tock. Whoever was watching must be sensing the delay.

His eyes swept the scene. *God, help me find an answer.* And then he saw it. Something that had a chance of working.

He spoke calmly to the ladder rig crew and other firefighters to the side of the church. There, in the small cemetery, whose ancient graves included Alexander Hamilton's, he had seen an open grave with the front-end loader that dug it beside the opening.

One, two, three … go.

If you want calm teamwork, call firefighters.

First, a firefighter cranked open a hydrant in front of the church, unleashing an unexpected geyser of water. A diversion.

At the same time, firefighters used prying tools to detach the pipe bomb packages from below the rear bumpers of the rigs and ran them to the open grave. Another firefighter had started the front-end loader, and as the bombs went down six feet, he drove the ton of equipment right into the hole, covering most but not all of the opening.

Dogu, on his e-bike two blocks away, saw the sudden column of water but missed his bombs' removal. The rigs shielded him from seeing what was happening in the cemetery. His sense was that this was taking too long, and he was in ever-increasing danger if he stayed.

He set a timer on his phone for remote detonation in ten minutes. That was enough time for the firefighters to finish at the church and turn back to their stations. He then zoomed away, using side streets instead of Broadway to limit any sight of him.

What could go wrong? He had done it.

Rivers was on the phone with Angelos, both monitoring the bomb situation at the church. No sighting of Dogu, although Xavier was with a driver, scouting the streets. The fire commander had largely buried the bombs but now was pouring a special sealant into the grave to help contain the expected explosion. The firefighters also were muscling in a heavy steel sheet from a road repair nearby to drop over a remaining small opening of the grave.

"That last item in Dogu's notes scares the hell out of me," said Rivers.

"Already on it. Security teams were sent as soon as I saw it," said Angelos.

Then, even over the phone, Rivers heard it: a sharp crack followed by a boom. He knew that unmistakable sound from his time in Iraq.

"Goddamn it," he heard Angelos say.

Angelos put the phone down and was gone for a minute.

Finally, he was back.

"The motherfuckers detonated a car bomb near the main gate," said Angelos. "We have to assume it was a dirty bomb."

Now Route 123 that ran in front of the CIA headquarters was closed and probably contaminated. It joined two bombed Metro stations in metro D.C. on a list of Dogu's and Umm's successes. Even his loss near Ground Zero couldn't erase the bitter taste of the day.

And it wasn't over.

79

Dogu's techs in Northern Virginia went about their tasks, buoyed by the early news of the bombings at the Pentagon and the other Metro station.

One group was on a soccer field at Idylwood Park in Fairfax County, ready to launch six commercial drones loaded with C4 explosives right down Route 66 toward the Capitol, all directed toward demolishing the dome of the building that housed Congress. One drone was fitted with a container of radioactive dust.

At 9:03 a.m., two Army attack helicopters swooped in and fired missiles on the drones, techs, and their van. A fireball flashed skyward, and the wave of air pressure blew out windows of surrounding homes. The traffic on Route 66 stopped at the spectacle.

Dogu's scribbled note had provided the timely clue.

Bombs at the Pentagon and in D.C., news flashes from New

York City, the massacre at Nashville—a holy hell had descended upon America. TV and the internet were filled with constant Breaking News bulletins. Fear rippled wherever people were, especially in the basements where many parents and kids huddled watching the news.

A few minutes later at 9:10, an attack helicopter reported six Switchblade drones in the air flying over the Potomac River toward Washington.

An EMP weapon fired bursts at two drones that turned toward the CIA headquarters, the electromagnetic pulses frying their motors and pitching them into the river. Two of the other four drones had been on the outer edges of the bursts and limped away, only to lose altitude and glide into the Potomac.

Two Switchblades remained on target: the White House.

As those two drones made a tight turn over the river toward the Washington Mall, a portable EMP weapon from an Army truck pulsed.

One drone spiraled into the river.

The remaining one—a silver slice of winged metal against the bright blue sky— tilted as if wounded. It flew for another few seconds.

It hit the top of the Lincoln Memorial, crashed onto the concrete concourse at the bottom of its steps and slid into the Reflecting Pool.

The crippled drone did not explode.

Rivers was on the phone to Raz.

"How are you doing?" he asked.

"I just want this to be over," said Raz. "Angelos called me. Security is en route, and my own bodyguards are aware."

"Be safe," Rivers said.

That last item in Dogu's note had chilled him.

It said: *Umm kill Raz Jak*

80

The door to Raz's hotel room at the Ritz slowly opened.

"It's her; no bomb vest but a handgun," a bodyguard watching the hallway via a video feed told Raz over her earbud.

"Come in, Umm or Susan, whichever you prefer," said Raz as the figure moved into the suite.

Raz wore a protective vest, but another bodyguard, who had stepped out behind Umm from a closet, was her real protection.

Umm smiled when she looked back and saw a handgun pointed at her head, her own weapon down at her side.

So, they knew she was coming.

"You never were one for a fair fight, were you?" Umm said to Raz. "Always had the CIA at your back."

"That always seemed fair to me," said Raz.

"It's been a good day—ISIS reborn," said Umm.

"But not a good end to the day for you," Raz said.

Umm didn't seem rattled that she was as good as dead, for

her end was clear: She would raise her weapon to kill Raz and a bullet from the bodyguard would strike her down first.

Umm's attractive face had aged, as the desert and the savagery of ISIS and Al-Hol and finally this mission of terror had chiseled it with hard lines. She was rail thin but with a coiled strength. Raz had the image of a placid snake that could lash out in a deadly strike.

"Don't see me as a monster," said Umm, seeing that Raz was sizing her up. "I am a creation of America."

"Oh please," said Raz. "Stop with the self-pity, blame-America crap. You are a monster who trained girls to be suicide bombers. That's all on you."

"These girls live a cruel life in a cruel world. I just make it shorter and give their lives purpose," she said.

"How noble," said Raz.

"Thank you," said Umm.

"What should I remember about you, Susan?"

She obviously had thought about it. "I grew up learning two things," she said. "I learned that I wanted— needed— the warm and safe embrace of a family, which my father did not give me, and of a community, which the self-righteousness of my church did not provide. The second thing I learned was an 'eye for an eye.'

"Ironic that I had to go halfway around the world to find my home with Omar and the true Islamic faithful. So, I should probably thank you, Raz."

"Yet, you want to kill me."

"An 'eye for an eye.' I can't kill the CIA, but I can kill you, for murdering my Omar."

There was then silence in the room.

Raz remembered Susan Owens in Cairo— the smart,

committed idealist who had helped the CIA monitor radical Islamists. Until she was soaked in the radical's commitment, enthusiasm, victimhood, and the community they offered. Finally, a love with Omar. A lot of what they said about the world's corruption was true, but the ISIS ideology to change it through murder and conquest was biblical evil in its own corruption.

"What would you say to Mary now?" said Raz.

"That I killed the son of a bitch who raped you, sister."

"You were the older sister. Couldn't you have saved Mary?"

Umm looked at Raz, her face recomposing before Raz's eyes into that of Susan Owens, a face with a gentle love for her sister, a feeling older and deeper than her hate.

"That is my only regret," Susan whispered.

Then she snapped out of it. "Let me ask you a question, Raz. How do you live with yourself, knowing your CIA manipulates people, sends people like me into harm's way, possibly to their death?"

"I simply don't lie to myself about it," said Raz.

At that, she lifted her handgun, and before either Umm or the bodyguard could react, Raz shot her once in the forehead.

Raz looked at Susan-Umm's body on the floor and said, "And I tell myself it's for the greater good."

She breathed out and was aware of a wave of conflicting feelings. Some small current of happiness— no, that wasn't the word —it was fulfillment, with the ending of this monster. A larger measure of sadness for Susan the idealist. Raz had spent years thinking, or trying not to think, of killing Umm. All she knew now was that it had been necessary, and it was done.

Raz laid the handgun on the floor at Umm's feet. She had never killed anyone before. She hoped she never would again.

81

Eight Days Later

"Y ou've played your cards masterfully," said Kate Milano to Harry Dalton. "I wouldn't be surprised if you have my job before this is over."

"I hope not. We make a good team," said Dalton, the CIA's new acting director.

"Will the air strikes this morning calm the waters?" asked Milano.

"It'll be a start," Dalton said.

They were drinking coffee in her office with CNN on the wall screen, listening to Jake Tapper broadcast that U.S. bombers were engaged in a massive raid on the Syrian coast.

America had counted its dead, which now stood at 203 from the Nashville, the Pentagon and L'Enfant Plaza metro stations, and the CIA front gate carnage. Nearly three dozen were in intensive care. Far below the nearly 3,000 fatalities of 9/11. However, the terror of radioactive poisoning, though limited from the dirty bombs, was widespread. Millions of people were demanding testing at hospitals and doctors' offices, some as far away as Houston and LA.

Huge areas of metro Washington looked like ghost towns. A cleanup was underway, but way more important, payback was at hand.

"Your biographer will write after your papers are unsealed in a generation that you were key to keeping this from being a total shit show," said Milano.

"No papers exist or ever will," Dalton said.

He had kept his own counsel, except for some conversation with Milano, and worked the situation like the polished spy and operations professional he was.

First, he had maneuvered to become the CIA's deputy director with a promise to then director Richard Harwell to help launch the scheme to oust the Saudi crown prince, for the profit of oil and pressure on Iran.

Then he shoved Harwell aside by confronting him with evidence that his communications with Steve Cohen could link him to murders in France. The old man who liked to be called "senator" wanted to keep his prized reputation intact and resigned that day, for health reasons.

"First Harwell and now Assad," said Milano. "I'd hate to be on your bad side."

Dalton had quickly identified the murderous Syrian leader Bashar al-Assad and his secret police as the villains who bankrolled Dogu Matsoy's attacks. There was some logic to it, as his regime always tolerated ISIS in Syria and would love a weakened America in the Middle East. As would Assad's supporters in Iran and Russia. Bank records in Cyprus now seemed to prove it, with the money from the narco-state's Captagon trade.

In wartime, on a battlefield or in Washington politics, it pays to act first. Dalton had leaked Assad as the villain to the *Washington Post* and got it to the president's attention before anyone could promote the Saudi story to him.

The tailored, seasoned Dalton sold his Syrian fiction well, a calm presence in the boiling waters of blame, backstabbing, and self-promotion playing out in Congress and the media. The only thing that could be agreed upon was that someone had to pay—quickly. The malignant Syrian dictator and his regime fit the bill.

"There's still Dogu Matsoy," said Milano. "No one can afford to have him alive for the next ten years with rumors that he's still planning from a cave like bin Laden."

Dalton looked at his watch—a theatrical gesture—and said, "Give me another twenty-four hours and there's a good chance our Dogu worry will be put to rest."

Dalton visited Angelos's office at the Operations Center, a trip that set gossip buzzing but was interpreted as a sign of respect for Angelos. Dalton was coming to him, not demanding his presence at the top-floor director's office.

That was how Dalton wanted it to be seen—respect. Even if the visit was to push Angelos out.

"I understand some heads have to roll," said Angelos. "I didn't see the attacks coming, I didn't stop it, and I got caught dressing up Rivers with fake credentials. So, I've got to go."

"The attacks getting through was a team effort," said Dalton.

"Yes, but while there's no *I* in team, there are three in *investi-*

gation, and that has to be short-circuited at all costs," said Angelos.

"An investigation wouldn't be good for you or the CIA," said Dalton. "A few quick cuts, fair or not, will show the agency is cleaning house and help keep the jackals away."

"Time to fall on my sword," said Angelos. "At least you got the scheming Harwell out the door. A win there. And I do admire the way you set up Assad as the villain."

"That means a lot coming from you," said Dalton.

"As it is, you'll be able to retire with all benefits. You earned it," Dalton continued. "I can't promise that you won't be dragged before a congressional panel, but I don't see that in your future. I'll make sure Harwell is front and center for such a show. His old comrades and current schemers won't want that."

"Well, full retirement works under the circumstances," said Angelos. "We're paid to protect our country one hundred percent of the time and prevent a terrorist from getting through once. These damn people got through. That casualties were limited, that just doesn't cut it."

"Stay in touch," said Dalton, rising to leave.

"Will Cowen take my job?" asked Angelos.

"Acting, of course," said Dalton. "But I think there's a stronger candidate in the wings. After all, Cowen may have advised you against producing fake credentials, but he wasn't forceful enough to stop you. That's a concern. He's a good hammer in his current job, though."

"Rivers?"

"Quite a remarkable young man," said Dalton. "He can stay if he wants to, after all he's done in the past weeks. But he has to survive the next twenty-four hours, doesn't he?"

"A good bet," said Angelos. "He's lucky that way."

82

L*et's get this done*, Rivers thought.

He was with Jack Rojas, the CIA paramilitary officer who had rescued him in the desert a few weeks back, and a team from Delta Force. It was a few hours before dawn, and they had silently filed off a launch at a rocky inlet and climbed a steep path beside a cliff facing out to sea.

They now had a field of large, wind-smoothed rocks between them and a few lights marking Dogu Matsoy's compound a mile away.

They were on the remote Greek island of Antiparos, a playground for the superrich who wanted peace and quiet instead of the rush and crush of Mykonos. Tom Hanks came here; Jeff Bezos visited. Now there were more guns on this speck of volcanic rock than since the Nazis used it as an observation post looking into the Mediterranean during World War II.

Satellite and drone imagery had painted a picture of a curiously almost abandoned compound, even as other intelligence suggested Dogu was there now. Could Dogu have men and weapons secreted in tunnels under the building? The island was known for its caves. Was there radioactive dust present?

All fifteen men on this raid hated the plan, which they felt put them at unnecessary risk. But orders were orders, and their task was to try to take Dogu alive. Some advisers on the National Security Council and top congressional leaders had sold the president on the idea of a show trial. The men on this raid preferred to missile the terrorist and any fellow travelers from an attack helicopter and then shoot anyone who came running out. Let DNA identify Dogu.

Delta also wasn't happy to have Rivers and Rojas along, but that was another order. At least it seemed clear the two knew what they were doing and weren't just along as tourists.

If things went wrong, additional Delta teams were ready on helicopters on ships hidden behind a close island and could arrive within fifteen minutes.

They were attacking a fortified position, and they knew Dogu may have set up video monitors and, perhaps, IEDs.

To try to avoid these defenses, Delta had decided on a challenging route fit only for mountain goats. They moved single file on the very edge of the ragged cliff, stepping over rocks and onto slick stones and moss in places. One step at a time.

Rivers was tugged by gusts of wind and felt the emptiness at his elbow and a horror at being one misstep from falling 100 feet onto the rocks below. He strained to decipher each footfall through the weird green light of his night vision goggles.

He was covered in sweat on a cool night.

He had a sense that his luck was played out.

Stay calm, calm, breathe, Rivers kept repeating to himself. *Just do your job.*

And for now, that was not to fall off the cliff.

At last, they were at the edge of a concrete balcony jutting off the cliff over the rocks and cold, swift water below. There was no sound or sighting of guards. They slipped onto the balcony.

It was time to go to work.

Dogu was sitting in the dark on a sofa in a bedroom with a huge expanse of windows overlooking the Mediterranean. Yesterday was his first in this compound after exhausting days escaping. First the cargo ship, then a pickup by a fast boat out of the Azores, a flight to Beirut and then a small boat to Antiparos. He didn't believe anyone knew of this hideaway.

He had seen when he arrived that light from the rising sun reflected on the cold water out this window and turned it the color of turquoise as the night chill was heated away. Dogu never had noticed that type of thing before. Maybe it was because he was so unsettled now.

Dogu the Chechen. A world-class terrorist. A hero to billions. His face on T-shirts that everybody was making money selling. He had earned that celebrity status.

What was he going to do now, though?

He had arrived at this compound expecting to see the dozen employees who operated a computer command center here, as well as guards, a cook, a house manager—all former ISIS or recruits. Only three guards remained.

"Where did they go?!" he had yelled at one.

"They are scared the Americans will come," Dogu was told by another.

He already was stunned in Beirut when he talked to a top

Hezbollah commander who had welcomed him in the past as the guy who paid extravagant prices for supplies, even though he was ISIS. The man gave him barely five minutes this time and then told him to take his boat from the port and leave.

"We did not support such an attack," the commander said. "We cannot be seen with you. You are not welcome here."

Dogu had planned to spend some wild days and nights in a discreet Beirut villa, partying with some of the most beautiful women in the Mediterranean. But the commander said no, and it sounded permanent.

He had received a message from a Matsoy cousin in Odesa congratulating him, but in the back and forth, his cousin said it would not be wise for Dogu to return because of the constant surveillance. "It's killing our smuggling more than the murder of Raglan," he said. "Maybe later you can visit."

Visit? Maybe he'd want to rebuild the smuggling enterprise to make it a Dogu empire. But they were scared and distant now, not offering to protect him or ask what they could do to help the most famous bearer of the Matsoy name.

He thought of taking a boat to Athens and hitting some of the wild clubs in disguise, but an old companion in such adventures did not answer his texts.

Dogu had thought the world of terrorists and dissidents and rebels would open their arms to him, but he was finding doors slammed in his face.

A friend in Paris texted, *Maybe later but you're radioactive now.*

Americans were bombing the hell out of Assad's Syria, and everybody knew the Americans wanted Dogu Matsoy even more.

For years his days were filled with fighting for ISIS,

surviving Al-Hol, planning to attack America. Now he sat alone in this new day.

Well, not alone.

A woman cowered in a corner. A pimp on an adjacent island was paid well for a woman who was OK with rough play. Last night he had perhaps been rougher than usual. He would have to consider how to handle this, for killing the woman and the pimp was bound to be big news on a small island. Or money could solve the problem, but only temporarily. Word would get out to pimps and women not to deal with him, and to local police, who didn't like prostitutes nearly murdered.

What was he going to do to get women? Where would he go?

The dark of night began to change to the purple of an arriving morning.

Open to him, of course, was the route of his father, Omar. To turn to the desert and the hiding places in Syria, where ISIS was resurging.

That might be his only choice, but the thought of the dirt, heat and smells disgusted him.

Delta had the advantage of satellite and drone imagery and sensors scouting the property, so they had a detailed look at the exterior layout and its lack of activity. Curious. Although someone had arrived by boat a day earlier. A guess was that it was Dogu.

There was a large main building and two smaller ones, one of which housed quarters for staff and a garage, the other some sort of computer operation, now seemingly powered down.

The soldiers were scattered on the balcony as one of them

drilled a small hole through a glass door and sprayed a sensor with a chemical to disable it. They had judged it wasn't a vibration sensor or the wind would always set it off.

Inside was a vast, open room with sofas and tables for entertainment and a massive, open-concept chef's kitchen. Delta split into three teams, with two moving rapidly down a corridor and then outside to the other two buildings. A four-man team stayed in the main villa.

Rivers and Rojas trailed that main team as they cleared rooms. No use getting in the way of soldiers with their practiced ballet of movement. Little by little the teams cleared spaces and reported their progress.

A winding staircase went upstairs in the main building, and Delta stepped up with their weapons targeting doors, open and closed. Rivers and Rojas followed.

They heard sobbing from a room, and a Delta soldier quietly twisted the door handle and nudged it open, careful not to be framed in the doorway. There, in the green light of their night vision goggles, was a woman trembling in a corner and crying as if she was choking on her tears. She did not look up as the soldiers entered.

Suddenly there was gunfire from one of the other buildings.

———

Dogu's phone buzzed when the soldiers first moved onto the balcony, compliments of secreted motion sensors that activated at night. He did not call his guards; one was possibly awake as a sentry watching the only entry road, but two others were snoring in another building. They could entertain the U.S. soldiers a bit and distract them from their search for him.

He had moved from the bedroom with the sobbing woman to a small storage room at the end of the hall, where a slim section of the wall held shelves of towels and bath supplies. He pulled the section gently toward him and a doorway was behind it, the opening now allowing cold air to seep slightly into the room. He entered and pulled it closed behind him.

Dogu was on narrow stairs that ran through the stone walls downstairs right into a cave underneath the house. He flipped a switch there and a tunnel was visible in a soft light. It would eventually bring him out to a small cove behind an easy-to-miss slit in the cliff, a hideaway at least a half mile from the compound.

He wouldn't be able to get away during the day but could take the small boat hidden there out at night. If he hugged the coast, he'd have a good chance to escape.

Delta had finished searching this last floor and now moved to where the gunfire had come from. "Three down, all clear" had come over the Delta comms. So much for the guards.

"Let's go and follow them," said Rojas.

But Rivers was leaning against the wall in the landing by the bedrooms. He felt spent and said, "I need a second."

Leaning there to catch his breath, he felt just a whisper of cold air and slowly turned his head toward a door at the end of the hall, which was left open after Delta searched it.

"I want to check something," he said to Rojas.

Rivers moved to the room, which had some boxes of toilet paper and such. He saw some shelves on the wall. Nothing interesting.

But wait … a slight flow of cold air.

Rivers took off his goggles, warned Rojas to do the same and turned on an overhead light. The faint stream of cold air guided him: There was a slight gap between the shelves section and the wall. He tugged at it while Rojas covered the space with his weapon.

A slim door to a slim staircase.

Rojas began to call it in to Delta while Rivers plunged down, ignoring Rojas's shout to wait for him.

Down, down. His shoulders rubbing against the rough walls, winding up in a cave that was the source of the upward breeze. Dim lights were on in a tunnel that led to an end unknown.

Weapon ready, Rivers moved at a quick pace down a straight-away, then around a curve, then another small cave into a curve, then straight ahead.

Now a curve ahead, and something told Rivers to pause. He had pressed his luck in an adrenaline rush but now his brain was kicking in and warning him that he was a lonely soul. *Wait for Rojas*, he thought. He hesitated and heard Rojas somewhere behind. But impatient, Rivers turned the corner, moving low.

No one around the curve.

He looked ahead and saw dim early morning light.

Rivers pulled up at the tunnel end, leaning into the rock for cover. Ahead was a rocky inlet into which he could hear waves crashing. There were shadows as the inlet had a shield of rock protecting it from the sea and easy sight. There was too much sunlight to take out a boat now with the Navy out there.

"Surrender, Dogu. You can't escape," yelled Rivers.

Rivers heard Rojas coming down the tunnel, getting close.

Dogu answered in a gravelly voice, "I give up."

Which certainly didn't sound like the Dogu who Rivers had been hunting.

Dogu could have heard Rivers trudging down the tunnel and had time to set up a deadly response.

Rivers leaned out just a little and saw Dogu standing near a rock that was up to his waist.

A hand was behind it.

Rivers took a quarter step out of the tunnel and centered his weapon on Dogu's chest.

"Hands, let me see both hands."

Dogu looked shocked. This was the CIA man with the jagged cut on his jaw, now a mean purple line. He had killed this man who killed Raglan in his apartment in America.

"You are a hard man to kill," said Dogu. "But now I will."

Rivers slid fully back into the tunnel, but the shock wave from the blast of a suicide vest lodged against the cliff slammed him into the tunnel's rock wall. Dogu had had a detonator in his hand.

Rojas checked the prone Rivers and then stepped out to Dogu; weapon ready.

Dogu was lying sliced badly by shrapnel, breathing in gasps.

"Is he dead yet?" Dogu choked out the words, pointing weakly toward the tunnel.

But Rivers had struggled up and limped over so the dying terrorist could see him. He pointed his weapon at the suffering Dogu, but after a moment moved it away, declining to finish him. No mercy for Dogu.

"Go to hell," he simply said.

EPILOGUE

The president called the head of the Delta team to say job well done.

Rivers and Rojas, as CIA, were happy to be unmentioned and out of the limelight, although the Special Forces guys and sailors on board the carrier off Antiparos treated them royally after hearing they were there at the death of Dogu the terrorist.

The black bag with Dogu Matsoy's body was now in the ship's morgue. A DNA sample would be taken. And his remains would be dumped unceremoniously in the Atlantic.

A Navy corpsman bandaged Rivers's bruised ribs from bouncing into the tunnel wall and gave a concerned look at his ragged jaw and at the multitude of fading purple and yellow bruises. "You know, Tom," said Rojas, who stayed with him, "you might consider getting a desk job. You've got to be running low on your nine lives."

Rivers's phone buzzed and there was a text from the new acting CIA director, Harry Dalton: "Good work. Take some time off and then come see me. I have a job that might interest you."

Then a call from Angelos.

"I'm glad you're OK. I heard you got hurt but are walking wounded," said Angelos. "You and Rojas did an outstanding job. Your country and the CIA are proud of you both."

"Thanks, Mr. Angelos. It's been a strange couple of weeks," said Rivers. "I could never imagine something like this could happen when you sent me to Paris. It's going to take me some time to process it all. Maybe when we get back, we can have a coffee or a beer."

"Maybe," said Angelos. "But I won't be at the Operations Center. I'm retiring. I've had a good run, but my clock hit midnight. I think I'll have a beer—or two or three—watching the top fools in Congress and their broadcast buddies pontificate on this disaster. Look me up when you're back."

Finally, the call he wanted.

"I heard you got hurt again," said Raz. "You keep this up and there won't be anything left for me."

"I'll always be there for you," said Rivers.

"That's what I like to hear." And then Raz said something that pierced to the heart of Rivers: "Come home."

———

He first made a stop in Athens to have lunch with Daryan Nuri and his son Ali, who ran some of the business operations for his father, the Kurdish magnate, with construction, oil, and financial interests.

They hugged on meeting, the greeting of an adopted father for an adopted son.

"The last time we met, I said to take care of yourself," said Daryan, who made a show of examining the wincing, limping young man. "You need to do a better job at that."

They were sitting at a small restaurant on a hotel rooftop, the Acropolis in sight upon its hill, the mighty building a ruin that was still a wonder of the world. A perfect place to wax philosophical.

"History comes and goes, and the best and worst works of man turn to memory," said Daryan. "I lost a son against those ISIS beasts." He paused to reach over and take Ali's hand. "How long before we can put this evil to rest?"

"Never," he whispered in an answer to himself. "ISIS eventually will fade away, but the evil of men remains.

"For now, some of the kids at Al-Hol and other festering places are already wearing Dogu T-shirts."

"Dogu and Umm lost their lives," said Rivers. "But the truth is we all lost."

Rivers thought of Alex, Nadia and the UN translator, and Paul, of the dead and terrorized Americans, and even the women and kids behind the wire at Al Hol, some ripe for recruitment to ISIS. So much loss.

They were quiet then, Daryan and Rivers solemn, and Ali moved them away from the serious moments by raising a glass to toast "To the best of us."

"I have an offer," said Daryan to Rivers. "One that will help me. I need someone who can explain American culture to my own and colleagues' businesses and explain our culture to American firms. It'd mean more business, more money."

A sly way of making a job offer; Daryan was making it for his own profit.

"You could work from Athens, even Paris if you chose," he said with a smile.

Rivers looked at Ali to see if he was on board with the offer and saw that he was.

"I'm fortunate to have you as my friend, Daryan," said Rivers. "I will consider your generous offer. But first I need to rest, and to see a friend in Paris."

"You are a lucky man," said Daryan. "May it always be that way."

After landing in Paris, Rivers made two stops on his way to Raz's place in La Marais: one to a liquor store and the other to the old man at the Dudayev Centre.

Musa Gugaev was sitting in the musty room, his two canes propped against the table that held an open bottle.

Rivers stood over him, smiled, and said, "Perhaps you remember me. I came with Paul Laurent a few weeks ago. I've brought you a present." A bottle of his favorite bourbon.

"Yes, I know you," said Gugaev, who gestured for Rivers to sit.

Coming here was in some small way an act of remembering Laurent, whose gallantry in pursuing life and of connecting with others inspired Rivers. He missed his smile that was a laugh at the absurdities of the world.

"I was sad about Paul," said Gugaev. "He was good, and I don't see that in many people. Over the years I've seen so much death. But you took my advice: You killed them before they killed you."

"These ISIS terrorists killed a lot of people," Rivers said.

The old man replied, "That is what they do."

Rivers got up to leave and Gugaev halted him. "Give me a kiss on both cheeks like a good Frenchman. I need to teach you some manners."

Which Rivers did.

"I see a lot of Paul in you," said the old man as Rivers turned to leave. "Now go to that woman I hear you have and don't become a lonely old man like me."

"Come home."

The words were magic to Rivers.

He didn't know what life held for him, but he knew he wanted to hold Raz in his arms.

The car left Rivers off in front of her imposing stone building with her living quarters on the top floor. Her bodyguards—new ones, he saw—knew who he was and nodded as he passed by.

He walked out onto the terrace of her top-floor quarters with its view of the sky over Paris, and Raz was at the railing.

She turned, and he remembered how she took his breath away at first sight, and she still did.

Rivers moved close, and Raz took his battered face in her hands and leaned in to kiss him and said softly, "What am I going to do with you?"

"To kill terrorist leaders without addressing the despair of their supporters is a fool's errand and produces more frustration, more despair, and more terrorism."

—ARI AYALON, EX-ISRAELI SECURITY OFFICIAL

ACKNOWLEDGMENTS

This is a work of fiction. All the names, characters, businesses, places, events, and incidents in this book are either the product of my imagination or used in a fictitious manner. Still, this novel rests on a foundation of reality: the Al-Hol detention camp, Omar the Chechen, ISIS brides, Western converts to ISIS, and the threat of radioactive caesium chloride dirty bombs are real. As is the resilience of ISIS and its aim to terrorize the West again.

Many helped this author get to the point of writing this book. Among them are my parents, Charles and Marie McQuay, who encouraged my reading of thrillers from a young age. Jesuit teachers lent a hand. And the support and happiness of my family — Cathy (a marvelous editor) and son Mark, and sister Peggy Hauf— anchors me always. My first editor was Steve Cohen, a family friend, who was essential in getting a failing effort back on track. His reward: A spy-cad in the novel bears his name. In addition, a special thanks to authors Tim Wendel, Peter Prichard, and Sean Carberry for their support.

I was fortunate to have a long career as a journalist with USA TODAY and then as an editor and report developer with SIGAR – the Special Inspector General for Afghanistan Reconstruction – and the Lead Inspector General for Overseas Contingency Operations/Department of Defense, where I was managing editor of its congressional reports on the wars. It was an honor to work with people devoted to doing the job right and to witness the professionalism of our military and civilian personnel. Even if overall policies were SNAFU.

In 2012 in Kabul, I asked an old hand what he made of our efforts in Afghanistan. He replied, "Vietnam all over again." And Iraq was a separate self-inflicted challenge. Maybe administrations, Congress and our vast bureaucracy can learn some meaningful lessons to make the United States smarter in a dangerous world. What are the odds?